Scatter the Mud

Scatter the Mud
A Traveller's Medley

by Nancy Lyon

NUAGE
EDITIONS

© 1995, Nancy Lyon

All rights reserved. No part of this book may be reproduced, for any reason, by any means, without the permission of the publisher.

Cover design by Terry Gallagher/Doowah Design Inc.

Acknowledgments
Abbreviated versions of "Inish bó finne" first appeared in *GEO Magazine*, 1982; "Death Valley Daze," in *The New York Times*, 1973; "Wine for Soap," in *Ms Magazine*, 1984; "My Friend the Witch Doctor," "The Straats of Amsterdam," "Nashville Brash, "and "Alien (Vac) Ation" appeared in the *Montreal Mirror* in 1995; "Adios Muchachas!" "A Jaunt Around the Lakes" and "Irish Pub Etiquette" were originally commissioned by the U.S. edition of *GEO* (before its demise). "Adios Muchachas!" later appeared in *INDEX*, December, 1994, "A Jaunt Around the Lakes" in an abbreviated form in the *Montreal Mirror;* and "Excavating Arthur" in *en Route*, 1995; "Bilingual Love in the Uh oh! Zone," "Tennessee Mountain English" and "The Ultimate Travel Adventure" appeared in the *Montreal Gazette*; "Pies," written for *In Dublin* magazine, was published in *The Urban Wanderers Reader*, Hochelaga Press, 1995 and broadcast in part on CBC's "Daybreak."

Published with the assistance of The Canada Council.
Printed and bound in Canada by Les Ateliers Graphiques Marc Veilleux.
Dépôt légal, the National Library of Canada and la Bibliothèque nationale du Québec.

Canadian Cataloguing in Publication Data

Lyon, Nancy
    Scatter the mud : a traveller's medley

ISBN 0-921833-42-3

    1. Lyon, Nancy—Journeys. 2. Street music and musicians. I. Title.

G180.L96 1995   910.4   C95-920872-0

Nuage Editions, P.O. Box 8, Station E
Montréal, Québec H2T 3A5

For my dear parents
 —Peg, who started it
  —and Elmer, who said yes

Contents

Runaway Beginnings
Adios Muchachas! 1982 8
Fun City, 1969-1979 16
Death Valley Daze 1973 29

Irish Roving
Round and Round: A Primer of Irish Pub Etiquette 1982 38
Pies: A Farce 1979 42
Inish Bó Finne 1982 52

The Great European Busking Tour
The Straats of Amsterdam 1995 74
Wine for Soap 1984 77

Montréal-Montreal
Bang 1994 90
Coup de Foudre 1993 94
Bilingual Love in the Uh oh! Zone 1993 98
Busking To Death 1986 100

Spooked!
My Friend the Witch Doctor 1995 112
Excavating Arthur 1995 117
The Ultimate Adventure Travel 1994 127
Alien (Vac)ation 1995 131
A Jaunt Around The Lakes 1983 135

Homecoming
Gotham, My Ex-beloved 1992-94 142
    Take The A Train… 143
    Hell's Hot Kitchen 144
    SoHo Sass 145
    Life's a Knish 146
    Under the Boardwalk 147
Tennessee Gothic 1992 150
    Mountain English 150
    Nashville Brash 152
    The Gospel According to East Tennessee 155
Back to School: David Letterman Country, Indianapolis 1995 158

Runaway Beginnings

Adios Muchachas!

We called it Indian-No-Place and snickered to think it could actually be the "Crossroads of America" like the radio announcers said. Indiana was a country for hogs and soybeans, and its capital was a "crossroads" only because you had to drive through it to get to someplace else.

Indiana was flat, boring and lakeless, except for those muddy man-made things. But for the thrill of an occasional tornado, a summer in Naptown was a string of hot drippy listless afternoons that began with cars screeching at the Indy 500, and ended with pigs squealing at the Indiana State Fair.

That's how I saw Indianapolis in 1961 when I was 13, and that's how my mother saw it too. I was a renegade cowgirl in a buckskin jacket who hated dolls and adored Nancy Drew mysteries. She was a rebel New Yorker who hated the Midwest and housework, and was decidedly inept at the social role of a tax attorney's wife.

When all the other mothers on North Delaware Street were ironing the smocking on little organdy dresses or making civic chit-chat over tea and Girl Scout cookies, Peg Lyon was making us pirate costumes, inventing toys and gluing *National Geographic* photos onto plywood and cutting them up into educational puzzles with her jigsaw.

It seemed perfectly natural that she should want to get away from Naptown for a summer. Perfectly reasonable that she should ask Dad for the Shell Motor card and an advance on her grocery money so she could drive me and my three sisters to Mexico. And perfectly normal that he said yes.

It must have been the neighborhood scandal when Mrs. Lyon piled her four girls aged 13, 10, 9 and 3 into the powder blue Ford Woody with enough jigsaw puzzles and Cheese Nips to make it to the border, said *adios* to her husband for the summer, and *vamos!* took off... Leaving the pallid moon on the Wabash for a fiery tropical moon, the flat stubby cornfields for the Sierra Madres and the muddy man-made puddles for the boiling Pacific.

All these years later, the enormity, the impetuosity of it hits me. The breakdowns at night in the Sierra Madres...the four bald tires...the shattered car window...losing my sister in a tortilla factory...that incident in the waves at Pie de la Cuesta...the red-haired prostitute with the pistol. That summer we chased iguanas, split coconuts, ate mashed beans, wrestled waves and climbed to the top of the Pyramid of the Sun. I learned to navigate and translate and appreciate that a woman could go anywhere—even to Acapulco—with no man, no plan and no Spanish.

Del Shannon was singing about Peg on the car radio. My lit-tle Indianapolis runaway...run-run-run-run run-away! I slept through all the CHEW—MAIL—POUCH plastered barns and BURMA—SHAVE signs from Kentucky to Tennessee; I knew them by heart from hundreds of family trips to visit relatives. It wasn't until we saw savannahs and swamps and signs announcing "Whites Only" that I could really believe this wasn't just another trip to Granddaddy Lyon's farm in Midway, Tennessee.

I perked up to my duties as co-pilot to read maps, figure mileage and keep Peg awake. Life in the back seat was simpler for my little sisters, who seemed happy to be going nowhere in a snug nest of pillows and blankets, candy wrappers and peanut shells. Our blue wagon hummed and rolled over the world. Life outside was a passing picture show.

Every so often Peg stopped to ask for directions and forage for provisions—Cokes, Cracker Jacks, maps, Chamber of Commerce brochures and cans of Sterno. If we got lost on one of these diversions, if I read a map upside down and we missed an exit and went a few hundred miles out of our way, then so what. Anywhere was somewhere else and might be an adventure.

"We fired our guns and we began a-runnin,' down the Mississippi to that sweltering Gulf of Mexico..." I was singing with Johnny Horton as we pressed onward to New Orleans. There we swam in Lake Pontchartrain, which the next day was declared polluted and shut down. We spent a gloomy afternoon reading crooked tombstones, until lightning flashed behind a huge grave with stag antlers and made us run in fright. And my sister Pat, a ten-year old entomologist, captured praying mantises and skittering chameleons to keep as pets.

I could hardly wait to get to San Antonio, to see the Alamo where the historic frontiersman born in my daddy's neck of the woods, Davy Crockett, King of the Wild Frontier who kilt him a b'ar when he was only three—had fought so bravely for the Republic of Texas in the Disney movie. I was all moony over Fess Parker, in his buckskin jacket and coonskin cap, and I kind of blurred the handsome star with Davy Crockett. I wanted to touch the walls of the old fort where Fess had been. But once we got to Texas, and the excitement of seeing my first tumbleweed and first cowboy hat wore off, Texas became an endless smoldering highway. I sat for hundreds of miles with my feet stuck in a plastic tub of ice water, chattering to Peg so she wouldn't sink into a trance.

We finally made it to good old San Antone. The Alamo looked a lot smaller than it did on TV. It was hard to believe Davy was really dead. The movie showed Fess heroically fighting till the credits came on. But after reading the plaques about the 1836 attack on the Alamo, in which Davy Crockett was felled by the Mexican soldiers of Gen. Antonio López de Santa Anna's armies, I realized Fess was dead. I stood in tears in front of the old mission and sang every verse of the ballad I could remember.

Somewhere past Cotulla, Texas, Peg shook me awake. Something on the radio sounded like a gargling match. It was loud, excited Mexican voices. "Ye gods! How will we ever communicate with them?" she cried. Our five hearts pounded as the border advanced.

All I knew of Mexico was from Hopalong Cassidy films, so when we crossed the Rio Grande I expected some kind of excitement. But the sleepy looking border guard looked dully at our tourist cards, stared at the mess in our car and waved us on. Suddenly pedestrians were *peatones*, the hit tune "Never on Sunday" was "*Nunca en Domingo*" with trumpets and brass, and *Bebe Coca Cola!* signs were everywhere. Like a cowboy movie set, dry and dusty Nuevo Laredo had rutted streets, goats and bony dogs, burros carting bananas and whiskery men in wilting sombreros. We tanked up with Pemex *gasolina* and hit the open road.

If Texas put us to sleep, Mexico kept us on the edge of our seats. The Sierra Madres had real hairpin curves and there was always a gaily-painted semi-truck snorting behind or wheezing in front. Every *curva peligrosa* had a gory crucifix splattered with red paint to commemorate the travellers killed there.

My sisters and I hung out the windows sniffing the tarry creosote and gaping at the strange prickly vegetation, and the purples, greens and blues layering the mountainy horizon. The cacti looked spiky and mean, and I knew there were tarantulas and scorpions lurking in the dust beyond our car. Vultures drifted hungrily in the yellow sky and I was so glad to be away from Indianapolis.

Having such a wad of pesos made us all feel rich, so we picked our motels by the looks of their swimming pools. My sisters and I would loll by the glittering pools of the Motel Cactus, the Motel La Siesta, the Motel Maguey, pretending to be rich actresses on holiday, (I in my new Jantzen fake tiger skin suit) while Peg cooked our TV dinners two at a time in our portable Sterno oven. Then at the Motel Tuna in San Luis Potosi I got a thundering earache. The dirty Lake Pontchartrain microbes had landed.

The owner of the Tuna found us a translator—a woman with big jangly pineapple earrings who reeked of Tabu and lived in a high-walled villa built like a prison. She went with us to the hospital and explained my problem to a nurse. But the only other words the translator spoke to me, after the doctor took his picador or whatever it was and lanced my eardrum and I had stopped shrieking and wailing were: "Theese may hurt." After that I studied our phrase book in earnest.

    We got into Mexico City with the help of a hitchhiker we picked up at night at a Pemex station, a stringy, greasy, toothless young man who said his taxi broke down. Ignacio was great at rounding curves while talking with his hands. He sang Mexican pop songs in a high wispy voice that made us laugh. He drove us through the honking, blinding lava flow of traffic to a cheap old hotel, where he jumped out and called, "Adios muchachas!"

    Then Peg got sick. I thought it was the piles of bite-size finger bananas and powdery pastries we'd been eating, but it was Montezuma's Revenge—altitude sickness, with a dash of Turista. She said it was her punishment for being a wayward mother and bringing us so far away from home. She awoke in the middle of the night dizzy and breathless from nightmares. I crawled over my sleeping sisters to comfort her.

    How would we ever get back home to Indianapolis, she sobbed. What if the Cuban Missile Crisis blew up and we had another war? It occurred to me that she was right, that it was a crazy thing to travel like this. Anybody else would have gone camping at Turkey Run State Park, and brought their husband.

    I always had a secret scorn for people who lived in tornado magnets—trailers—who couldn't afford a real house. Trailers were flimsy tin cans with chintzy windows. I laughed to imagine them whirling through the sky in a funnel cloud. So how did we end up at the Buena Vista Trailer Court in the suburbs of Mexico City, in a pink Winnebago owned by missionaries from Moundsville, Ohio? We met them on our way to the floating flowers and singing boatmen at Xochimilco. They were moving into a house in Mexico City, and their trailer was vacant for the summer...

    Once we got the hang of trailer life, converting the table into a bed, and sleeping head to foot, Peg made sure we saw all the cultural attractions of Mexico's great capital city, including the 22-ton Tiffany glass curtain depicting Mexican volcanoes at the Palacio de Bellas Artes. On afternoons when we didn't take a picnic to Chapultepek Park, or go to a museum or market, or exhibition of native dancing, or for a hamburger at Sanborn's, Peg and I took a long siesta. Pat chased the long-tailed pistachio-ice-cream-colored Luna moths, and Susie and Jan visited the family that lived in the wall.

    The wall around the Buena Vista trailer park was five feet thick with broken bottles cemented into the top of it to keep out bandits. Near the entrance gate, the wall was hollow and a whole Indian family lived inside, in a windowless room with a dirt floor. The mother pressed clothes for the Buena Vista residents with an old iron she heated over coals. The father peddled hand-carved wooden marionettes outside the entrance gate. And the seven barefoot children ran around hounded by flies.

    The big brown mother was always smiling, even in the sweaty dark of their little cement room. One day she showed Susie and Jan how the saber-like tip of a maguey leaf could be used as a needle and thread. She broke off the tough thorny tip of the plant, and trailing behind it was a long stringy fiber she could use to patch her husband's pants.

My sisters loved watching her make tortillas, slapping the lumps of dough on a rock and throwing them into the air. One day they brought me one crowned with a wrinkled thing that looked like an olive. I popped it into my mouth. *Caramba!* A hot tamale! I stuck my smouldering mouth under the faucet of our trailer, but it was hot and dry. My sisters giggled as I gasped. They had been eating those things. Like *natives*. Like a good fireman, Peg ran for bottled water.

One night we got homesick for America and went to a Gary Cooper western at a drive-in theatre, to hear some English for a change. Cowboy movies were silly enough, but this one was even sillier with dubbed Spanish that didn't fit the faces, and a live soundtrack of Mexican horns and whistles from the rowdy crowds perched on the fence and nearby rooftops for a free show.

Just as the movie bad guys were winning it started pouring, and Peg said we had to remove the speaker from our car so the lightning wouldn't strike it. But we kept nagging at her to stay, even though the windshield was just a big watery blur. And in the confusion of hollers and boos and soaked Mexicans running for cover, we drove off with a big crunch as Gary Cooper fired at the *hombres* and the speaker ripped the window out of our car.

Another day we went to a bullfight, and it was just our luck to see a matador get gored. The bull hooked him in the stomach and tossed him in the air like a sack of hog feed. A hush fell over the mob but I could tell they were really enjoying it, like the crowds at the Indy 500 who secretly hope for a crash to make their day worthwhile. We mourned the matador for days—he was so young and handsome—until we saw in the newspaper that he had lived.

The gore of the bullfight made me sick, yet I was fascinated by the Aztecs and their gory human sacrifices. Their monster goddess Coatlicue was something to admire, with her face covered with rattlesnake fangs, her navel bulging with human skulls and her huge breasts bloody with the hearts of sacrificed victims. According to Aztec legend, the place where the gods had gathered to plan the creation of the world was only 28 miles from our trailer court: Teotihuacán.

The only pyramid I'd ever seen was the Indianapolis Circle Tower Building, the fake Babylonian ziggurat where my father worked. Now before us was the colossal and weathered authentic ancient Pyramid of the Sun of the Plumed Serpent god Quetzacóatl. The guidebooks explained that it was 2,000 years old and 20 stories high. I could see some colored dots moving slowly over the top of it. I walked through the heat toward it in a trance. Peg clutched little Jan, but Pat and Susie tagged along with me to the pyramid base.

The broken steps were barely the width of a tennis shoe. One slip and it would be a quick tumble to a split skull. My sisters and I climbed sideways, hunched over and hugging the crumbly rock. We didn't look down to the vast plain receding below. We didn't look up to the empty sky. We kept climbing through the strange powdery air, until the Pyramid of the Moon at the far end of the Street of the Dead seemed miles below. Then the ledges vanished. There was only a huge mound of loose stones, and we had to crawl on our bellies to make it to that place where the priests with obsidian knives had ripped the still beating hearts from their victims.

From the top, dazed by the eerie clarity of that Mexican sky, I could see thousands of dark men in Quetzal feathers, carrying fires, while the ceremonial drums beat louder and faster until—someone flicked a lit cigarette and it bounced down and flew off into the hot wind.

The guidebooks called Acapulco a "jet-set playground," a "real hot spot" and it didn't really sound like the sort of place a mother should go to. But one day while we were admiring the mosaic murals of Mexican revolutionaries on the University of Mexico campus, we met an American named Barbara. Barbara was looking for a ride to Acapulco, and we were getting pretty sick of trailer life, always finding tomato skins in the bedclothes...

On the way to Acapulco, we spotted a gang of skinny boys by the side of the road. They were grinning and holding some horrible lizardy things by their scaly tails.

"Uggh! What are those?" I said.

"Iguanas," said Barbara. "They eat 'em like chickens around here."

Barbara looked like she ate iguanas, I thought. Her flesh jiggled and her eyelids were a kind of lizardy green. She never smiled and her short dry hair looked like it came off a coconut shell. I wondered why she didn't like America, or had to leave it. And most of all I wondered why she had no suitcase, and what could be inside the woven cactus bag she was clutching.

She seemed to know the seamy side of Mexico. She probably went to cockfights and drank Tequila in those cantinas where loud men knocked each other over the tables. But she was helpful with driving and directions, and we left it at that. We landed in Acapulco, and she took us straight to the Hotel Sans Souci and we never saw her again.

The Sans Souci was truly "without sadness." It perched on the side of a fragrant jungly cliff overhanging the gaudy Acapulco Bay on one side, and La Roqueta Island and the boiling Pacific on the other. The lush hill side below hid thatched native huts and dry slithering things. We took a cheap airy bungalow with a hammock-slung verandah overlooking all of it, and found paradise.

Mornings we spent at Caleta Beach, frying ourselves in smelly coconut oil and eyeballing hermit crabs as they peeked out from their sandy holes. We haggled with men peddling stuffed armadillos, and a fisherman wearing a necklace of shark's teeth gave Pat a jar of sea life—tiny sea horses and porcupine fish—which she kept in a pan of sea water under her bed. Afternoons we'd spend making the rounds of the big resort hotel pools, having a dip, sipping Cokes, looking for movie stars.

At night the soft winds huffed against our bungalow screens, making the clinging geckoes cheep, and the waves shushed us to sleep. Sometimes a coconut fell with a comical *whock!* or creatures in the brush thrashed and screamed. One evening the sky turned the color of avocado flesh, the moon eclipsed and the hills went red with native fires and drums. At dawn it was all ashes.

The Sans Souci was a beautiful old place, but like Barbara it was kind of mysterious. It wasn't just how the moon shadows of the nodding palms crept across our beds at night. Or what we heard through the taco-thin walls. It had something to do with the skinny woman with the painted purple lips and hair dyed the colour of rusty tin cans. One night we saw her slinked in the hammock of the Sans Souci patio—with a pistol in the pocket of her pink capri pants.

Those torch-lit Acapulco nights, with bronzed-gods divers at La Quebrada plunging from the cliffs, brought out something wild in all of us. Pat went from chasing Luna moths to chasing five-foot iguanas with evil leathery eyes. Susie befriended a native girl who showed her how to slide down the liana vines to the cliff's sea-sprayed rocks. And little Jan fell madly in love with a young resort hotel owner named Carlos, who let her sing Elvis Presley songs over the microphone with his hotel Mariachi band. Peg was like a Mayan goddess now, her wonderful aquiline nose the colour of baked clay, and I felt restless and ached for romance.

Yes, Acapulco was a place for romance—not a place to be seen with your mother and sisters. And one fateful day on the diving board of the El Presidente Hotel pool, I met tall, dark and handsome Armando. Not a beach boy or gigolo, I could tell by his respectful looks. He said he was an *abogado*—a lawyer!

Armando invited me to join his friends Mario and Frankie, to go see the famous sunset at Pie de la Cuesta. "Ees fantastico!" he exclaimed, describing how the sun plopped into the ocean "like a beeeeeg eggg plopping into a frying pan."

Around and around the hairpin turns, chasing the blazing ball before it sank too low. I'd be back at the Sans Souci before Peg even knew I was gone. Just in time to see Acapulco lights blink on in the bay. To stand on our bungalow balcony all rapt in the afterglow of what I would proudly call my first date.

With the rays of a mauve sun shooting through them, the monstrous waves at Pie de la Cuesta filled and burst like gigantic luminous lungs. Truly it was, as one guide book said, "the most spectacular sunset in Mexico." It was also, as Fodor's called it, "a death trap," with 20-foot-high waves, a deadly undertow, and sharks...

How they let me wade out so far, I don't remember. All I remember is having my legs yanked out from under me and being sucked down into the dark. Churning and foaming like a rag doll in a Maytag. Being smacked hard and lifted up, and thrown close to shore. Standing up stunned, salt-blinded and trying to walk. Being dragged down again and coughed up, until I felt my arms being pulled off my body and the sand scraping my belly...

I should have been grateful to be alive. But I stood before Armando, Mario and Frankie, my handsome rescuers, all skinny and prickling with goose bumps, with sand in my teeth, my tangled hair, my burning nose, and a huge humiliating lump of it hanging down from the crotch of my fake tiger-skin bathing suit.

We finally made it back to Indianapolis, after crossing the border at Matamoros in the middle of a drug raid, and getting stuck in a sand trap in Texas. I felt proud riding up North Delaware Street and into our driveway in a station wagon all loaded down with Mexican pottery, piñatas, tin pineapples and rebozos, and a limey-green sweater for Dad. I was feeling worldly and grown-up and excited to start high school. But the festive green sweater we'd bought at the market in Cuernavaca, knit by hand with nubby wool, never fit Dad.

I wrote a letter to Armando. I picked the Spanish words out of Cassell's dictionary, blissfully ignorant of such things as conjugation and syntax.

September 3, 1961

To desire Armando,
    How to be your law to go? I to start to tall school and to be aroused. But we all sisters to get sad surprise when my father to leave my mother. I to have fear of to divorce.
    I to miss you very much, and to want to come Mexico some day.
All my love,
your Nancita

Fun City, 1969-1979

> BUSK v.i. Brit. To entertain by dancing, singing, reciting, or doing tricks on the street or in a pub; to perform plays in rural areas, esp. with simple theatrical equipment and in make-shift theatres; to travel to rural areas to swindle the inhabitants.
>
> —*Random House Dictionary*

Blame it on that cheap piece of tin with six holes. It caused my downfall, from an Upper East Side brick-walled one bedroom with wood-burning fireplace, and a swinging single life dating *New York Times* editors and free-lancing for top national magazines—to a West Side Story tub-in-kitchen tenement, with professional hotel thieves, pimps, junkies and transvestite-prostitutes for neighbors, and an Irish bagpiper and his vacuum cleaner of an instrument as intimate companions.

Blame love. Insomnia...butterflies...a feeling of wild rapture and boundless energy—I had all the symptoms. But it wasn't a man.

That tin whistle had looked like a kid's toy—a plastic mouthpiece stuck on the end of a piece of metal tubing punched with holes. But the music it made was a bewitching siren's song. After I first heard it, I didn't sleep for three years.

I first became unhinged by the sounds of Irish traditional music in November of 1973. On an impulse one night I went down to Greenwich Village and ended up at a concert in the Washington Square Methodist Church. A tatterdemalion band filled the stage, playing strange instruments that looked like hat boxes and vacuum cleaners. The music was wild, ethereal, lonely and playful, and it hit me with an odd painful force. The concert started at 8 p.m. and was still going strong at 1:30 a.m., but I had to leave. I was completely and utterly overwrought by the sounds I'd been hearing for the first time.

And as I was to find out later, I wasn't the only one. There were concertina players of English sea chanteys and Old-Timey bluegrass fiddlers discovering The Music too. They found it so melodically challenging that they abandoned their other musics, and with the fervor of born-again converts, packed off to the bog to learn tunes from the source. It was happening on the East Coast. It was happening on the West Coast. It was happening in St. Paul and St. Louis. It was an epidemic. In New York, a small group that called itself *An Claidheamh Soluis* /The Irish Arts Center was coalescing around the idea of spreading an awareness of Irish traditional culture outside the Irish community. Its zealous founder was Brian Heron, the grandson of James Connolly, the Irish Republican hero and leader of the Easter Uprising, executed in front of the Dublin General Post Office in 1916. Heron wanted An Claidheamh Soluis to be a "Sword of Light" reviving an interest in the Irish language, but it was the wildness of the music that drew people to the organization. Hundreds of us. Heron and his friends were the raggle-taggle band on that stage.

Mattie Haskins' Gift Shop on Second Avenue was one of the few places in America that sold Irish records not plastered with silly shamrocks. Somebody at the Irish Arts Center concert had told me "Get The Chieftains!" and so I found them, albums with pagan-looking inkblot renderings of scenes from the Gaelic epic the *"Tain Bó Cuailgne"* (The Cattle Raid of Cuailgne) and dance tunes with names like *"Pis Fhliuch* and *An Falaingin Muimhneach"* and "The Lilting Banshee" and "The Munster Buttermilk." On the backs of these albums were pictures of penny whistles, wooden flutes, fiddles, concertinas, Irish harps, sheep's bones, goatskin drums—bódhrans—and *Uilleann* pipes, the cantankerous bellows-blown Irish bagpipe that resembled something an octopus would copulate with, and sounded like "a hive of honeyed sounds" when its reeds were well tuned. And when they weren't—like a sack of roosters accompanied by an old Edsel horn.

Mattie Haskins also sold tin whistles for $2. I greedily bought one and tried it out in the shop. I couldn't believe it was the same instrument I'd heard the night before, sweetly chirping, sadly keening, wild, sassy and bold. When I blew it, it screeched like a scared bat.

I rang up the handsome bearded fellow I'd seen playing it at the concert and pestered him to give me lessons. The next week I was down in Little Italy in his storefront littered with bamboo shavings, fumbling with the notes of the jig "The Blarney Pilgrim." Bill Ochs from West Orange, New Jersey had given up theatre directing when he'd heard Liam Og O'Flynn playing the Uilleann pipes. Now, when he wasn't scraping and shaving bits of cane into what he hoped would be the perfect Uilleann pipe reed, he was hollowing out pieces of bamboo to make flutes to peddle on the New York streets. Even in winter, you'd see him playing his penny whistle or bamboo flute to attract customers, a Dickensian figure of tattered elegance in an old blue greatcoat, wearing gloves with cut-off fingers.

Bill's passion for the Uilleann pipes bewildered his parents, but not those of us who gathered around him to learn this music and tap our feet on his sawdusty floor. There was an Irish-American carpenter who wanted to learn the fiddle; a Polish lad who sang English sea chanteys, did Balkan dancing, coaxed tunes from a tent pole, and was mad to learn the concertina; a young Irish-American woman who wanted to play Irish airs on the flute she'd found in a trashbin, and me. We destroyed ourselves with late nights in Irish bars, playing tunes until our fingers ached, and hung out together to reinforce our new habit—mainlining jigs and reels.

I felt like Pinocchio skipping school to run off with the fox and the cat. Bill the Whistle Master made that little tin whistle do rolls and cuts and double-cut rolls and cranns, and all sorts of ornaments that thrilled me and made me jealous. I practiced my whistle while waiting for my tea water to boil, and for the subway rats scampering along the tracks while I waited for my train, coming home from music sessions in the Bronx at 2 a.m. I played it for hours and hours a day, until one day it dawned on me that learning "The Cow That Ate the Blanket" was more important to me than getting published in *The New York Times*. In my heart of hearts I knew it was much more than tunes with silly-sounding names that I was embracing, and that I had to follow this obsession wherever it would lead me. But I had no idea that it would be to a tinker's camp in Dublin, a steak-and-kidney pie factory job, a stint as an Irish traditional music columnist for *In Dublin* magazine, a haunted cottage on a primitive Irish island, and the streets of Paris.

Irish traditional music was causing chain reactions in my life. The spring of 1974 I found myself at another concert where a raven-haired, electronic-age Celtic bard in a white gown, with a gold triskell medallion flashing from his chest, held the audience enraptured. Alan Stivell had come all the way from Brittany to play on a medieval harp strung with bronze wire. He plucked the glittering strings, making wild music of satyrs, like chimes in a marble cave. It wasn't the saccharine, simpering sound made by the classical concert harps strung with gut. The sound of fingernails ringing on this harp's wire strings was bold, blood-stirring. I craved one of these instruments like a hot kiss. But I was disappointed to learn that they hadn't been made for a thousand years, except by the father of the New Age Breton bard himself, M. Cochevelou.

Around this time, the sensual dark-eyed piper with whom I'd immigrated to Hell's Kitchen, whom I'll call Hornpipe, got the urge to learn wood turning, to make Uilleann pipe chanters. He enrolled in a free woodworking class at George Westinghouse Evening Trade School in East Flatbush in the back-of-beyond of the Borough of Brooklyn. After he dropped out in frustration, I picked up the pieces.

I didn't know a spokeshave from a battering ram. The Italian teacher with eyebrows like turkey feathers had never seen a harp, except Harpo Marx's glissandos on TV. Other students were making stereo cabinets, bookcases and baby cradles. I, the female, had this cockamamie project to build a copy of the harp pictured on the Guinness bottles, the 14th century harp with 30 wire strings preserved in Trinity College, Dublin. The teacher thought I was nuts, but his male ego was ready to take me on.

Gepetto was alternately helpful and obstinate. Great with his mortis and tenons but stupid about acoustics. To him, an Irish harp was a just piece of fancy furniture with a lotta holes. And so after I'd spent nine months poring over Armstrong's *Irish and Highland Harps* and letters dated 1785 describing the inflecting and tending forces of the latitude of the pulse of musical strings; and after chiseling, shaping, sanding the pieces of wood on the subway ride from 49th and Broadway to Bay Ridge, Brooklyn and back—when I had finally joined the neck and forepillar to the body, Gepetto doggedly insisted that I glue in the tuning pins.

"You can't glue them in!" I shouted over the buzzsaws. "You have to turn the pins around—to tune the harp!"

"Trust old Gepetto.. I say glue 'em in, and you'll be set for Carnegie Hall."

In June, 1975 the Board of Education of The City of New York awarded me a diploma for the satisfactory completion of all 120 hours of the course in Advanced Cabinet Making. I carried the new-born instrument that Derek Bell, harper with The Chieftains, would one day admire, back home to 46th Street, strung it up with brass and bronze wire, tuned it, and tape recorded its first ringing cry.

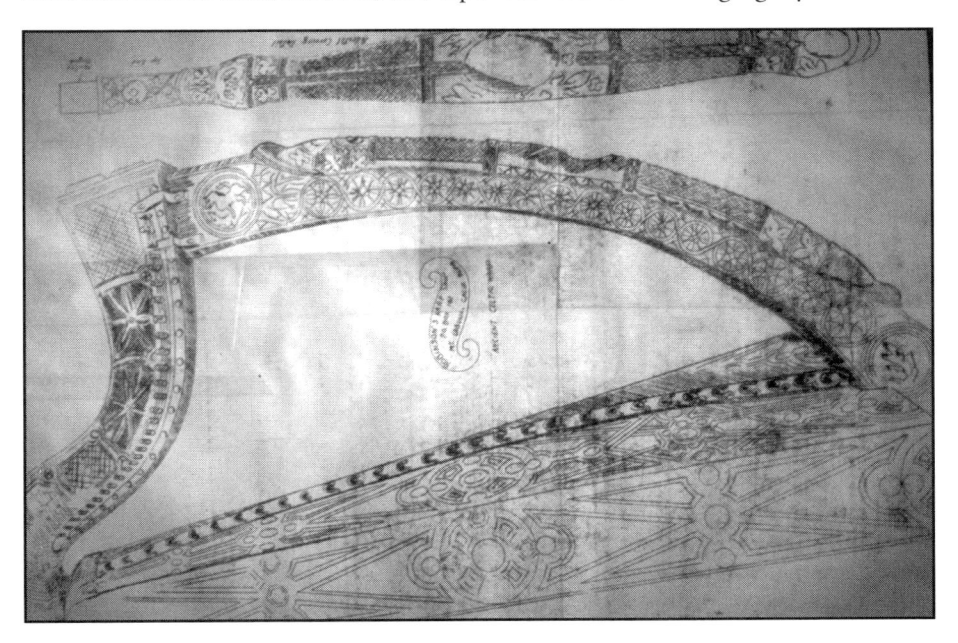

Honest to God, this street troubadour business really started out as a lark. I'd been playing my harp for only three months when Hornpipe dared me to play it on Fifth Avenue.

"I might get arrested. I...I've only got three tunes, " I protested. "The old harpers apprenticed for seven years before they plucked even a single note in public!"

"You're not playing for lords and ladies for God's sakes. And you won't get arrested."

So one muggy July afternoon, I put on a dress, slung my harp over my back and walked over to Fifth Avenue. At 53rd Street, on the steps of St. Thomas Episcopal Church, I unfolded the bright orange canvas camp seat sure to attract cops like a bull. I tugged my harp out of the patched canvas case I broke 23 sewing machine needles to make, and timidly sat down.

Lordy! I felt like an elephant in a zoo, waiting to be thrown peanuts. A duck in an arcade waiting to be hit by the ball. With a goofy plastic smile and shaky fingers, I started up the frisky jig "Scatter the Mud," and hoped that Denis Hempson wouldn't curse me from his pine box for desecrating the old tunes like this.

Denis Hempson, the last of the old Irish harpers to play upon a wire-strung instrument, expired in 1807, at the age of 112. He died with his dear old harp, solace and bedfellow, in the bedclothes—after playing it for a hundred years. The only noises Hempson had to put up with at those castle banquets were the snores of the listeners whom he put to sleep with his gaily tinkling strings, and their groans as they tumbled from the table onto the floor. What would the blind old harper say of my efforts to bring forth the noble strains of the ancient battle march of King Brian Borumh, Ard-Ri slain in the Battle of Clontarf in 1014—against the wails and bus exhaust of Fifth Avenue?

"Daft! Ye's 're all daft!"

It was daft, and people stopped and stared, dumbfounded to see a 14th century harp alongside a 20th century pretzel vendor. It most certainly did not have the effect upon the listeners that 12th century ecclesiast Geraldus Cambrensis had described, of exhilarating dejected minds, clearing the clouded countenance and removing superciliousness and austerity. But these people *did* toss me coins. Who cared if I only had three tunes. Nobody stayed for more than a few bars. And in the tumultuous roar of the city rushing to get home, the tunes sounded alike anyway.

"Thirty dollars!" Hornpipe exclaimed when I got home and hour and a half later.

It was beginner's luck. If I had been moved by a cop that first hour, I would have quit there and then. But after that first jackpot day, I bought a little amplifier and was in business, Tuesday through Friday from noon to 2 p.m. on Fifth Avenue. For two weeks I didn't see a cop. Then the merchants started cracking down on the street sellers and vagabond troubadours, and I was forced to play a game of musical pitches. When I got moved from the great glass wall in front of Alitalia at #666, I went across to the Spanish Tourist Office. When I got moved from there, I set up in front of the Tishman Building. And when they wouldn't have me there, or when the lady bagpiper got there first, I went down to Scribner's Bookstore, which I loved for its literary aura and great acoustics.

Under the striped awning in front of the glass window, I perched my amp on top of the brass fire extinguisher outlet. I'd chat with the Irish guard stationed at the building next door, and got friendly with the book-delivery men. The guard kept a look-out for the cops, and the book delivery men warned me about the deliveries. Every pitch has a kink or two. At Scribner's, when it wasn't the menacing blind man with the rattling tin cup and the German shepherd who growled in my face, it was the metal hatch door I was sitting upon. Every 30 minutes it opened up to receive book deliveries. I had to move off it or else be lowered into Scribner's basement. Some days I thought it mightn't be a bad idea to end my meager set of tunes with a vanishing act.

Every day I marveled at my new income. It was friendly, virgin money compared to plastic credit cards and computerized checks. Busking was honest work and it made perfect sense. Up to now, I'd been splitting my head juggling articles on a variety of topics including vitamins, rock climbing, sex therapy, non-sexist toys, blue-collar resorts, and yodeling.

Why slave away at freelance magazine assignments that took months to research and get paid for and always involved compromises—

> "Our *Town & Country* readers are glamorous people. Remember to bring in some movie stars and fancy Upper East Side doctors when you're writing your story about the cholesterol controversy... infidelity... jet lag... dog health"

—when I could make thirty dollars instant tax-free cash in an hour?!

And not only cash! Jelly beans, joints and love letters; Cracker Jack toys and bouquets of daisies; sketches and Polaroid photos and poems scribbled on the spot; roasted chestnuts and Jesus bumper stickers; theatre tickets, party invitations, porno club tokens and Grand Marnier crepes. And sometimes extraordinary things, like the keys to a thatched Irish cottage in Connemara for three months, and an invitation to play for Jacqueline Onassis and friends at a private cocktail party for patrons of the Metropolitan Museum.

One day on Fifth Avenue, a public relations firm manager came up and hired me on the spot to provide music to celebrate the opening of the Metropolitan Museum's Exhibition of Irish Art. At the noisy party, at which I was barely audible, I spotted Jackie O. through the gladiolus leaves and Nelson Rockefeller by the punch bowl. After the $250 Ritz gig I hopped a cab back to Hell's Kitchen, threw on jeans, and ran around the block to teach my $25 tin whistle class at the old garage on 51st Street, formerly used to bullet-proof Mafia getaway cars, which was now reincarnated as the Irish Arts Center.

Denis Hempson's 18th century patrons had been the Anglo-Irish gentry, merchants and landholders who lived in elegant country demesnes. My patrons were ex-first ladies and billionaires—and Chinese waiters, financiers, hardhats, ballerinas, editors and wrestlers—the Greater New York populace! They lived in penthouses and walk-ups, condos and tenements with cockroaches, but the only land most of them held were the sacks of earth they bought at Woolworth's to pot their fire-escape geraniums.

My father would say I'd taken a tragic 17-story fall from grace. My mother would say I'd come up in life, having found my passport to adventure. However you saw it, down or up, there I was on the streets of Manhattan, soliciting coins. Sitting with my knees squashed under a portable camp stool in front of the Corning Glass Building, the very same building I'd worked inside on the 17th floor ten years before—for Marion Gough, the travel editor of *House Beautiful* magazine.

A pratie is an Irish spud—a good old Gaelic potato—and "The Gander at the Pratie Hole" is a great old Irish jig. But I bet Marion Gough never heard it on a press trip to Ireland. Sitting there plinking out this plucky tune, my fingers warmed by cut-off gloves against the November chill, I half-wished the worldly traveller would come back from cruising the Amazon or shooting kangaroos in Australia and see me. I loved the irony, but I could hear Elmer's dismay. Yeah Dad, your daughter started her New York City career in a fancy Fifth Avenue office building, and finished it as a street urchin ragamuffin busker...

I never imagined that I'd stay in New York City for 15 years, or that I'd take up with street gypsies when I seemed bound for the editorial heights. Fresh out of Indiana University that summer of 1969, I'd landed a job that jump-started my writing career. I was one of 33 journalism students across the U.S. chosen by the Magazine Publishers Association for a summer magazine internship in New York City—a five-week editorial stint at *Forbes* magazine, followed by five weeks at *House Beautiful*—with a weekly salary of $77.52, airfare to New York, and swanky cocktail parties and tony lunches at the St. Regis, the Plaza and various other ritzy New York hotels, hobnobbing with editorial luminaries of *Time, Look, Newsweek, Harper's, Cosmopolitan,* and *Esquire*.

The foyer of the elegant old *Forbes* building on lower Fifth Avenue housed a tycoon's private museum—Malcolm Forbes' collection of fabulous Fabergé eggs. I loved to dawdle in front of the cases of luminous jewels on the way up to editorial, where, because of my lack of business acumen, I didn't quite fit in.

My first week as an intern I spent lots of time getting my hands dirty reading *The New York Times,* going to the bathroom to wash the ink off, and staring at the coffee stains on my blotter. At last I took it upon myself to come up with a story idea. I noticed that *Forbes* hadn't done a story on the funeral industry in quite some time. I stumbled on a news item about how cryogenics was being used to quick-freeze bodies for suspended animation seconds after death. I thought this was odd and provocative, but a top editor said "Just because we haven't done a story on the funeral industry in the last ten years doesn't mean we have to do one now."

On Malcolm Forbes' 50th birthday, he walked around the office passing out crisp $50 bills. I took mine and invited an intern from California for drinks at the posh Tavern on the Green in Central Park. Sitting under the Perrier umbrellas, sipping whiskey sours, we felt almost like famous published writers...

After *Forbes*, it was *House Beautiful* magazine. My first day there I arrived panting—having taken the subway 55 blocks out of the way, and a swerving rush-hour ride back uptown to the Corning Glass Building, where I was deposited without a penny of lunch money. Then I was sent to Marketing Research, where I was taught how to put gnat-size pencil dots onto yards of paper. After that my letters back home began... "Life is getting duller and duller as I record the numbers of adult, female purchasers of washing machines in the last year who own Frigidaire separate home freezers."

Other interns were getting by-lines in *Newsweek* and their names on their magazine's masthead. One even got to work on the *Time* magazine mafia cover. She scoured the city picking up brass knuckles, switchblades, bludgeons and bombs, and a sawed-off shotgun—to use as for props for the cover shoot.

I was fed up alphabetizing filing cards at *House Pitiful* and started wandering around editorial on my lunch hours. One of the editorial ears I bent belonged to a matronly buxom blonde, who happened to be the travel editor. Just my luck—Marion Gough was looking for a full-time assistant. Sitting on a white kid sofa in her office crammed with travel books and souvenirs from every continent, discussing the job in detail, I felt I'd finally arrived.

Every morning after that an avalanche of travel press releases awaited my trusty letter opener. Zip, zip. Ireland by bicycle. Zip, zip. France by balloon, the Amazon by raft, the Rhine by barge. Zip, zip, zip China...Cuba...Mozambique, and honeymoon specials to the Seychelles. Honey, be a travel editor, and we'll give you the whole planet.

I expected to hate New York City, but I loved it. It was friendly, dangerous and alive. All of us magazine interns, wide-eyed ingenues in Fun City, were lodged in Columbia University housing up on 116th Street and Broadway, on the spooky edge of Harlem. My spartan little writer's garret with a grafitti-carved desk overlooked the bright lights and traffic streams of The Great White Way. Every morning I'd eagerly put on pert a Midwestern suit, stick a subway token in my shoe in case I got mugged, and join the sweaty mash of commuters on the grubby Broadway IRT downtown. From my Harlem aerie over the Hudson I wrote letters back home about New York's extremes—underground, a drunk mumbling to a subway candy vending machine "Mirror mirror on the wall, I am the ugliest of them all" while on the street above, a slick blonde *Vogue* magazine model posed for a fashion shoot at the Plaza Hotel. And I wrote about the subway that brought all these people together, for better or worse.

One day at Astor Place I'd watched as 20 people put their tokens in slots, then rammed against the old wooden turnstiles which *wouldn't* turn, because the token slots had been jammed with wads of paper by a wiry young con. And I chortled watching him go from token slot to token slot, bending down and SUCKING out each token—*upffp! upffp!*—without choking himself!

On Moon Day, July 21, 1969—the day I gathered with thousands in the romantic twilight in Central Park's Sheep Meadow to witness Neil A. Armstrong and Edwin E. "Buzz" Aldrin, Jr. taking "The Giant Step for Mankind" on drive-in-movie sized screens—I had been saved from hopping to work on one shoe. That day all the subway cars were over-crowded and delayed. As I was squeezing out the subway car at Times Square, my red Papagallo slipped off my foot and the subway doors closed. I hopped around on the chewing-gummy platform, waving my arms at the crowd inside the car. Then, as the train pulled out of the station, I watched my shoe sail out the car, fly over the platform and slap an old Italian man on the cheek.

    I had planned to stay in New York City only a year, but after a few months at *House Beautiful*, I stumbled upon a copy of *New York Magazine* featuring a Bowery bum on the cover. The bum was actually a writer who had dressed up like a bum and lived on the Bowery streets without money for two weeks—just to see what would happen. That night I wrote an excited letter to this daring new incarnation of the old *Sunday Herald Tribune* magazine, asking for a job.

    A month later I was on the masthead as editorial assistant to Executive Editor Sheldon Zalaznick, going to work in a funky fourth-floor walk-up on East 32nd Street, where hot-pants were acceptable office attire and joint smoke went unremarked. I felt lucky then, as I feel lucky now, to have been on the scene in the magazine's heyday, with visionary Editor-in-Chief Clay Felker directing a cast of soon-to-be celebrity writers—Dapper Tom Wolfe in his summery white suits and spats, the Kandy Kolored Tangerine Flaked King; the flaxen-haired Gael, Gail Sheehy, checking the emotional pulse of our lives; Street-Talkin' Tough Jimmy B. the Breslin, Scandalous Detail-Junkie Julie Baumgold, and my Gotham City heroine, lanky gorgeous Gloria Steinem in her tinted aviator glasses, Superwoman *Savant* who founded *Ms.* magazine.

    It was genial teamwork, made all the more fun by the staff champagne breakfasts at the Four Seasons, lunches at Maxwell's Plum, glamorous movie premieres, press trips, parties at Clay's penthouse, and miscellaneous perks. I still have the certificate from the Ringling Brothers Barnum & Bailey Circus bestowing on me the coveted title of "Elephant Equestrian Extraordinaire" after my successful trek from the Circus Yard to Madison Square Garden—"Perched Precariously on a Ponderous Pachyderm"—riding a bare-backed naked elephant through the streets of Manhattan. "Hang on to her ears!" the Dutch trainer screamed to me from very far below at an ungodly early a.m. as my renegade beast named Efa twirled her two-ton head and refused to grab the tail of the old gray one in front.

    At *New York Magazine* I graduated from fact-checking 5,000-word Julie Baumgold social exposés to writing "Passionate Shoppers." I greedily collected bylines. "Where to Buy Your Bird"..."Homage to Fromage"... "What's Open on Sunday." But after three years of writing about where to rent a gorilla suit; where to buy organ-grinder monkeys and desert tarantulas, and how to bid for 500 pounds of confiscated bean curd and 162 dozen door peepers at a U.S. Customs Bureau auction—I flew the coop. I went freelance.

When my mother was a little girl, street performing was a fact of New York City life. In 1923, there were 800 organ grinders and 800 other varieties of musicians licensed to play on the streets. When my mother heard that organ grinder grinding up Riverside Drive, she'd hang out the window of her first-floor apartment and wave a peanut in the air. The memory of that monkey's hairy paw snatching it from her little palm makes her giggle to this day.

In the early 1930's, when Central Park was a shantytown for the homeless, busking was one of the best ways to survive the Great Depression. Manhattan streets were filled with gleemen and minstrels, troubadours and jongleurs who danced, sang, juggled, conjured, told stories, twanged on guitars and mandolins and lived off their piles of nickels and dimes.

In 1936 Mayor Fiorella LaGuardia put an end to it all. He signed a law forbidding street performing. Buskers became objects of pity and scorn. The only ones who ventured into the streets were the "legless, armless, blind and maimed," who played on cracked violins and wheezing accordions and used their poor shabby instruments as an excuse for begging.

Now it was different again. The 70's folk music revival had turned the street into the New Age Vaudeville—the place to learn the ropes and get discovered. I wrote about it for the Sunday *New York Times* Arts and Leisure Section on August 17, 1975. But the version I gave them, featuring James Grasek, a classical violinist earning money to pay for his concert in Carnegie Hall, wasn't all there was. The New York City streets, the cruelest stage in the world, were also a very forgiving stage for weirdos.

There was the wild-eyed, shell-shocked opera singer on 57th Street, who made dramatic sweeping arm gestures in between stomps of his combat boots, and crooned into his army canteen "microphone." And the guy in the Greenwich Village doorway trying to get music out of an empty anti-freeze container. He blew it, plucked and strummed it, beat it like a drum, totally lost in himself. And the black Evangelist who shimmied around with Vicks inhalers hanging out of her nostrils. And Gypper the Gypsy with the dirty noserag, in his greasy black pantaloons, big earrings and a bandanna tied over his brown forehead like a pirate. Conning crowds with fast talk and smutty humor, cheap magic tricks and demonstrations of how he picked pockets.

In Central Park I watched a man direct a turtle race with 15 turtles of different sizes and colors that had never heard of a straight line. At least it was livelier than the show I'd seen at the market in Portland, Oregon—a guy performing a "Trained Sponge" act in which he tried to coax a square bathtub sponge to jump over a broom.

After my first month of playing my harp in Midtown, I started recognizing the cops on their beats. They were usually courteous, but they treated me like a little girl who should know better than to use the nice Fifth Avenue for begging. One crisp September morning I was sitting all alone in front of the Alitalia Building with two lousy quarters in my harp case. I was bored enough to be playing the shoe game I'd invented to play when I got bored. Sitting only two feet from the ground allowed me to see a lot of shoes. Stilettos, combat boots, jelly sandals, nurse's whites, smelly gym shoes, spikes, platforms, shiny, scuffed, curled at the toes and down at the heels. As people walked by, I tried guessing their ages, faces and professions by their shoes. As I was playing my little game, a shiny black pair came over and stopped. I looked up to see a night stick and a gun.

"Are you soliciting money, ma'am?" said the young rookie cop in a wooden voice, as if quoting scripture.

"Nope, I'm working. This is my job."

"I got a job to do too, ma'am. Soliciting is against the law."

"But officer, I've only got fifty measly cents in my case. Will you lose your job if you don't move me?"

"Now, now—don't you have a big pile of quarters hidden away there somewhere? You people must make hundreds a day, at $20-$30 an hour...Let's see, that's $240 a day, $1,200 in five and—weekends you must really haul it in."

"Oh yeah, maybe those mean steel drummers haul it in, but I'm just a poor struggling 14th century Irish harper. Besides—nobody's got the finger stamina to play music eight hours a day. And you don't give them a *chance!*"

"Got a problem, Arnie?" said an older cop who had strolled over from his side of the street.

"Officer," I said politely. "Could you please tell me once and for all, what are the laws against street musicians in New York City? You guys just move us whenever the whim strikes, whenever you're bored or feeling testy, or—"

"—Whenever there's a crowd blocking pedestrian traffic," said the sergeant.

"—um..." I said, looking around. "Where's the crowd?"

The sergeant looked quizzically at the young cop, who shrugged.

"Or when merchants complain it interferes with their trade," explained the sergeant.

"So if someone gives me a quarter, he won't go buy a shirt at Bendel's?"

"Well..." muttered the sergeant. "uh, the New York City Administrative Code requiring licenses of street musicians was repealed in 1970, so now you're all lumped together with peddlars, itinerants and beggars as 'undesireables.' Technically, there's no such thing as a street musician's permit, but if you really wanna play in the street, you need three kinds of permits."

"Excuse me?"

"Yeah, I know it sounds contradictory. But you need a Street Fair Permit from the Office of Neighborhood Government, and then a Sound Device Permit from the precinct you want to play in. And then you gotta get a permit from the Department of Welfare allowing you to solicit funds for a worthy cause, which I guess could be paying your rent. But even if you got all these, the merchants of the Fifth Avenue Association have their say..."

"Which is to say...?"

"They don't like buskers."

"Thanks for enlightening me."

"Look, Arnie, I'll let her play on my side of the street...."

Fancy this, cops turning rivals on my account.

"Thanks guys. I'm much obliged, but I can tell it's gonna be one of those days. Naw, I won't break my fingernails for a few lousy dimes."

Luigi and Arnie had become downright jovial. It must have been when I turned around to pack up that they slipped the bills into the pocket of my harp case. I found the two fivers the next morning.

After a few months of playing on Fifth Avenue, the noise and bus exhaust were giving me colossal headaches. One Sunday afternoon I ventured down to Greenwich Village in search of a quieter spot. I felt nervous in new territory where the cops were used to wilder goings on, and there were spaced-out freaks to watch out for. But I felt encouraged to see, as I emerged from the stinky bowels of the West 4th Street IND station, a plump grandmotherly black woman sitting on a lawn chair with a small stack of children's books spread at her feet. Her life was piled beside her in a bundle, and her sign CLEAN HUMOR FOR ALL AGES announced her trade—a storytelling busker peddling children's stories and clean jokes!

After I played in the Village, I never wanted to play Uptown again. It was looser, friendlier, slower-paced, and I met some unforgettable characters—long grey-haired Silverbell, a gentle aging beatnik who played plunky old-time piano sitting on top of his pick-up truck; James, a black bassist who took me up to Harlem to the Showman's Café, where the jazz band invited me to play some Irish tunes on my tin whistle with them. And Julio, a Latino guitarist who took me to his Spanish restaurant to watch him work the tables. With sweaty passion, he swept from paella to paella, singing sentimental or rowdy Spanish songs that had the diners all wringing their tomato-stained handkerchiefs or slapping their shoes on the table tops.

Greenwich Village was a real stage. Instead of throwing me quarters and passing me by, or asking me stupid questions like—

> "Please miss, how do I get to the Statue of Liberty?
> "Say lady, where can I buy an I LOVE NEW YORK bumper sticker?"
> "Uh...duh... What's a good hard-on porn theatre on 42nd Street?"

—people actually stopped to listen. I was terrified at this rapt attention, but I was thrilled that my music could enchant these strangers. At the end of my little alfresco concerts under the awnings of Baskin and Robbins ice cream shop and various sidewalk cafés, or on Eighth Street late at night, my harp case was bulging with coins, and other forms of appreciation.

One deliriously sunny Sunday, I had a dozen red roses laid at my feet by an Asian woman. Shortly thereafter, I was served a steaming Western omelette that someone in the crowd had flown upstairs to his flat to cook for me. Then a man jauntily crossed the street to a cash machine, and came back to lay a new $100 bill in my case, with good luck wished scribbled on his business card: Editor of *The National Lampoon.*

Death Valley Daze

Did God make this land? Warped, slashed, torn, squeezed, pounded, twisted, scoured, then set afire? Or was it, as some say, conjured by the Devil himself? Bleached skulls, gliding greedy buzzards, flesh shriveled in the sun. Death Valley has a morbid reputation, which its place names seem to celebrate. In the 1900's, newspapers syndicated a photograph of one J.R. Wilson, who worked the graveyard shift at the Coffin Mine near Tombstone Flat in the Funeral Mountains on the eastern rim of Death Valley. The map of Death Valley shows Hell's Gate, Poison Spring, Devil's Golf Course, Bloody Gap, Skeleton Mine, Desolation Canyon, Starvation Canyon, Coffin Canyon, Suicide Pass, Deadman's Pass, Deadman's Gulch, and the Last Chance Mountains. Not exactly names to entice a three-children family in a Nimrod camper!

My first travel article had a kind of Dantean ring to it. Rather hellish for *The New York Times* travel section in November, 1973. But Death Valley's satanic beauty and killer heat scalded the senses, and its morbid reputation fascinated me.
    It was ghastly how you could shrivel with thirst in Death Valley. But even stranger how you could drown here within minutes. Death Valley's annual rainfall was a paltry 1.68 inches, but it could come all at once in a summer cloudburst. With no vegetation to absorb the downpour, it caused flash floods—stirring up a lurid frothy soup of mud, rocks and tangled brambles that avalanched down the mountains, and careened in high walls across the valley floor. Rolling bathtub-sized boulders, wiping out roads

or blocking them, blanketing everything in mud, and making any creature stuck in a canyon a water-logged corpse in minutes.

There were lots of ways to die in Death Valley. But going there in November seemed pretty safe. Even strapped into the cockpit jumpseat of a DC-8 cargo jet loaded with footballs. What a way to greet the west! From the cockpit of the Flying Tiger jet, I devoured my first views of the eerie Nevada badlands and that symbol of Flower Power, the Golden Gate Bridge. My airfare from Newark to San Fran had been a dirt cheap $49 because I'd flown as a courier on Flying Tiger Airlines, carrying a precious hemoglobin sample for an experiment at a San Francisco teaching hospital. To keep the blood cold, I transported it in an ice-filled styrofoam wig stand I'd hollowed out with a knife and spoon. But the joke was that the blood was fake, and so was the "experiment." A hematologist I knew had slipped me a faked letter and an ounce of dog blood. Flying Tiger calculated your airfare according to the combined weight of your body and your cargo, and blood was about as weightless commodity to transport as there was.

After landing in Frisco, I spent a few days soaking up my first views and smells of the Pacific from the pounding edge of Golden Gate Park, reading Frisco poets in the City Lights bookstore, and watching a sage old soul with one-stringed Chinese violin busking in Chinatown. Then I hopped a Greyhound to L.A. for $16.50, to meet up with a *Travel and Leisure* editor with rented wheels, an expense account and a curiosity about Death Valley National Monument.

> Entering Death Valley is intruding upon some Paleolithic time, into a prehistoric loneliness unknown to man. The dried river beds hide dinosaur spirits in their folds, and there is only the sound of a million-year-old wind... Color is this desert's only clock. The travelling sun turns buff mud hills to champagne, then saffron, then streaks them with cinnamon. Salt flats dazzle platinum, then tinge with pink. Mountains marble blue to purple. Dusk opalesces the sky. And on days when clouds shroud the sun, time disappears. In winter, the clarity of the undusted sky extends the vision for hundreds of miles. From Dante's View, the valley's eeriest landscape, you can stand on a cliff edge gazing across to Death Valley's highest mountain, the snow-capped Telescope Peak in the Panamints, 11,049 feet above sea level, and down into the salty carpet of Badwater a mile below, and the Devil's Golf Course, the lowest point in the Western Hemisphere.

The only images of Death Valley I had in my head before going there were from the old TV series "Death Valley Days" with Walter Brennan, sponsored by Twenty Mule Team Borox, and Michaelangelo Antonioni's *Zabriskie Point*, the 1970 pretentiously political film about student angst and revolt. The TV series and the film did nothing to capture the spirit of the place, its awesome silence and astounding geography, but banalized it with gee-haw wagon trains and sex. Antonioni's film made Death Valley look like a neat place for an orgy. Watching actors Daria Halprin and Mark Frechette, you'd never guess it was hot in this 190-mile long, 20-mile wide trough 282 feet below sea level, because they never take a single drink of water in the whole two-hour film! They scamper hatless under the noonday sun, making merry love on the blinding white sand dunes, as hallucinations of other love-making couples with sand-powdered faces fill the screen.

But the Shosone Indians named the lowest point in the Western Hemisphere *Tomesha* "ground afire" because blazes to hell it was. "Hold your hand out in the sun," a grizzled old prospector said, "—and when your fingernails bust loose at the back end, it's 158°F." Death Valley's kind of heat singed the hair off your arms, burnt wings off flies, fried scorpions in their shells, thickened the blood, caused fever, delirium and bizarre hallucinations. One man was found dead with his arms over his head and his hands clutching his shirt and jacket—as if he'd been imagining himself wading through deep water. Another died of dehydration right beside his car stocked with cans of soda.

Tomesha became known as Death Valley after the Bennett-Arcane wagon party of 100 gold-seekers set out from the Midwest in December of 1849 with Bibles and banjos, seeking a shortcut to the El Dorados of California's Gold Coast. The "Forty-Niners" didn't cross Death Valley in murderous summer. But as many as eight of them died and the rest barely escaped two months later, on foot, with a little dried ox meat. Their shortcut to the gold-rich streams of the Sierras had resulted in nightmarish lost wanderings and a horrendous living death. As they crossed over the Panamint Mountains, "Heartbreak Ridge," one of the women looked back and cried "Good-bye Death Valley!"

Death Valley is hyperbolically hot because the Panamint and Funeral Mountains barricade the rainfall out and the heat in. Summer air temperatures have been known to fume at 135° in the shade and the ground temperature recorded in 1972 at the palm-fringed oasis at Furnace Creek was 201°. But at the center of the 200 square-mile shimmering white crystal salt pan—8,000-foot thick—that was once a salt lake, it could get even hotter.

Hot. As. Hell. So you can imagine my shock to learn that a preposterous stunt-mongering Brit had actually jogged 130 miles over this blistering Hades on earth, in the daytime in the 130°F summer heat, in 58 hours and 30 minutes—wearing a black bowler hat, vest and a dark blue pin-striped suit and a Thames Rowing Club tie. How in hell did Kenneth Crutchlow do it?

I was lying on the Murphy bed of my newly-rented San Francisco apartment on Powell Street right on the cable car line. As the cable car was clanging by with tourists staring in my window as they did every nine minutes, I was staring at Crutchlow's photo on page one of the final edition of the Monday, December 11, 1972 *San Francisco Chronicle*.

In the photo, Crutchlow looked like a walrus in a Colonel Sanders Kentucky Fried Chicken cap. Closer inspection showed that it was a black- and-white striped convict's cap on his head, which was sticking out of the 50°F water of the San Francisco Bay. Under an ornery east wind, with the ebb tide and white caps moving at one knot, he was swimming to shore from "The Rock"—Alcatraz—the notoriously nasty escape-proof island federal prison which had held the country's hardest cons until 1963. Page three photos showed Crutchlow's limp, exhausted blue body being supported by the men who had followed him in the rowboat. But what grabbed me was the mention that Crutchlow had "hobbled across Death Valley as temperatures in the 120's were being recorded there." This crazy guy had walked across Hades in July when I had been nervous driving through it in November, especially over the rubbly road through Bloody Gap and the 1,000-foot deep Titus Canyon, barely as wide as a car. I had to meet him.

I'd met some of Death Valley's other eccentrics, including Death Valley Helen (alias Diamond Lil Wallace) from Wilmington, California, who was going on 80 but still had her figure, and 20 pairs of high-button shoes, 100 antique dresses and a blue net sequined coat, which she wore only a few minutes at a time. She wasn't wearing it the cold November morning I met her—shivering in bare arms on the Death Valley sand dunes in a short dress of fuchsia satin and ostrich feathers, high-button shoes, black lace sequined stockings and red corkscrew curls crowned by a diamond tiara. Paunchy male Forty-Niners were stretched on their stomachs to photograph her in the dawn's early light, while their jealous pot-bellied wives in Capri pants, white heels and jangling ear baubles looked on. Red-head Diamond Lil was back for her yearly appearance at the Death Valley Forty-Niners Veteran's Day Encampment. Over 35,000 trailer owners mobbed the National Monument's nine campgrounds for the celebrations at Furnace Creek, which featured hootenanny breakfasts, chuck wagon lunches, flap-jack eating, burro races, desert hikes, fiddler contests and square dancing under the stars,

Later Death Valley Helen told me that she had once been a sad and lonely person. Then she had learned to sew, and started making her own costumes, embroidering sequins on everything she made by hand and performing (at what I wasn't sure) in Beattie and Calico. "Write to me honey," she said. "Here's my card. I have so many people writin' to me honey, you wouldn't believe. Authors, ministers... God bless you, honey."

>The Forty-Niners and the rip-snorting one-blanket prospectors who came after them raped Death Valley for its gold, silver, copper, lead, talc, asbestos and borax, leaving isolated desert graves and ghost towns in their wakes. Rhyolite, Panamint City, Leadfield, Skidoo, Bullfrog, Chloride Cliff— these were the roistering, brawling boom-or-bust towns attracting gunslinging saloonkeepers, prostitutes and preachers and thousands more. Today's more civilized rock hounds prospect for moonstones, geodes, onyx, agate, turquoise, obsidian, pyrite, jasper, honey opal, tungsten, calcite and a variety of fossils in the nearby Owls Head Mountains.

>Leather skinned Shoshones, glassy-eyed grubstakers—they possess this land still, for they met it on its own terms, fighting its heat delirium and sand storms, gagging on its briny water, eating its insects and piñon nuts, bedding down with its scorpions. Who would live here but misanthropes, heliolaters, mad geologists and jackass prospectors?

I found it amazing that Death Valley had a phone book. I still have the copy of the 1972 edition that I filched from my room at the luxurious Furnace Creek Inn and Ranch. The directory was a 6" x 9" tome with five and a half pages and 62 addresses that included the towns of Baker, Shoshone and Tecopa. I figured that the best way to find out why anyone would choose to live in the most desolate area in the U. S. (even though the U. S. Post Office actually bestowed it with a zip code: 92328) was to ring them up and ask them.

>The first person I called was a man named Tom Williams. And the first thing he said to me was "The people don't pick the desert—the desert picks the people." Five years ago this New York advertising man had been en route from New York City to Las Vegas with his wife Marta Becket, an artist-dancer born on Bleecker Street, when they had a flat tire at Death Valley Junction, pop. 16. "Marta saw the deserted old movie theatre," says Tom, "and within hours we had made up our minds to settle here. The people living here are all mutually dependent on one another, running the hotel, gas station, café, general store and beauty parlor. We just have the same old $5 bill that goes round and round."

Marta Becket was a visionary. Despite the fact that in the desert there was no one for miles around who could serve as an audience, this lithe brunette wanted an opera house in which to perform her modern dances. So while she and Tom lived in a cluster of adobe buildings they rented for $50 a month, and he worked as a job printer and she sold her paintings, they transformed the crumbling movie theatre into the Amargosa Opera House.

The curtain went up in February of 1968 with Marta as dance-mime, comedienne/tragedienne, and Tom as manager, emcee and stage-hand. Marta practiced every day, performing her one-woman show with 15 costume changes three nights a week—often to an empty hall. Then, so she wouldn't feel lonely when nobody showed up to her performances, she painted her own audience—a magical mural of colorful spectators—on the rear wall of the opera house.

> An opera house on the edge of a desert may seem strange, but a grandiose castle—with 18 fireplaces, 50-foot ceiling, a jasper fountain, goatskin curtains, Mediterranean tiles, ornate tapestries, a chiming clock tower and a 1,600 pipe organ rigged up to play duets—smack in the middle of the desert, is even stranger. Death Valley's best-known eccentric is the flamboyant character who built the castle, Death Valley Scotty. Walter Scott was a Kentucky-born lad who left or ran away from home at age ten somewhere around 1878 and headed for the mining towns of Nevada. After working with a desert survey crew and mule team drivers, he became a cowboy in Wyoming, then took up with Buffalo Bill Cody's Wild West Show as a trick rider. Twelve years on the road with Cody, travelling around America and Europe, gave Scott a taste for the fabulous. After he left Cody's show he headed for Death Valley to go prospectin'. Some time after that, he was seen throwing silver dollars to astonished crowds, and hiring a whole Santa Fe train to run him from Los Angeles to Chicago—in a record 44 hours and 54 minutes. What was that Chicago connection all about? In 1922, Walter Scott and the Chicago millionaire named Albert Johnson, whom Scott lured into the desert to improve his health, built the fabulous Moorish mansion with battlement towers and buttressed walls that today is known as Scotty's Castle.

Most of the phone numbers in Death Valley's phone book belonged to the people who worked at the Furnace Creek Inn and Ranch and the Stove Pipe Wells Hotel, and the Death Valley park rangers in straight-brimmed Stetsons.

> "Death Valley is one of the best assignments in the National Parks system," says ranger Frank Ackerman. "There are things to learn here that can't be learned anywhere else on the continent. Death Valley is the largest single desert unit in North America. If you wanted to cover the geologic span represented here, you'd have to make separate trips to the Grand Canyon, Salt Lake City, Craters of the Moon, Glacier National Park, Mount Rainier, Crater Lake and then Los Angeles."

> Death Valley's geological formations may come nearer to revealing the mystery of the creation of this earth than any other group of mountains

and chasms. With buttes, alluvial fans, sand dunes, volcanic craters, playas, and fault scarps, no other place on earth gives so many clues to the natural forces still sculpting the earth. Death Valley is not really a "valley" carved by river action, but a trough-shaped "graben" formed when the mountains raised up and the earth below them sank, scarcely a million years ago. That's only a second in geologic time, yet the rocks here reflect two billion years of the earth's geologic history.

Sandstorms, heat funnels, water spouts—Death Valley has some pretty peculiar natural phenomena, but the strangest are the moving rocks. On a two-and-three-quarter mile long cracked mud playa called "The Racetrack," 600-pound boulders mysteriously zip across the ground by themselves, furrowing straight, curved and even zig-zag tracks 200 to 800 feet long, and ones that even double back on themselves. The geologic explanation is that a slick, wet or frozen surface on this very flat dry lake bed and a gust of wind 100 miles an hour are enough to send these rocks skidding.

It went without saying that Death Valley was hardly a jogger's paradise. Nobody could tell you that better than Kenneth Crutchlow. Crutchlow was not hard to track down in San Francisco. The *San Francisco Chronicle* article stated that the 28-year old, six foot tall, 154-pound English adventurer was the director of the Cathedral Hill Medical Center's Abortion Clinic. I rang up the clinic and arranged to meet Ken there after hours. Post-Alcatraz, this tall thin walrus-moustached Londoner with the cockney accent was looking and feeling pretty good. He seemed easy-going yet enigmatic. In the small clinic room that seemingly contained the entire contents of his life—a cot and a scrapbook of newspaper clippings—he told me about how he came to jog through Death Valley, from Shoshone to Scotty's Castle.

Kenneth had been having dinner on some continent or another with his friend John Fairfax, who did many dangerous things, including wrestling hammerhead sharks bare-handed and stabbing them to death with a knife. John had been boasting "Though I walk through the Valley of Death, I fear no evil, as I am the biggest son-of-a-bitch in the valley." Ken liked the ring of that sentence and tried to repeat it, but he garbled it by saying "Though I walk through Death Valley…" Then and there he decided that he had to take on Death Valley. He would do it all alone, without anyone trailing him with supplies. He would bury water jugs five miles apart before starting out, marking the spots with Union Jacks, and carry salt tablets, snake bite kits and as much food and water as he could in a backpack. And being a dignified Englishman, he vowed he would not remove his suit coat along the journey…

Just listening to Ken's stories made me feel I could almost go anywhere and do anything. His James Bond escapes, ingenuity, bravado and sheer experience were very strong aphrodisiacs. He showed me the clippings and photocopies—from the *Teheran Journal, Malay Mail, Fiji Times, The* (Singapore) *Straits, El Informador,* the *Sydney Herald Sun, Los Angeles Times,* London's *Daily Mail, Daily Sketch,* and the *Pakistan Times,* to name a few. It was shocking how anyone could have packed so much life into 28 years, and do it in style. He knew the dope smuggling scene in Morocco, and the Black Market in Bombay, and had passed as a journalist by printing up his own fake press cards. And once, to stow away on board *The Bremen* luxury liner from New York to Cherbourg, he had taken his belongings to a fancy Fifth Avenue shop, had them gift-wrapped, then walked jauntily on board, announcing to the pursers that he was a visitor taking Christmas gifts to certain passengers. And when climbing up Japan's Mount Fujiyama, Ken told me how at the 8,000 foot mark he had fallen and slid 250 feet—onto a dead body!

He was in deep shock, wondering how he would ever get back down, especially with his shoes in shreds. Then Ken had what he thought was a bright idea. He took the good boots off the dead man's frozen body, and thought he should collect the poor man's passport and wallet as well. But at the very moment he was doing this, he was being surveyed by the Mount Fuji Mountain Patrol—through their telescopes. On his way down the mountain he was met by the Japanese police, who accused him of murder.

I never imagined meeting such a world class adventurer, and in such a place. It was Monty Pythonesque. But it was San Francisco in the early '70's. Looking back on it, I remember thinking that knowing someone who had done all these amazing things—swam from Alcatraz, jogged across Death Valley, climbed Mount Fuji, shot kangaroos and dug for opals in Australia, done time in an Indian prison after being accused of being a Pakistani spy, stowed-away on a ship to New Zealand, been shot at by Indonesian gunboats, bicycled from Los Angeles to Mexico City, and thumbed more than 100,000 miles—once around the world in 97 days with only $24 in his pocket, just to win a pint of bitters—might be the closest I would ever get to doing it all myself.

Irish Roving

Round and Round
A Primer of Irish Pub Etiquette

You offer him another pint.
He says, no he's all right thanks, and sure America must be a grand place.
You say, are you sure you won't have another?
He says, no, I won't.
So you signal to the barman for one refill instead of two, and suddenly the gush of chat and charm slows to a thin miserable dribble. The man at your sleeve looks balefully at the rings of foam in side his empty pint glass, and then petulantly at the television. You were just getting ready to tell him about your Irish roots, the Caffertys of Tooloobawn, Kiltulla—but his stool is now empty.

You blundered. You committed the deplorable, the unforgivable, the greatest offense and atrocity against Irish pub etiquette. You didn't ask yer man a *third* time if he wanted a second drink, and with boldness, joviality and dash.

Sure you didn't even give the man a *chance*. He was only waiting to be asked again, having twice refused so as not to seem too eager or, God forbid, an alcoholic, and he intended all the while to relent on the third time and say with shyly downcast eyes, "I don't mind if I *do*." And then the chat would have bubbled on, exploding with a newfound, profound effervescence.

Now you know. A night in an Irish pub can be a madcap display of wit and malarkey, or funereally sodden, morose and boring. One night a cozy turf fire, a jovial publican, jigs and fiddles, singsong and yarns. The next, a row of old necks craned toward the flickering gozzlebox for "Dallas," with nary a word spoken, grunted or hurled.

The Irish psyche is more tangled than the knotwork in *The Book of Kells*. You will never, ever unravel it, but knowing something about Irish Pub Etiquette will enhance your enjoyment of pub life, for many the only life in Ireland.

A Glossary of Terms

ROUNDS

A group insurance policy against sobriety; a highly complicated ritual involving any number of people, in which drinkers who are pub-crawling together, or those collected within a certain "circumference of attention" each buys a round for the group. Everyone is expected to drink at the same pace—age, fortitude or gender notwithstanding. And everyone must buy—even the ladies. (These days, women are expected to buy back drinks, although men usually buy the *first* round.)

The lofty price of the pint has worked to reduce the size of the once epic-size round these days, but we still hear reports of 30-person rounds, and there are even those who would snigger at this low figure. If you prefer to drink "on your own," neither accepting nor buying drinks, be prepared to be regarded as "mean"—stingy—aloof or ignorant, and henceforth left out of any decent conversation.

HOLY HOUR

"They had to call it something comical," says one about the hours (2-4 p.m. Sundays) when pubs close to wash up glasses, sweep out cigarette butts and throw out drunks. This tragic policy of closure pertains more to the cities of Dublin and Cork than to small towns and villages.

STOUT, PORTER, GUINNESS AND "PINT OF PLAIN"

These names all refer to the same drink. As well, a "half pint" is the same as a "glass," and a "small one" (small'un) is the same thing as a "whiskey" or "half un." So don't make the faux pas of sauntering up to your publican to order two pints of porter, a stout and a Guinness, a glass and a whiskey, a half pint and a small one and a pint of plain!

JAR AND JORUM

These slang terms for a pint originate from the days when a pub was just a room with some old barrels of porter, and you had to bring you own "jar" or "jorum" from which to drink. It should be noted that these terms are applied only in tweedy-capped chat about drink, and discussions of bouts and binges and such. So don't ask the barman for a jar or jorum unless you want to be taken for an ee-jit silly Yank.

COLLAR

This is not what you wear around your neck, but the head of foam on your pint of Guinness. If it's too thick, it's a "bishop," and if it's too thin, it's a "cardinal." Remember to use these terms when registering your complaints with the barman.

ON BUYING

A pint buys jokes, preposterous yarns, false compliments, genealogical info and sometimes even friends. As we have said, always offer at least *three* times. If you should feel intimidated by this little game, and lack the native poise and charm to play it, then forget about asking at all.

Simply note when yer man's or yer woman's drink is three-quarters gone, and nod or shout and roar and wave your arm to the bar man for another round. Timing is critical. If you wait too long to make your move, the man at your sleeve will be pressed to buy your round himself, and this is utterly disagreeable. But what do you do if you have three pints going flat in front of you, and he's drinking so fast he's down to the foam on his fourth? Let the chancer buy his own!

ON ACCEPTING

When being bought a drink, it is appropriate to appear surprised, pleased and grateful, even though you know the drink is only offered as payment for the one you bought, or in anticipation of the one you will buy. But false sincerity makes what is really a crass tit-for-tat appear to be a form of gift giving. It is an Irish pretense you would do well to master.

ON REFUSING

To refuse a drink, protest at least three times and show good cause, i.e. you have seven drinks in front of you already, you are already drunk, you're a lorry driver off to France in the next fifteen minutes, or a champion step dancer off the stuff for the week. If you don't drink alcohol, drink something—*anything*—and try to keep up with the pace of the round, lest you miss your turn.

At an uproarious Irish wedding, the father of the bridegroom offered a pretty woman a glass of scotch. She declined, exhibiting her glass of soda and lime. She didn't drink alcohol, she said. "Well you aren't fit company for a *bullock!*" he raved at an embarrassing decibel.

Yes, some drinkers will be offended if you are teetotaling. Say you're an alcoholic, or already have a hangover or drink Kalibur—the non-alcoholic beer created by Guinness for these situations. (It fizzes like real and only your publican will know for sure.)

Do's And Dont's
For Men:

It's not the done thing to drink Guinness from a glass. Order up pints, men, the only size vessel worthy of your fist. Drinking stout from glasses is a feminine practice, and even the women are giving it up.

For Women:

Ladies are allowed into all Irish pubs these days, city and country, day or night, alone or accompanied by men or children. But this doesn't mean that you will always feel welcome in every venue or comfortable in every pub situation. Big lounge bars, music pubs and venues with "pub grub" are well trafficked day and night. But in certain rural places you're likely to be the only female in the place during the day and early evening.

It's typical for a hush to fall over an uncrowded pub whenever a new person enters. Don't mind the stares and ensuing mumbles. Head straight for the bar like you mean business.

For All:

A pint of Guinness is a thing of beauty to be poured with decorum. Pulling it properly is at least as great a ceremony as pouring Japanese tea. Never, ever display impatience at the necessary pumping, scraping, topping and leveling, and never stare inquisitively at the performance. And when you have your pint in your paw, show due respect. Don't jostle or bruise it or swish it around in the glass. And never, ever ask for ice cold Guinness or beer, or a mug with a handle.

A Final Word About "Closing Time"

The high price of drinks these days has forced Irish people to delay their nightly pub forays until an hour and a half before the closing time of 11:30 p.m. in summer and 11 p.m. in winter. Why? Because they can't afford to go any earlier. Because they want to drink at the pace they are accustomed to, not sit there sipping sappily, measuring their money against the clock face.

Closing time is a variably timed event. Until you are hoisted out the door by your breeches, don't be bothered by shouts and roars of "Out now, ladies and gents! Finish up there!" But do stand for the singing of the national anthem.

Pies: A Farce

1st November…Dublin

Dear Billy,

    Well my friend, summer's last swallow is still here, chasing tunes and elusive music sessions. After my traveller's checks ran out, I took to the streets with my harp. I was doing okay until the arthritic damp set in. (Trying to pry jigs from cold cramped fingers was hardly attracting customers.) So with my fake student work-permit, I went looking for a real job.

    One frosty October morning I borrowed an old black banger of a push-bike and pedalled twenty miles out of Dublin, to Keeling's Apple Orchard to answer their ad for pickers. But when I got there the foreman looked me up and down and said, "Oh, now we don't hire *girruls*. We wouldn't have *girruls* working in the same field with the men." Then I answered an ad for a photographer's model. But it didn't take me more than a few sips of a Guinness to figure out that he was up to something kinky.

    Remember Paul MacDonald, the tall, lanky guitar player with the frizzy Harpo hair? He's started up his own business. Bought a pack of old brushes, strapped them onto his old black bike, made up some funny business cards that say Sam Hall, Chimney Sweep, and set out to seek his fortune in soot. Somehow, he talked me into knocking on doors to look for dirty chimneys at 50 pence a chimney. Anyway, Billy, after three days of knocking on doors—"Wouldja like yer chimney swept, missus?" in my best fake Dublinese (God forbid they should guess I'm a Yank, for they think all Yanks are rich)—I could not find one dirty bloody chimney.

Finally I saw an ad in the *Evening Press*...
> Help Wanted On Pastry Bench
> No Experience Required

Ah, I thought. Peaceful work in a warm place...

I went to see the owner, a surly-looking Frenchman. He asked me if I liked to bake pies, and I said, "Of course." He asked me if I liked to eat them, and I said "Oh, no." Two right answers landed me the job, as a "pastry cook trainee"—at age 32, Billy!—in a steak-and-kidney pie factory right in the grimy heart of the old Dublin Liberties. I went out and bought one of those white nylon frocks, a hair net, and some crummy second-hand shoes. The next morning I showed up for work and was greeted with a doughy handshake and a lump of puff pastry to pound. None of that polite orientation stuff. Only 15 minutes on the job, and I'm rolling pork into little pie-size balls and slopping steak-and-kidney stew into aluminum tins in a place right out of a Dickens novel.

The *A La Français* factory is on Blackpitts Street, still cobbled and overrun with Dick Whittington's cats, rats and forlorn junk shops with dingy windows. It's a small gray building on a grim empty street. I learned from Willie, one of the workers who knows all about Dublin's history, that when they were excavating Blackpitts to build these factories, they found the mass graves of some medieval plague. (Charming site for a bakery). And the old River Poddle, mostly filled in a hundred years ago after it went out of use as an open sewer and repository for tanner's and butcher's wastes, still trickles above ground close by.

All I see of Dublin now, Billy, through the smudgy grilled windows of our pie factory, is rows of chimney stacks and a garbage dump. I bicycle to work in the dark and bicycle home in the dark. But the work is so new for me it's kind of fun. Squishing soft margarine onto trays, rolling sticky sausage into links, fluffing feathery grated cheese. At certain times of the day the place is a frenzy of pounding, poking, rolling, whirling, whisking, heaving. Then we rush to the oven and heave a big sigh.

The other workers are great. Putting out pies is only incidental to the *craic*—the good times. There are seven of us—eight if you count the cat that lives in the oven. A cocky, sinewy Malaysian lad who attacks the dough with Tae Kwon Do blows; a real Dublin woman who should have been in vaudeville; a choleric Frenchman whose two comments through a day are *merde* and ees no funny; a solitary Sligo man who eats his lunch alone among the pigeons on the gray rooftop while dreaming of kinder days gone by living at the Brazen Head; Georges, a cool handsome Austrian; a quiet young Dublin woman newly betrothed, and me, The Yank. In our various Sligo, Dublin, sing-song Malaysian, Alsacian, Austrian and Indiana English, it's a wonder we can communicate at all.

One morning I'm weighing up the ground ham for the quiche and find a big bone in it, and Miss Mullen, the woman I work under, says "Oh! A hambone!" and Jacques says "Hambone? *Jambon!*" and Won howls *"Jambon?* In Chinese that mean loo bowl!" And then Georges, the stiff Austrian, is yelling at me for cracking *fifty* eggs into the quiche wash, when he had said *fifteen*. And sitting around the breakfast on a cold damp morning, Jacques asks me if I miss the comfort of the "central hating" we have in America. Billy, I think this job will be great. Just the pure and simple Zen of Dough. Dough and only Dough. With this I can keep up the writing and the music. And hey! I have a new nickname—Buns!

"Mornin', Buns…"
"Bonjour, Buns…"
"Howeyhyah, Buns?"
"Hallo, Buns…"

After two weeks on the job Buns is starting to get the hang of it: clock in, change into old shoes, throw on coveralls, put up hair and tie on scarf; up the narrow staircase, say hello and grab hunk of marge. Grease the quiche rings, grease the trays, grease the tins. Roll sausages, weigh ham into six-ounce balls, fill steak-and-kidney pies, put hats on the bouchées and fork them, egg wash on sausage rolls, and fork the sausage rolls.

By the time she finishes on the quiche rings, a smudge of rosy light is just breaking through the window, thawing the cold slab of broken marble and softening the neon overhead. Seagulls squawk in the new day and Jacques is at his croissants, folding them into skinny crab shapes. Won is whipping huge vats of cream. Mary is chopping apples for the tarts. Georges is doing his fancy cake batter. Willie is sobering up to the shock of cold trays plunging into scalding water. And Miss Mullen is fussing over the day's orders…

"Fifteen dozen small boo-shays, lordy, five dozen small steak 'n kidneys, mercy, three dozen large steak 'n kidneys, twenty quiche—'is the ham up yet?'—five cheese flans, six doz sausage rolls, well, we has three leftover from yesterday, and eight doz cheese rolls."

"Hang on, Miss Mullen, we'll get it all done. Not to worry, you have me working for you now."

"Youse a good worker, Buns," Miss Mullen says. "Child, youse catch on fast. A few months here, you'll be taking over my job. God knows I need a break after twenty-six years," she sighs, throwing a flap of dough over a quiche ring and pinching it down.

"Twenty-six years! My God, that's a lot of bouchées, Miss Mullen."

"Here's your tea, ladies," mutters Willie. "Buns, yours is schtrong as you like it, but mind yourself, it's schalding."

"Ah thanks, Willie, I'm freezing."

"Trays washed yet, Willie?"

"In a minute, Miss Mullen." Then Willie pauses, eyelids fluttering as if to steady himself, and looks searchingly at Buns. "There must be more to life than this," he sighs. And when he arrives at the sink on the other side of the room, he adds, "To live…is the rarest thing in the world."

Buns can read Willie's mind. She knows he is only counting the minutes until morning break, when he can open the roof door and gaze through the tangled coils of barbed wire, to the wild gray clouds scudding over the cityscape, and the silhouette of Christchurch Cathedral, founded in 1038 when Sitric MacAulaff was Viking King of Dublin. A few inches to the right, five or six rooftops maybe, he could see the old Brazen Head Pub off Merchant's Quay, the most decrepit and most loved hotel and public house in Dublin, whose walls have stood since 1198. Willie must have known more about Dublin than all the journalists of Dublin put together, after living there for 13 years. Why he had to leave he would never say.

"*Schnigffl!*" A rainburst from Miss Mullen. A snifffle quick-doused with flour. "Oh me dead sister. Was sendin' out the Christmas cards last night, but I can't send one to her this year because she's dead."

"*Dead*?"

"Ten months ago. She was just home to us on a visit from Africa—was a missionary over there. And a month after she went back we got a letter that she was dead. Fell down the stairs and broke her hip and died in hospital. Lordy, the cards we got, she was loved I tell you. Hand me up more quiche rings, will you now?"

"I'm so sorry, Miss Mullen."

"I dunno what people's born fer anyway. Might as well die as soon as we're born, for the hardships we goes through in this life," Miss Mullen says, settling the scalloped rims onto the bouchées. Like little sand dollars they bask on the tray. Then she stoops down to the fridge below the bench and grapples, as if with an octopus, to haul up a giant lump of dough. It drapes itself in eight different directions, but with a determined grunt she lands it on the marble. She spreads it out and whacks it hard with her rolling pin. Then she nudges Buns and says, "Oh, child, go fill up the pail with steak-and-kidney. We'se got five doz small today."

"Yes, Miss Mullen, I will of course."

Down to the big dark fridge goes Buns in search of steak-and-kidney. Groping, sniffing in the dark, she bumps into bald ogling turkeys strung by their feet, dangling yards of sausage and sad ear-hung rabbits. Uncovering this tub and that bin, she wonders "where the hell is it?" when her nose detects urine fumes wafting from a big vat, smelling of foul cat. She sloshes up the steak-and-kidney with a big spoon, and pail filled, turns to go, when GLONK! she's locked in. Ten minutes pass…fifteen…

"Oh, Miss Mullen," says Buns, returning breathlessly to the bench. "I had a fright down there. The fridge door shut on me and I had to pound and scream to get Monsieur Quidenay to open it."

"Lordy, woman, no wonder you took so long. I got me a fright too just now. Georges is just after sayin' the health inspectur's visitin' us today. With a mice-scrope, you know, that thing that brings up the germs. We'll all be in trouble if we don't pass inspecshun."

Buns smiles, remembering last week and Miss Mullen mixing up a batch of dough. While the woman's head was turned, the lump of dough climbed up the arm of the mixer and lept onto the floor. Not to worry. Miss Mullen brushed off the sawdust and hairs and droppings and heaved it back into the mixer.

"Well, what will happen if we don't pass inspection?" Buns asks, concerned.

"Monshur Kidney will give out to us. But don't you worry, this place won't never shut down. Kidney's got a deal or somethin' with the inspecter."

Jacques, reaching over Miss Mullen to weigh crumbles of yeast, huffs "Ah, mon Dieu! You would *naever* see place like zis en France. *Naever*…"

"What do you mean?" Jacques, asks Buns.

"Ah, *merde*. Cheap ingredients. Poison food dyes banned in France. Rush rush and no care for *la qualité*. The mean way he treat us—*naever* in France. *Naever!*" he shouts over the whirring blenders.

Jacques, who was lured from France for the job of pastry chef at £130 a week, is sorry he came.

"Oh, my *gawd!*" says Won, joining in with hearty disgust. "Yesteday you know what that mean boss man do? He accidentally step on my fut, and I pull my fut out from unner his fut to get away, you know? And he lose his balance and then he say to me—to *me*—'Won, don't you apologize?' I no take that. I say to Mr. Steak, 'Solly, but you step on my fut. You can apologize to *me*.'"

"Great schtuff, Won," cheers Willie from the sink. "And what did he say to you after that?"

"He said, 'I'll sack youse!'"

It was a mystery to Buns why Won put up with Monsieur St. Quidenay's abuse for his measly wages of £15 a week. His parents owned a rubber plantation near Penang, he said, and sent him plenty of money to live on. Won's father still worked the family rubber plantation, even after Won's grandfather was eaten by a 145-foot python. Yes, it was hard to imagine, but Won had explained that his grandfather was tapping a rubber tree at dawn one morning, right beside where a mother python was guarding her babies, and the mama snake socked him in the head with her head to knock him out, then squeezed him to death, and swallowed him up to his shoulders. Won was happy to be in Ireland, where, thanks be to Saint Patrick, who ran the serpents off the island in the 5th century, there were no snakes of any kind.

"Why do you put up with this job and that man at all, Won?" Buns asks.

"You know, Buns. Because I lovvve Miss Mullen. Because she is so sexxxy. Miss Quiche of 1934. Ooooh!"

"G'won, Won, you cheeky boy."

"Buns, when I finish my fashion design study at Grafton Academy, I go to Paris. You see."

"And you, Miss Mullen," says Buns. "You should be running your own French bakery, for all you know about pastry now. Why do you stick it for 43 quid a week?"

"Because, child, it's close to me bedsitter. And I've worked in worse places. And what do I need more wages fer anyway? I'se got enough for meself. And no matter how much money we gets, we're all going to die just the same."

Miss Mullen takes a flap of dough that she has secretly been lace-poking with holes and places it on Won's black head. "There! a lovely hat for Won. Oh, doesn't he look *lovely* in it?"

"Miss *Mull*-en!" shrieks Won. "Mind the dough! You can't use it now, with my hair in it."

Childlike, wounded, Miss Mullen takes back the dough. She brushes the black hairs off, says "nice hat" and puts it back on the marble slab. A few minutes later, Won pokes Buns and shows her what he has made with a lump of puff: a puppet of Miss Mullen. Won waves the effigy in Miss Mullen's face. And the woman crows with glee and clowns around, strolling with her rolling pin like a flapper with her beads. Then Jacques hears heavy feet on the stairs and whispers "Watch out! Here he comes!"

Monsieur St. Quidenay strides into the room and in a big voice sings:

> Monsieur St. Quidenay's Good Morning Song:
> Ten Black Forests and a 'Happy Birthday, Pappy'!
> Nice and moist—and make it snappy!
> Yesterday's quiche crusts were layered with patches—
> What we're doing here, mending *britches*?
> > What is the *meaning* of zis?!
>
> Complaints about the sausage rolls again:
> The crust's too flaky, the dough's too thin.
> And if you think these scones attractive,
> Wrong you are—my God, I'll *sack* youse.
> > What is the *meaning* of zis?
>
> Won—You sneaked in late today—
> I'll dock ten minutes from off your pay.
> These steak and kidneys are a mess—
> Broken bottoms, ugh—they're *use*less!
> > What is the *meaning* of zis?
>
> And here we are—now don't lie—
> Who puts the steak and kidney in the steak-and-kidney pie?
> Miss Mullen? or is it this Yank?—Fie!
> Look! Can't you read a scale?
> You've put in too much meat!
> How can I make a sale?
> I've got to make my profits
> To pay you all—you *dossers!*
> > What is the *meaning* of zis?

The room is silent as Monsieur St. Quidenay pinches, sniffs and measures his way around the room. Then he is gone.

"I knew he'd give out to you about the steak-and-kidney. What'd I tell ya? Saturday after you all left, he yelled at me, sayin' he'd sack you for fillin' 'em too full. But I says to meself, 'if she goes, I'll go, even after twenty-six years, because we works together.' Lordy I prayed all weekend he wouldn't sack you."

"You prayed about that Miss Mullen?"

"C'mon, child! Grease those rings and fill those tins and hide those broken bouchées so he doesn't see and hand me up three dozen eggs and beat the marge into the puff and fork the pork pie hats and I need four dozen sausage rolls and go ask for more cheese. Jesus Mary and Joseph—hurry, please!"

"Yes, Miss Mullen, I will of course."

"Twenty-six years here—you think I don't know that man! He'd go through you for a shortcut—or steal the steam off yer peas, me god! They'll burn! Jacques!"

"*Merde!*" screams Jacques. "Miss Mullen, you crazee por zee bouchées, always zee bouchées. You want a heart attack por zee bouchées?" Only minutes later, just as Willie has thrown the last of the soggy quiche crumbs to his birds, and Buns has smuggled some more sausage rolls, cheese scraps and a fruit cake into a big straw bag kept for this purpose in the loo, the health inspector arrives. Notebook and magnifying glass in hand, he begins at one side of the room, peering into bins, taking flour samples, flashing his torch into the depths of the fridge, studying the floor on his hands and knees, and glaring critically over each shoulder. An hour later his report is circulated for the workers to read.

Miss Mullen studies it thoughtfully for a moment, then she reads to all gathered around. "Let's see. We'll have to get rid of the cat, it says. And Georges can't use the lightbulb anymore to roll out them sugarcrust rose petals with. And there's something here about not sneezing onto the cakes. And them rotten eggs—I *knew* they'd give out about the rotten eggs—St. Quidenay buys 'em cheap that way—the rest of it says what it always says, we just gotta get rid of the dirt. But this time of year's bad enough just gettin' th'orders out. No time for cleanin'!"

Miss Mullen goes back to her dough, cutting out hats for steak-and-kidneys. She pricks them with forkholes and carries them to the oven. But oops—she slips on some unmopped slop and her dear little pies go flying. They veer and careen, spin and roll on their slick little bottoms, blackened and old. But swoop, she's down like an old mother hen, folding them tenderly to her breast, and then flicking off sawdust, droppings and mould, they look just like new if the truth be told. A touchup job with eggwash slosh will cover the lingering debris. And who will be supposing that the flecks of brown reposing on the steak-and-kidney closing aren't grains of bran or wheat?

A week before Christmas, Dublin's bright shop windows are filled with Black Forest cakes glistening green and red with angelica and cherries, plump friendly fruitcakes, merry Nollaig logs, and jolly marzipan Santas. But the light coming from the smudgy windows of the pie factory where these delicacies are produced has no festive hue. It is a sickly gray ghoulish beacon in the depths of the Liberties blackness. And it glows long, longer, before dawn and after dusk, as the workers inside race to feed a gluttonous oven.

"Mornin' Buns. My—youse the early worm."

"Early bird you mean."

"No, I changed it. Terrible morning—would you look at that mess outside. Mother of God, didn't get a wink last night. Me hot water bottle burst in the bed."

"Oh, Miss Mullen…"

"I brung you more chocolates, downstairs in me bag, don't let me forget. Is the ham up yet? Monshur Kidney was givin' out to me about the sausage rolls bein' too big. You'd think they was fairies buyin' em."

"I don't care, Miss Mullen. About the ham I mean. I can barely stand up. Just came from The Embankment—after-hours jigs and whiskeys. Didn't even see a bed last night."

"Lordy, child! Ye'll destroy yourself. Is the ham up yet?"

"Miss Mullen! Lay off the ham situation! Let's talk about some thing else, like baseball."

"Baseball?" mumbles Miss Mullen, her mouth crammed with bread. "Now neither you nor I knows anythin' about baseball. But hurlin's a good game. You know with them white knee things."

Miss Mullen peers through a hole in the smudgy window and jumps in alarm. "Mother of God, he's in early today. Quick, Buns! Hide those broken steak-and-kidneys on the floor and stand in front of them so he doesn't see—we'll scrape the stuff out of 'em after he leaves."

Obediently, Buns takes a wide stance in front of the tray of steak-and-kidneys, spreading her bell-bottomed jeans as wide as she can to hide the broken pies. Monsieur St. Quidenay strides into the room and when he walks by she pretends to look busy, though she is greasing the same quiche ring over and over again because she cannot reach the other rings without moving her legs. Monsieur St. Quidenay calls over to Georges from across the room. "Georges, have we seen any more animals today?" he asks politely, referring to the rats. Georges says no and Jacques says yes and it is discussed. Ten minutes pass. Twenty. Twenty-five. Then Buns moans. "Miss Mullen—my legs!"

"It's all right now, he's gone," Miss Mullens whispers. "Jesus me nerves. Buns! Pick up that and put 'em on those. Put it on the thing and bring me some of that and hurry don't you know, child, and pile it on and count them out and send it down, g'won woman!" Miss Mullen gasps.

Buns pulls herself together but while crossing the room for eggs she is nearly beheaded by a speeding tray, nearly walloped by a wooden paddle bearing hot fruitcakes. Stunned by these near-collisions, she soberly begins cracking 72 eggs into a pail and prays that she will make it back to the bench without tripping with 72 eggs. As she is cracking the last dozen, to the tuneless symphony of trays banging, tins clanging, blenders roaring, rollers droning, she hears the most wonderful sound of all: "Breakkkkkfassssssssssst!"

Broken scones
And pots of tea
And sausage rolls
And lumps of cheese
Second-hand eggs
Runny quiche, fine but soppy
Cups of cream
Fractured tarts
More rounds of tea
Marzipan hearts
A feast!

BUNS: Willie was saying that at last year's Christmas party for the staff, Monsieur St. Quidenay charged you each six pounds, then served sandwiches, bananas and Orange Squash. How could anybody be so mean?

MISS MULLEN: G'won Willie's oney coddin' ya. We hadda nice party, in a room in a little hotel in town, and Monshur Kidney gave us a pound back each.

BUNS: Willie! You sly old scoffer you! But he charged you for your own Christmas party? He charged you?

WILLIE: It was a schplendid occasion.

JACQUES: Merde.

WON: This year we get turnips and Coca-Cola.

GEORGES: Well I'm sorry to say there won't be a party this year. Monsieur Quidenay, unfortunately, was not able to book a room.

WILLIE: Ah, do tell us—sure the grand Shelburne Hotel was booked out and he couldn't get the proper champagne from France.

BUNS: I can't believe it! No party? After how hard we worked? But it's Christmas!

ST. QUIDENAY'S VOICE FROM INTERCOM: Cut out the noise up there! And send me down 16 dozen large bouchées!

JACQUES: (*Inspired.*) I know what we do. Tomorrow I bring in beeg amplifier and we hook it up to everything, so he can hear better the eggs breaking, trays banging, mixers roaring. (*Howls of laughter.*)

ST. QUIDENAY: Shut up up there I sayyyyyy! Or I'll sack youse!

MISS MULLEN: Jesus Mary and Joseph, Christmas is upon us! Me bouchées!

10th January, Dublin

Dear Billy,

    I hope you've recovered from your crazy New York holidays. I had the worst Christmas in my life. The pace at the pie factory got to be hideous. Twelve hours a day in the cold and dark turning out Black Forest cakes for the bourgeoisie of Dublin. How could we feel like Christmas at all? And after giving up our Christmas week so that man could stuff his shops with fancy pies, he didn't even give us a party. Party, ha, there wasn't even a meal break on Christmas Eve. And he even made Miss Mullen, who should get a medal for all her years there, pay for a fruitcake and a turkey to take home to her family. Well, she was the only sign of Christmas in the place, bringing in presents for everybody, cigars for the men and a green plastic bubblebath apple for me.

    I guess it won't surprise you to hear that I quit the job after New Year's. I feel sane again, but I miss them all. The other day I went back for a visit. Won had been deported for stealing fancy nightgowns at a department store. Jacques was there swearing at his croissants. Willie was still hunched over that manky sink. And Miss Mullen was at her bouchées. Ah, that woman. Revering those bouchées like they were the Pope's holy wafers. Well, I guess after twenty-six years, you'd see life through a forkhole, too. I felt my own vision of the world shrinking there day by day. That's why I had to get out. But it was easy. I'm only a tourist.

Inish Bó Finne

I love being here, but last night I went berserk. After ten shuddering hours of trying to light a fire in this dark howling cottage—after stacking the clumsy damp sods of turf and throwing on parrafin fire lighters and butter wrappers and scraps of old Wellingtons and plastic bottles belched by the sea onto the strand outside my door; after huffing and blowing and choking on ashes and singing my hair, and the hail whistling and cracking the windows and the wind strangling the candles, and after all and all, and only two beady coals leering out of a steaming black cave—I went berserk.

I took the tongs and beat the sods and shrieked and beat and screamed and crushed the glowing lumps until they spattered over the stone floor in a lurid wet mash. My blood felt like murder and I didn't care if I set the house and my own self on fire, only to have light and heat. Cold, scared, furious and helpless, I met the Furies of Inishbofin.

This is what my love of Irish music has led me to: a sea-torn island with no electricity, minimal plumbing and a tiny potholed road not fit for donkeys. Inishbofin, County Galway: a speck in the Atlantic six miles out to sea from the village of Cleggan on the bald rocky coast of Connemara; a crusty weathered hunk of land five miles long and three miles wide, population 200 and dwindling.

Strangely, this largest island of a tiny archipelago consisting of Inishshark, Davilaun and Inishlyon is the only one of Eire's 300-odd islands that appears on a 1912 map drawn up by Thomas Johnson Westropp titled, The Legendary and

Sunken Islands of Ireland. These enchanted lands were said to have rivers of fire, wine and milk, sea strands made of dragon stones and crystals, magic fountains and wondrous psalm-singing birds. They had been doomed to drift eternally after the vengeful sea god Mannanan MacLir ordered the waves to cut their roots and whelm them beyond the gray and endless deep. But they rose up from the sea god's realm every seven years, to be sighted by a rare few and to sink again beneath the waves.

Islanders say that Inishbofin's enchantment was broken one night when two fishermen lost in a swirling fog landed upon its shores. The fishermen lit a fire and the island stood fixed, and through the rising mists they saw a red-haired shrivelled hag driving a milk-white heifer into a lake. They caught the cow by the tail, but the tail turned into a root, and the hag and the cow vanished under the lake. Seven years hence, and for every seven years after that, the cow was seen to rise up out of *Loch Bó Finne* and wander about the island. And so the island was named *Inish Bó Finne*, Island of the White Cow.

Summer visitors swear that Inishbofin is still enchanted. The very rare and lucky white heather grows on the island's wild northern slopes, and magic mushrooms sprout up queerly through flaps of cow dung. Not the towering variety that shelter fairies and elves, but the hallucinogenic psilocybin. Those with psychedelic appetites have been known to see white cows after eating platefuls of Inishbofin mushrooms.

Bofin people don't like to talk about magic anymore. No, the only myth talked about on the island these days is the old White Cow legend printed on wooden plaques and sold in the lobby of Day's Hotel. Storytelling, other than gossip, is "dead out." It died along with the house ceili dances when the spark of social life flew out of the cottage hearth and into the pub. It died when Irish pound notes replaced kettles of fish and drops of parrafin oil as means of barter.

A few island place names like *Gap na Síog* (The Fairy Gap) and *Aill a' Phuca* (Cliff of the Fairies) belie the old superstitions. But you mention fairies and banshees today and the islanders scoff and snicker. Yet when walking back to Rusheen along the low road on a moonless night, they'll turn at the crossroads by the old derelict two-story house to take the high road, even though it weaves a longer path and will tumble you about. The low road is sheltered and more direct. But it passes within spooking distance of the ancestral graveyard.

I was first tempted to go to Inishbofin one sodden afternoon in a Dublin pub banging with fiddles and banjos. Paul MacDonald, a guitar-playing friend on his fifth pint of Guinness was rhapsodizing about the terrible beauties of the West of Ireland. I told him about meeting the writer Sydney Smith the week before, and how Sydney had raved about this place called Inishbofin, where he'd lived and wrote plays and pageants for the islanders to perform. But it was primitive, he said with a twinkling grimace, recalling the morning he'd dumped the contents of his "chemical toilet" into the sea, only to have a wave lash it back all over him!

"Bofin's cursed with magic!" Paul laughed, twanging the top E on his guitar. "Once you get out there you'll lose your head, wish the fog would come down so you'll never have to leave. The islanders still ride donkeys to the bog and to 'town'—a pub and a phone box. And everybody on the island's related to everybody else—third cousin or half-sister or great uncle, or whatever-you-like half-removed—so island life is communal. And there are no *gardaí* to police the island, so the pubs never have to close," he said, licking the foam on his Guinness.

I said I'd been surprised to hear of other Irish islands besides the Arans.

"My God, yes!" Paul jumped. "There's Inishshark, and Cape Clare and Tory and Inishturk, Sherkin, and Valentia and about 300 other odd bits of land. But you and lots of other people haven't heard of 'em because they aren't tourist traps like the Arans. I know people in County Galway who've never even heard of Bofin, or they think it's somewhere in the Hebrides.

"The Aran Islanders speak Gaelic, the sacred native tongue," he continued, "so they've gotten government subsidies for electricity and tarmac roads and crafts shops and horse-drawn sidecars to haul the tourists around, and a secondary school so the kids don't have to emigrate at age 12 to get higher education on the mainland.

"They've got big ferry boats that can cross in gales, and airstrips to fly you in and out as you please sir, and a pub the call the American Bar. Bofin was settled by English monks and Cromwell's soldiers. The last Gaelic speaker on Bofin died over a hundred years ago, so the island is an unwanted orphan of the Irish Government. Bofin's got no electricity, except for the generator at Day's Hotel, and the shops haven't got much beside tinned peas, candles, bananas and stale Easter eggs," Paul went on. "The little post boat won't cross to the mainland in a rough sea, and the sea could be rough *any* day of the year. If you go in, there's no telling when you'll come back out…"

On a balmy morning in late May, I hitchhiked from Dublin to Galway and then out to Cleggan, a scattered harbor village with a few houses, a shop, a pub and a crowd of peeling boats. A fire crackled over the mumbling voices in the Pier Bar, and I fell into chat with the people waiting for the post boat to Bofin: a veterinarian going over to test the cattle for brucellosis, an Electricity Supply Board agent going over to peddle electricity, a country doctor making his weekly call, the island priest who looked too young for the part, and a salty islander who'd seen the world in trawlers.

The harbormaster and his oilskin-clad crew waited at the side of the *Leenane Head* with the cargo: cases of sliced white bread, bulging sacks of coal, barrels of Guinness, a limp mailbag, a roll of flowered wallpaper and a ton of cinder blocks. After an hour of heaving and hauling the cinder blocks, we pulled anchor on the creaking craft and set off for our six-mile slurp across the sea, with only the priest's Hail Mary's to save our lives lest we sink.

Gray sky and gray waves closed in around us. We rolled and slapped for an hour, when suddenly a hunk of land rose up like a scaly dragon and then vanished in a thick green mist. We glided along until looming darkly on the cliff over our heads was a jagged shape of rocks and broken towers with windows like the hollow eye sockets of a skull.

"Don Bosco's castle," shouted the old seaman. "The Spanish pirate in cahoots with Gráine Uaile, the feisty lady pirate who terrorized these coasts from Kerry to Donegal in the 16th century."

The boat steered around the tip of a boulder that jutted out like a shark's fin. "That's Bishop's Rock," the seaman roared. "In the old Irish penal times, Bofin served as a prison for Catholic priests. On this very rock Cromwell's soldiers chained a bishop at low tide and stood watch as the rising tide crept down his throat to drown him."

The boat's prow circled a tiny islet strewn with the stony carapace of a fish curing house, skeletal remains from the days of the big island fisheries when a hundred 100-ton ships would harbor here. And then out of the mist broke the pale green sweep of Inishbofin—mountainy, voluptuous, stark and frightening.

I climbed out of the boat and trundled up a hill and found a road such as I'd never seen: four feet wide, with dips and pits and ruts and bumps, squeezed between the blackberry hedge and the stone wall—fine for a donkey but ridiculous for wheeled conveyances. I set out to look for a camping spot with a spectacular view.

I passed hay mounds and potato ridges and a long-faced Morris Minor with four flat tires; stacks of turf set out to dry under sheered clouds of blue-stained fleece; idle donkeys, new caravans and rubbled cottages with gouged windows, a lake with drifting swans, the ruins of a 14th century stone chapel and the lone stone *bullaun* left from the plundered seventh-century monastery built by the island's first known inhabitants The sea followed me everywhere—rising, tilting, stretching beyond bogs and cliffs and the rock-scabbed hills.

By and by I passed a little man in a big-shouldered wool coat tied with a string. He offered me a camping plot near his cabbage patch for the night, but I declined. I thanked him and kept on walking, past piles of handmade lobster pots, a bramble-tangled graveyard and more donkeys, until I saw a pale stretch of sand and a lone curragh lying overturned like a skinned mackerel, with its black tarred canvas rotting away from its wooden ribs.

Here I camped, on a goose-feathered field overlooking the Atlantic and across from an islet which the Irish Ordnance Survey Map called *Inis Laighean*—Inishlyon. I passed a calm night dizzy with stars and roving satellites and awakened giddily to bright warming sand dunes.

The next afternoon a fierce wind blew up. I took a long roaring walk against it down to the pub, which looked like ski lodge with high-sloping walls. I sat myself down next to the only other female there, a squat matronly woman in her fifties whose weathered face, windblown hair and worried eyes were hardly in keeping with her stockings and polished high heels. Lena remarked about the weather and the fact that I was here too early to appreciate the island in its full-blown summer madness.

"In July this island will be well and truly packed!" she cackled. "With campers and daytrippers and cottage renters. And my house'll be stuffed with Germans and Dutch and French and Americans, and bird watchers and botanists and divers and painters and hikers and neurotic writers," she fired breathlessly.

"For some queer reason I can't figure, my dear," she said gravely, "Bofin has a great attraction for neurotic writers. I had a guest once—a learned professor from that Trinity College in Dublin—who paced and muttered around his candle all night long, about his thee-sus. Woke me up at 4 a.m. in the dead of a wet morning with his rantings and grumblings and I demanded to know what he was about at that time of night! 'Oh, it's nothing,' he says to me. 'I always write this way.' 'Well you can't write that way here!' I says to him. Go rave at the moon or the geese in the bog, or I'll put you out tomorrow!'"

I couldn't get a laugh in edgewise. Lena told me how the professor did leave the next day—without paying her the week's rent he owed. And he left behind a huge old tome on Joff-ree Chaw-ser, just the thing Lena wouldn't know what it in the world to do with.

"And then we had a poet on the island, a Yank who got the writer's block so bad he filled a bottle with sand and hurled it at some men digging a grave. Ye can see a bronze plaque with some of his poetry on it over there. Theo-dore Roeth-ke. Won that Pew-litt-ser Prize. Came here in the summer of 1960, and was writin' about how the Bofin landscape reflects a state of mind. I guess he went mental doin' it. They carried him off to the Ballinasloe hospital in a straitjacket.

"And now we've got a psycho lady in from Paris. I call her The Screamer because she tromps for six hours a day and screams over the cliffs whenever she can't sort out her bloody French sentences. A film critic from Paris, Luh Fig-a-roh, sealed away in a damp cottage to write an eggsus-ten-shull novel I suppose. But she'll be gone after the first gale hits."

It hardly seemed the opportune moment to mention that I was a writer, so I told Lena about the great camping spot I'd found—across from the islet bearing my family name.

Lena downed her hot whiskey and slammed the empty glass on the counter. She grabbed me by the arm and pulled me out the pub before she could explain that she'd seen my tent that afternoon. With gales forecast for the night, she knew that if I stayed in it, I could be blown out to sea, or smacked against a stone wall and torn to shreds. She'd seen tents with people in them blown away before.

"Blown away?" I gasped.

"Where do you think you are, girl! Around here they still talk about the night of The Big Wind like it happened yesterday, even though it was the sixth of January, 1839. The sea went lunatic and hurled monster boulders against the cliffs. All the houses on Bofin were blown away but one. By dawn that house was filled with twenty baby cradles!"

Lena led me to the top of the little hill behind the pub where she'd parked her old car. She started it with a can opener, and then we took off toward my campsite, bumping along the road in the dim purple twilight. By the time we reached the beach near Inishlyon, the wind was truly wild. We caught the billowing tent and flung it into the car and rode to her cottage in blackness with the wind heaving us over the tiny island road. When we arrived at her tidy place with a turf fire burning and a bare gaslight hanging over the kitchen table, I was in a daze. But I heard her say I could stay with her for the week and not pay her "a single shilling."

This is what my curiosity has lured me to—a vicious and sublime piece of land where 200 islanders live tenaciously and despite demoralizing odds; a community in bewilderment, between the old life of work-sharing and storytelling and the new life of electricity and television. Where life teeters between the profound and the monotonous, the zany and the tragic.

In the long days at Lena's I heard island tales of pirates and smugglers and sunken Spanish Armada ships, and stories that impressed on me just how much the islanders' precarious existence was at the mercy of nature. You might laugh about the islander whose false teeth were grabbed out of his mouth by a wave as he was picking winkles at high tide, but not about the fisherman castrated by a kicking horse one week after his wedding or the woman still bearing the scars after being attacked as a little girl by a donkey in heat.

The old people remember all the stories, the capers and the strange changes they've lived through. The self-appointed island genealogist and historian, the octogenarian Michael Cunnane, known as Mick the Roux for his shock of flaming hair, was eager to tell me the whole history of the island in one gulp, one night at his lonely cottage. Since he was a gossun at his grandfather's knee, he'd taken it upon himself to memorize the histories of the islanders for two hundred years back. By modern standards it was impressive, but compared to the recall of the ancient Celtic *fili*, it was a mere scrap of time.

Like the best of the few remaining Irish storytellers, Mick could tell the history of Inishbofin as if he'd seen it all with his own eyes. He sat there in trance-like concentration for four hours, with the candlelight flickering eerily on his face, and the wind howling outside the cottage door.

"The first documented inhabitants we had on this island were Irish and English monks," he began. "They came here in 665 A.D. with Saint Colman, bishop of Lindisfarne and Northumbria. Them monks knew the island as *Insula Vitulae Albae*, or Island of the White Heifer," said Mick, demonstrating his Latin. "Yer man Colman had a dispute with St. Columcille about settin' the day for Easter Sunday to please Rome. He refused to abandon the old Celtic church practices, and left the island of Iona and came here with some dissenting Irish and English monks. They built a monastery, the ruins of which ye can see by the graveyard. Colman assigned the English monks to do the teachin' and cookin' and what have you, and sent the Irish monks out tillin' the land. That went on for a while, until a dispute arose between the English and Irish monks about the division of labor. Then St. Colman packed th'English monks off to County Mayo and came back and spent most of his life on Bofin, till he died in 676 A.D.

"Up until the 10th century, the only population that was ever mentioned in historical records was the monastic settlement. There's a big gap in the history of th'island until the 16th century, when it was taken over by pirates. The 26 ships of the Spanish Armada were wrecked off the Irish coast in the autumn of 1588, and the 300-ton pay ship, the *Falco Blanco Mediano*, with the admiral of the fleet Alonzo Bosco on board, broke up on the rocks near Davilaun Island. She'd be carryin' gold bars and 16 guns, includin' six copper cannons, which would be of good value today."

"Did anyone ever dive to look for her?" I broke in.

"They did. Some divers came in here four years ago. They found the ship, but we don't know what they got. The ship's still there. And as well as havin' the gold aboard, they had their war horses, Arab stallions. Some of them got clear of the ship and swam across to the mainland, where they mated with Shetland ponies running wild on Connemara. And that's where we got the Connemara pony...

"Anyway... Don Bosco and some chaps named White and Corbett got ashore to Inishbofin and settled a while. Bosco took up the life of a buccaneer and allied with that fierce Pirate Queen Grace O'Malley—known as Gráine Uaile, whose clan of sea mercenaries had captured Bofin back in 1380. For years until her death in 1603, she and Don Bosco controlled the harbour with a chain boom strung across either end from Don Bosco's castle to *Scealp na gCat*.

"The next crowd that came in here," continued Mick, lighting another candle, "was Oliver Cromwell and his men, in 1653. They turned Bosco's castle into a fort and Bofin became the place Catholic priests were sent to be executed. There's a deep chasm in the rocks on the northeast side of this island called *an prisiun*—the prison. Cromwell's soldiers would lay a plank across the cliffs over the chasm and force the priest to walk across the plank. When the priest got midway across, they'd flip the plank and watch him fall hundreds of feet to be shredded on the rocks."

Mick's storytelling could have gone on all night, so eager was he to have an audience. "The young ones here, they're all telly boys and telly girls," he muttered in a tired voice. "They only want to move to the cities. The life here is over."

The older islanders had grown up with dramas and crossroads dances and visiting and storytelling. But since the telly's debut, bringing greed from Dallas and speed from New York to the two hotels and few houses with electric generators, these amusements were "dead out." Now there was only the Sunday night Bingo emceed by the priest: Win a Tin of Biscuits. Or stay at home and watch a drama of embers and listen to the news on the wireless. There were still a few musicians on the island who knew the old dance tunes. But on an island of bachelors, why have a ceili when there were no single women to dance with?

Emigration was the specter that shadowed the past and future of every islander. It had created a lopsided population of 65% pensioners, 27% bachelors, 7% school children, and one young single woman. Until recently, unemployed single women in Ireland weren't allowed to collect the dole, and so they abandoned their islands to find work and husbands on the mainland.

The only hope for Bofin's economic future, some people thought, was tourism. Not so repugnant an idea, perhaps, when the island's spate of reasonable weather was at best eight weeks. But I thought of the brash, bronzed Californian who'd accosted me on the little island road. He'd spoken in conspiratorial tones of his Grand Plans for the island.

Geared up in a flashy red jacket and short-shorts that flaunted his thunder thighs, he'd hunched over his $2,000 custom built 100-speed pot-hole-proof bike, and squinted close to my face. He described his visions of lakes stocked with trout eggs—he'd single-handedly import fly-fishing to Inishbofin—and industrial washing machines. It was high time things got civilized here, he said, and he was just the one to do it.

Down at the pub I heard islanders referring to him as "Kojak" because he was the spitting image of the bald TV tough. He'd come to Inishbofin to buy some land, and the islanders were putting him on in the best of fashion. Drawing out negotiations as long as they could, so that Kojak would have to make several visits and buy the islanders endless rounds of drinks. But all Kojak's scheming would come to naught! Any Bofin man who sold his land to this ranting industrialist would promptly be lynched by an island mob.

The more I saw and heard, the more Inishbofin fascinated me. Its people wore modern clothes but farmed with donkeys and fished in boats of the most ancient kind to be found in Europe—tar-covered curraghs descended from the sixth century rudderless skin boat of Saint Breandan the Navigator. Here you could find economic gaps centuries apart: island houses with designer bathrooms with bidets, and houses whose toilet facilities were a shovel and a hole in the ground; a room lit with a 300-watt bulb and another with a tattered black mantle providing the wattage of a jam jar of fireflies; a woman who tossed her Switzer's designer sheets into the washing machine, and a woman who scraped dirty diapers and boiled them in an iron pot over a turf fire. And for recreation—one who traveled all the way to Dublin to shop, and another who stared at a fire and fumbled rosary beads. In the days when the islanders all lived in mud huts and fished and farmed for a livelihood, the Haves drank tea and the Have-nots drank water. But now the class differences were a third world apart.

The haunting remoteness of the island, so close the Galway Races and the seaside amusements at Salthill and yet so far, was compelling. But I didn't think, like some visitors, that it would be a shame when Inishbofin got electricity. Not for the mother of nine who ironed with a heavy old iron kept on the hearth, or the school kids who suffered eyestrain from flickering gaslight and headaches from the parrafin oil fumes. Or for everyone who feared those occasional accidents, tipped candles, kerosene fires and exploding gas tanks. Yet I knew that the coming of electricity would break the island's spell of magic. Gone forever would be the dead stillness of its night, the shocking brightness of a full moon shining on a dark world, and the running joke on Bofin that the greatest offense you could ever have brought against you was "drunk in charge of a torch." And so I decided to return in late summer, to live through Inishbofin's last winter without electricity, to teach the island children the tin whistle, and to perhaps count myself among the island's eccentric scribes.

In late August the island harbor was bobbing with yachts. The pier was littered with diving gear and a crowd decked out in flippers. Foreign accents percolated out of the pub, and the little road resounded with the crunch of bicycles. The bogs and cliffs were flashes of unruly color, and the lonely grassy field where I had camped before was like a regatta. Urbanites from everywhere had come to see the Ireland of the Welcomes—happy old men with their caps and their cows.

Since May, electric poles had sprung up like Calvary crosses all over the island. And soon the Great Generator would come and banish the batteries and the wicks and mantles, and there would be hairdryers and clothes dryers and electric fires and more television sets. But when, no one knew exactly. The contracts weren't settled. The powerhouses weren't built. The houses weren't wired. And the dirty weather was soon coming on, making all these jobs impossible.

After disembarking from the *Leenane Head* I had dumped my load of "tin whistles and birdseed," as my Dublin friends had called it, in the veranda of Day's Hotel. My island provisions consisted of 45 pounds of brown rice, beans, popcorn and garbanzos, books, typewriter ribbons, reams of paper and blank notebooks, hot water bottles and batteries, long underwear and Wellingtons, a bicycle, an oil lamp and an accordion, a pile of sweaters and tin whistles, and a goatskin drum. Who knew what you would need for five months on an island with no electricity, no library and a shop with only tinned peas and Easter eggs?

After getting my bearings, I set out for a long walk to Horseshoe Bay. The flute player I'd met on the boat had invited me to supper. When I arrived at the old cottage where he was staying, it was filled with tourists from Normandy who had been island-hopping all week long from Achill Island, Clare Island and neighboring Inishturk. They'd sailed their yacht to Inishbofin upon hearing reports of a cozy harbor and friendly natives, and now sat sipping Bordeaux before a hearth steaming with wet bathing suits.

The chef made ready the table and the old gas lamp and spread before us an island-reaped feast I would dream about for months to come: a wreath of fat crab just pulled from the nets, tender island lamb, a garden of island vegetables, and for dessert, a delicate flan made of carrageen moss laced with Irish whiskey. The wild pink sky was streaked with pewter, the sea lapped sweetly around us, and the French were rhapsodic. *"Quelle île magnifique! Et sans electricité, c'est si romantique!"*

After the feasting we floated down to the pub, which flowed over the rim and down the sides and out onto the pier with tourists and brawny fishermen from Inishturk, urban refugees from Dublin and Belfast, Electricity Supply Board lads working for the summer, and island children back home from London, Bermuda and the Bronx.

Fiddles scraped and accordions wheezed and the floor shook till the tables danced. By 4 a.m. everyone had evaporated but the musicians, who fortified themselves with bracing reels, and the doctor whose wife was expecting a baby any minute. He sat behind the bar in his pajamas and Wellingtons dispensing jokes and brandy.

This went on for another week. Then one day the island looked like the morning after a fancy dress ball: tattered and sad. The tourist season was over, and the island put away its dancing shoes for another year.

The island turned back into a pumpkin and I took up the life of Cinderella. I moved into a damp cottage a few feet from the seawall in the eastern village of Rusheen. No sink. No toilet. No bath. £25 a week—turf and milk included. Eighty years ago Rusheen was a swarming village of thirty houses with some nine people in each house. It had a jetty and a busy fish curing station. Now it was a shipwrecked village of cold hearths.

My tiny window stared out upon a circadian drama of changing tides, weather and people. One hour a grey sea flowed up to my door, and another hour a cold desert of sand and brown tangles stretched far across the bay. The distant peaks of the Twelve Pins of Connemara bleached and faded under the sweeping sunbeams, and blued with cold under the brooding clouds. For sound effects, the sea crashed and slapped over the rocks and they clattered like bones.

Coming and going were donkeys to and from the bog; kids in hooded wool coats like wet sponges, to and from school; squeaking bicycles to and from the pub; mothers and rattling prams with little ones bundled like mummies to and from the shop. Sometimes a lone figure crawled and stooped among the rocks, picking periwinkles from the seaweed for the plates of France. But the ruins of the fish curing house at the end of the quay, and the old broken hull beside it never budged.

I was happy. I shyly started up the whistle classes, and the kids eagerly flocked to my cottage in all kinds of weather. But I had one problem: I was always sleepy. I complained to Henry, a 10-year-old.

"'Tis the heavy air that makes ye dopey," he said.

"'Tis the salt that takes the puff out of ye," said his younger brother Francis.

I thought it might have something to do with the parrafin oil, turf, coal, sulphur and cylinder gas fumes I was inhaling. Outdoors I was breathing the purest air my lungs had ever known, but indoors the pollution level was staggering.

Coffee, tea, coffee, tea—I was swallowing buckets of it to keep from passing out. I was exhausted by the endless housework of dumping ashes and tea grinds and garbage pails and plastic toilets; hauling sacks of turf and filling and emptying tea kettles and hot water bottles and pans of dirty dishwater and plates of turnip peels; sweeping mud and turf crumbs and boiling sheets and blue jeans and filling oil lamps and building and blowing fires. And then one night something happened. I think the island was determined to have me reckon with its hypnotic air and its other forces as well.

I burrowed under my mountain of blankets, and fell into a deep sleep in a room so black there was no up or down. Hours later something jerked me awake. I felt a heavy presence breathing over me. I felt a needle pricking my left wrist and a dry scratchy thing being forced down my throat. I bolted up in the bed. I blinked in disbelief. The room was still black, yet floating over my head in a garish orange light was a puppet-like face with a hooked nose and slit eyes. Black tattered shapes hovered around it. I squeezed my eyes tight and saw reassuring darkness. But when I opened them again it was all still there. Frantic, I muttered some holy words to the dark. Then I watched as the orange light and the horrible things inside it dissolved, and the room became black and peaceful.

The next day a woman from a neighboring village stopped by with some turnips and two weeks' worth of newspapers tied up in a string. She wanted to know how I was settling in.

"I'm doing just grand," I said. "But last night I think I had a visit from the fairies."

"Faith, tell me! What is it?" she asked, sucking in her breath.

Over tea I gave her the full details. I wondered how fast they'd get around the island and into what fantastic shapes they would grow. But while I laughed, she stiffened.

"Well now..."she said hesitatingly. "I hate to tell ye this but...there is a thing about this house."

I lurched forward and clutched a turnip. Did I really want to know more?

"A man who was staying here heard a tap at the window late one night and a voice calling his name. He got up and looked out the window but saw no one. He was annoyed to be wakened like that, so he roused a neighbor and they went out fishing. They went out in two curraghs that night. But his curragh never returned."

My pounding blood stopped. I knew that I had come to a wild remote island with a dark history. An island where savage things did indeed happen. The Inishbofin nights had not been exorcised by electricity. Nor had the imagination of its islanders been tamed by technology. But it was hard to believe that I'd come all this way with my accordion and tin whistles to end up in a cottage that was haunted by fairies, or whatever they were. It felt stranger than fiction.

"And I dread to tell ye," she continued, "but a woman who lived here—her name was Nancy—was cooking over the open fire one night when the big cooking pot suddenly flew across the room. She's dead now. Died at thirty-four."

" That's my age!"

"You could change bedrooms," the neighbor offered lamely. "That's what the O'Malleys did. They were sleeping in that bedroom there, but after a week they moved to the other one."

"Why?"

"Faith, I don't know."

By now I was in stutters, and it wasn't the coffee. After the woman left, I pulled on my Wellies and walked straight to Lena's and told her my story.

"Faith, there're enough stories goin' round this wretched island,'" Lena said. "I never heard anything about yer house but that lightening came down the chimney once and fired the cooking pot across the room."

Seeing my collapsed state, Lena offered to let me stay at her place until I felt calm enough to move back into the cottage. Her husband Ned was sympathetic about my condition too. But he didn't believe in fairies and couldn't resist using the occasion to show me. I was huddled in front of the fire, still mulling it over, when he poked me on the shoulder. "There's yer fairy," he laughed, pointing across the room. On the table beside the teapot was a plastic bottle of Saxa-brand salt shrouded in a white tea towel.

Saturday brought a cold-blooded rain and Saturday's wind was a faceful of nettles. But Saturday night was a big night in the pub and only a hurricane would keep islanders away. The road from the east was a big mud pie, and the potholes gargled as we plodded, my Wellingtons and I. My oilskins slithered as I passed the graveyard and I gave a nod of respect. Then I saw a light bobbing on the road. As the two women approached the torch swept my face and one shrieked, "This one's not of this island!"

"I'm the tin whistle teacher!" I shouted into the wind and the woman recovered her senses. And two hills and three donkeys later I heard the great stuttering heartbeat of the hotel generator and felt relief to see the great light of the pub.

In one corner some gray and brown men were staring at the gozzlebox. Another gray and brown clump was reading the flickering fire and the *Connaught Tribune*. Another batch of bachelors was gambling at cards for stakes of chickens and mutton. And around the big U-shaped bar, like weary horses pulled up to a corral, were five brown foaming pints parked beside five old rusty bicycle lamps, the kind you crank to turn on.

"Now that's a fine old lamp," I said to the old man next to me, thinking with regret of the cheap plastic flashlight I'd brought to the island. More than once on the three-mile walk between my cottage and the pub, it had flown apart like a jack-in-the-box, its head popping off and its batteries rolling down the road in the dark.

"So 'tis a fine one," he said. "Bought it for two shillings twenty years ago. 'Tis the boy-o you need on a night like this, along with a diver's suit to get across them potholes. Ye'd have yerself drownt or kilt in them, surely. Or maybe break yer back. Ah, ye'd think the back was only an ould muscle and bone, but I seen skeletons in the graveyard popping up—'tis so crowded in there—and the back's a complicated ould piece'a work."

Just then an oilskin streaming with rain blew in the door. It slithered to the bar and a skinny old hand reached out and laid another fine old bicycle lamp on the counter. Mary was only down to buy fags and a bottle of orange, she said, for the pub wasn't the place for a family woman to be seen. But we fell into chat...

"I'm still recruiting for my tin-whistle class," I said playfully. "Would you like to join up?"

"Well, aren't you a great girl to bring music to the island—and in the furies of winter! If there's a purgatory, this place is it! Gales and storms and rain and rheumatism and colds and dirty old turf fires and hissing gas lamps and hail and flu and pneumonia and nothing to do for amusement. An ould Inish*coffin*. This weren't no place for holiday makin'!"

"Well, I'm not exactly on holiday," I said. "I'm here to pass a quiet winter and do some writing. Would you like to learn the tin whistle?"

"Well you reckon I could play it fer the donkeys on my way to the bog?...Heavens, child. I'm not a'tall musical, but I used to dance. Oh the dances we had here when I was young. From noon till dawn! There were twelve hundred people on Inishbofin back then, and four hundred others over on Inishshark. That's th'island ye can see over there beyant that strip of water we calls the Dirty Sound because 'tis so treacherous. When I was a courtin' the Shark people'd row over in their curraghs on Sundays for mass and to buy tea. But 'twas only an excuse for a hooley, a party. All the people's gone off Shark it now, moved off it by the government in '56. "Tis sad, really, to see all the cottages in ruin. Some German owns the island now. Says he's going to fix it up for tourists with an airstrip and all. But he'll have to bargain with Lucifer to change the weather!

"When I was a girrul 'twas so warm here we'd run barefoot all summer and there'd be fishin' up until after Christmas," she went on. "But we're shiftin' out of the Gulf Stream I do believe, and th'island's gettin' to be an ould iceberg. Bofin was like a gold rush in them days, with people comin' from everywhere to fish for mackerel and cod and ling and plaice and pollack and crabs and lobsters. Our harbor was one of the best in Europe, and many a stray ship would take shelter here."

"One of the best in Europe? Really?"

"I'm tellin' you!" she said. "Known far and wide. The world over. Them Norwegians would be comin' all the time with their fiddles—could they dance! And the French—you'd give 'em a bottle of milk, and they'd give you a bottle of Bo-jo-lay. But the Frigidaire got invented. Kilt the salt-fish trade overnight... In them days this island was self-sufficient, too. Every inch was farmed. We'd pull the grass from between the cracks in the stones to feed the cows. ''Twasn't anythin' we didn't eat that didn't come from th'earth or the sea. Now 'tis only an island of tin openers! Now 'tis only an ould Inish*dole!*"

I believed Mary when she said Inishbofin hadn't suffered as severely as Ireland during The Great Hunger between 1841 and 1851. The potato blights brought rampant misery and starvation to all on the mainland who'd been forced by government policies to depend on this staple crop. Inishbofin lost one-third of its population during this time, but it was to a cholera epidemic that started when a diseased corpse washed ashore on the island at *Scealp na gCat*. Despite Inishbofin's overcrowding during the famine years, islanders managed to survive because they knew how to live from the sea.

But did they now? With the sea all around me, I couldn't even get a fish. In 1820 Bofin was one of the biggest fisheries on the Irish coast, with 10,000 herring fishermen converging on the island all at once. Its harbor was a traffic jam of big masted ships, nobbies, rowboats, pucáns and curraghs. But now I had to pay a neighbor to bring me some mackerel from a shop in Galway. And I was thrilled skinny to receive a tin of tuna fish postmarked San Francisco, sent as a joke by a *Sunset Magazine* editor with whom I'd been corresponding.

A hundred and fifty years ago there were some 1500 people living on Inishbofin. The Irish Congested Districts Board considered the island overpopulated, yet on 3.5 acres of land, each family managed to grow enough oats, barley and rye to feed their fowl and livestock, and enough potatoes and turnips for themselves. Eggs were so plentiful they were exported to the mainland. Daring Bofin fishermen harpooned seven-ton basking sharks for the precious liver oil, burned in the world's lamps. Islanders managed fish-curing and kelp-burning industries. Women carded, dyed, spun and knitted. The island had a carpenter, blacksmith, boat builder, weaver, tailor, sawyer, one public house, and three small shops.

There were still three small shops, but what did they sell? Gray splotched carrots that looked like leper's fingers, whiskery turnips like shrivelled walrus heads, boxes of wallpaper-paste-flavored instant mashed potatoes, and real potatoes imported from Holland. It shocked me to see islanders buying white bread loaves baked on the mainland, eggs, butter, and onions from Galway, and Long-Life, evaporated and powdered milk.

A mother of five had tried to explain it to me by saying how there weren't the people to do the labor on the island now, with all the young ones gone off to the cities. But the logic failed. Did it really take that much effort to plant a few rows of squash or beans? Well, maybe. Planting beans would involve tying them up on strings and poles and looking after them. And xenophobia counted for something. Some French visitors had brought an *aubergine* to a young farmer I'd befriended. He'd laughed at the "vegetable from outer space" and thrown the eggplant to his chickens.

I stared at the wizened face looking out of the oilskin hood and I said again, "How can it be?"

"'Tis a queer thing all right," said Mary, "and 'tis even queerer that everybody on th'island *agrees* that 'tis a queer thing Some people say the growing season here's just gotten too short, and others says we're just too lazy."

She'd just come down to the pub to buy some cigarettes and a bottle of orange, and had been talking and dripping for over two hours. It was getting late. I reluctantly turned my thoughts to my cottage. A few more hot whiskeys and I'd throw the fairies out on their ears. I started to tell Mary about my visitation from the fairies when suddenly the pub lights went out. The generator had a coronary. The lads at their cards struck matches to see their hands. The beams of the old bike lamps dueled in the dark while the maid behind the bar fumbled for some candles. We stuck them on saucers, and suddenly the pub looked like an elegant dinner party! I told my story, now to a flickering face lurking out of a dripping hood.

"Well now, maybe 'twas a window peeker ye saw," Mary said.

"A window peeker? On Inishbofin ?"

"Don't be fooled. There's all kinds on this island. Ye'd want to keep yer curtains drawn and yer door locked at night. And if ye see any fairies or puppets or flyin' saucers, ye could always keep a night candle going and put a little holy water by the bed."

I left the pub in great form. I trundled up the hill, bid good-night to an old man mounting his old push-bike, and passed two glowing cigarettes mumbling by a stone wall. The next day I would move out of Lena's and back into my cottage. Fairies or no fairies.

Sunday morning was deliriously sunny. I awoke feeling courageous, but I took an empty bottle to the church anyway. After mass I sheepishly asked one of the little girls where I might find the store of holy water. She giggled when I asked, because she knew I was not Catholic. She'd heard about my troubles with the fairies, and pointed to a large stone urn.

I discreetly took out the empty shampoo bottle and thrust it under the holy water, coughing to muffle the gurgles. When I got back to my cottage, I nonchalantly sprinkled the water over my bed, over the windows, over the floor, over the geraniums, inside the drawers, just to make sure, then stashed the rest under my pillow. I felt sound. But as dark came down, I felt the willies coming on. Before I crawled into bed, I lit a votive candle, put on a tape of merry jigs and gulped a few whiskeys. I felt ridiculous. But you wouldn't know what there was or wasn't in the fright of the night on Inishbofin.

When I stopped groping for a light switch on the dark mornings and fumbled for the box of matches instead, I was settled into island life. But I still couldn't get the islanders' names straight. Because they were all related by blood or marriage, there were only 17 surnames on the island. But the variations on the first names had me perpetually confused. There was Michael Joseph and Michael John, but they'd be called Mickey Joe or Michael Joe or Michael or Mick or Micho or Joseph or Joe or John or Mickey John. And the women went by their married names and their maiden names and their nicknames, so the gossip was hard to follow sometimes.

I gave up contact with Dublin and Ireland and the rest of the world. The news on the wireless was only scratchy noise from a distant star. And the public telephone box two miles down the road was truly as someone described: "a fine toy for a child."

The telephone equipment was World War II gear and the weak radio signal was subject to weather interference. When the phone worked properly you'd wait up to half an hour for the Bofin post mistress to get you through, even to Galway. Then you'd have to bellow into the receiver, so that she and everybody passing by the road knew your business—if they weren't already listening in on one of the ten island phones all strung onto one party line. While waiting for a connection you might be privy to a cross-stitched conversation like this:

"Yes, send me out some bacon, please. I need fifteen pounds."

"Surely, and what color, green or blue? And with ruffles?"

"Why of course, like the last order...Tell me, they do be sayin' that last week there Henry was dreamin' he was kickin' a rat, and he broke his toe on the bedpost. Would that be true?"

"Faith, yes. 'Twas green, and it had ruffles."

I helped a neighbor dig potatoes and got the nickname "Slicer Lyon" for the method I had of cutting up the potatoes with the spade before I got them out of the ground. I took long walks in the mist, in the rain, in the sun, in the snow, to the tops of wild cliffs, looking out over frolicking dolphins, and down into the jaws of the rocks to watch seals diving for fish. One morning I walked to the edge of *Trá Gheal*, the bright pearly strand with a treacherous reputation. At this beautiful spot four different currents converge at 13 knots, and the sand is so quick it'll suck you in up to your shoulders in minutes.

On Easter Sunday, 1949, three Lacey men set out from this beach in their curragh to row the mile back home to Inishshark. They'd hardly gotten the boat offshore when the converging currents snapped the oars and dumped the men out of the boat. The quicksand did the rest. Only the shattered oars were found.

One evening I wandered down to the harbor and saw a solemn assembly of cows and men silently waiting for the tide to rise. The *Glorius* was docked by the quay and the harbormaster stood on board. After the tide had risen I watched a drama of agony as the farmers tied ropes around the cows bellies and a crane hoisted them high with splayed legs and gaping mouths into the crowded boat bound for market. The tension and silence was frightening, and the harbormaster stood with his arms outstretched as if giving last rites.

I hiked the island from one end to the other, making house calls as the itinerant tin whistle teacher, while the island's petty reigning monarchs, the priest and the schoolmaster, bickered over the after-hours use of the schoolhouse. One blustery night in a warm house filled with tin whistles and balls of wool, the mothers and I were discussing these "negotiations."

Brandishing her knitting needle one cried, " 'Tis ridiculous ye can't have the key to the schoolhouse for yer lessons! What'er ye goin' to do—go in there and steal the crown jewels? What's this about the priest havin' to ask the schoolmaster! Who runs this island anyway? I thought it was the priest! I thought *he* was head man!"

Despite the freezing damp of my cottage, I survived Granuaille's Curse, a three-week siege of flu, colds, tonsillitis, and wild stomach pains that had me crawling on all fours to get to the turf pile. Word of my malady brought a visit from Sister Reginald, the nun who was filling in for the island nurse while she was on holiday in America. She arrived with the priest himself, an affable young man with a Campbell's soup kid face who'd been sentenced to three years on Inishbofin by the parish in Tuam.

Sister Reginald came with ravishing energy, motherly love and a prescription for brandy. Father O'Gorman came with interior decorating hints. "You could move the sofa closer to the fire," he suggested, "—and hang a blanket over the door to keep out the draft." After studying the gaping space under and around the rotting door, through which the sea spray sneezed, he concluded, "What you really need is a snake."

The Sister grabbed the bódhran from over the fireplace and whacked an impish beat on its leathery skin. The Father blew his way through my arsenal of tin whistles. Then as suddenly as they'd come, they were off to pay another call. But halfway out the door, the priest offered his counsel. "You really ought to get off the island every week or so, even for a day. You can go a bit funny here, when all you hear for talk is 'Did the boat go?' 'Will she go?' 'Is she in yet?'"

It was easy for the priest to come and go off the island, and this offended the islanders who couldn't. He kept two cars, one on the island for short zips up and down the steep Inishbofin hills, and the other in Cleggan for his jaunts around the Irish countryside. He was never seen walking. Once, his speeding VW almost ran me down on my daily jaunt to heave the contents of my toilet bucket over the sea wall.

The miraculous lights of Renvyle and Cleggan sparkled across the bay like beacons of a dream world, but I never left the island for even a day. A day might end up being a week if the sea got rough. The boat and taxi and bus fares to Galway amounted to £20 one way, and hitching was tricky. On the lonely ten-mile road from Cleggan to Clifden, cars were as rare as sunshine. A ramble to Galway was like an excursion to Paris. That's why some islanders spoke of Ireland as a foreign country and didn't go off the island for years.

Inishbofin was tiny world but it was the whole world. Every single islet, rock and ridge and cove and cliff and gully and reef and blow-hole and scrap of bog and beach had a name, and each of the 300 names told a story. Oogh being the Irish word for cove, the map of Bofin had an Oogharlea, Ooghnastrappy, Ooghnacappul, Ooghnacronlach, Ooghnadoby, Ooghacat, Ooghnanunsa, Ooghnavaud, Ooghnagaragh, Ooghnageeragh, Ooghaveagh, Ooghnacronlach, Ooghnashinnagh, Ooghnagunnel, Ooghnacarrick, and so on. In the same spirit of grandeur, the five miles between the East End and the West End might have been the See America Greyhound Route for the way the islanders talked about the vast cultural differences between them—

"Ah th'east is more civilized, but 'tis not as friendly. The people there do be keepin' to themselves."

Here there were no secrets, and no escapes. You could find every quirk and caper of human nature if you looked for it. Island families who hadn't spoken to one another in generations, and others who hadn't gone from the West Village to Rusheen, or from Rusheen to the West Village in twenty years.

Inishbofin was psychically marooned by the formidable boundary of the sea. On its northeast cliff side carved jagged by ferocious Atlantic breakers, the known inhabited world dropped off into waves stretching to infinity. On its harbour side, another country lay not so far across the water, but the people who lived there had alien habits like riding in buses and eating in restaurants.

With its reputation for enchantment, and its gaudy harvest moon, Inishbofin seemed like the perfect place to celebrate *Samhain*, All Hallow's Eve. The island schoolmaster, a proper sort of fellow with 18th century sideburns and a natty tweed suit, was quick to advise me that Halloween capers had been dead out on Inishbofin for over 20 years. "There'll be nothing doing on the island—nothing at all," Eugene had huffed into his brandy snifter one night at the pub. So when the 31st of October came, I prepared for another night of writing. I popped a batch of corn, lit my host of candles and loaded up my typewriter with another piece of damp curly paper.

Between faltering taps of the typewriter keys I heard a tap at my window. The door blew open and my cottage was swirling with terrifying specters swinging carved turnips with leering fiery eyes.

My whistlers! They were reviving the Celtic New Year charade. I screamed with delight. I offered them popcorn. I blurted out, "Could you use a spare ghost?"

There was a long excruciating pause. The ringleader turned to confer with the others. Then, to my delight, one of the lads offered me his own refuse sack to use as a costume. I smeared Maybelline-blue rings under my eyes. I blackened my lips with eyeliner and pulled a green bathing cap over my scalp. Then off we went, tumbling along in the windy darkness, screeching our tin whistles to frighten or banish whatever else was on that road.

By and by, we came to a house with a great light. We rattled and banged on the door. The latch was turned, and through the half-open door we spied a roomful of souls bewitched by the eerie flickering of a battery-operated TV set. They slowly turned their heads to see who was at the door. They slowly turned them back to the Radio Téléfis Eireann special on the origins of Halloween. We stood there in the doorway, watching them watching the television. That was all. We left without a word. Without a toot from a tin whistle.

When the coldest temperatures on record in Ireland hit, and the egg yolks froze in their shells, I put on my hat and my mittens and went to bed with some poems and two hot water bottles for three days. Three days became three weeks. Christmas came and wild gales drenched the island in an icy depression. I would gladly have slept through December 25th and the Sumo wrestling wind and nails of hail. But I dragged myself out of the only warm place in my cottage in late afternoon to cheer a lonely neighbor with a special imported treat—a tin of jellied cranberry sauce. We celebrated a Tin Openers Christmas without tinsel or pretense.

What better cure for this mid-winter depression and social rigor mortis—a Bofin wedding! Since the day I arrived on this island, I have been hearing about the wedding in the same important tones the outside world reserves for coronations and inaugurations. A Bofin man is about to marry a Dublin woman—and despite the wretched rain and gales and 17-hour nights, the island springs back to life!

Oh the wonderful hysteria! The sewing, the run on eye shadow, lipsticks and stockings in the shop, the practicing of struts in high heels, the baking and the tasting, and the polishing of hotels. Supply lists are drawn up: more nylon stockings and more boxes of home perms and marzipan and RyVita crackers for the dieters, and cases of champagne and barrels of porter and a mammoth salmon and sacks of rice, and lace for the bridesmaids' dresses and smooth wooden planks for a dance floor!

The hairdresser arrives, and women with wet permed heads crowd into a makeshift beauty parlor to share one blow dryer. And the men are getting their suits pressed. And the boat flies back and forth from Cleggan packed with friends and relatives from Dublin, and island children back home from boarding school in Tuam and immigrants from everywhere!

The night before the wedding there is a stag party for the men and a hen party for the women, and at an appointed hour they mingle. Through this endless night I meet Esmeralda and Tony, the sister and the brother of the bridegroom, who talk with regret about their exiled lives in England and how they hate to see their island becoming a holiday resort. I meet the overjoyed parents of the bride, who've never been to Bofin before but have fallen in love with the islanders. I meet a Belfast architect with a holiday home here who is seeking a grant for a community hall for the islands, while his American wife envisions yoga and macramé classes. I dance with Andy, an effusive young Dublin journalist and poet who, after 24 hours here, is calling Bofin "Ireland's answer to Paris" and threatening to tie himself to the pier and never go back to "The Big Smoke."

Two hundred and fifty people are invited, but 400 show up at the bridal dinner. After a diet of turnips I go wild at the sight of pâté and roast duckling and

Charlotte Russe. After dessert, the dance floor is laid. Glamorous dresses and spiffy suits pour onto the makeshift ballroom. I don't recognize the islanders out of their oilskins and they don't recognize me in a dress.

Accordion bellows are unstrapped. Sister Reginald lashes into a wild leathery beat on the bódhran she has secretly been learning to play. The priest waltzes and sweeps his way around the room. And everyone is flirting with everyone! Never mind that after the fabulous wedding the couple will have to go on the dole to stay on the island—tonight is the happiest night of their lives!

We party for days and nights until the dreadful moment comes when the boat must carry the wedding guests away. The jobs back in London and Manchester and Belfast and Dublin won't wait. Standing on the quay watching the good-byes, I feel like I'm watching a coffin ship sailing off with famine survivors, such is their trauma at leaving the island.

Whatever the hard life on Inishbofin, the treachery of wind and fear of sea and small world monotony, this piece of land wrenches these exiled hearts like the vision of stars sprinkled in a pothole puddle. As I fix on the tear-stung faces I wonder how I will ever be able leave. Will two more months of turf fires and eyestrain and risk of hypothermia cure me of this island infatuation once and for all? Will I be ready to say of Inishbofin, "It's the most beautiful place on earth, but it's not enough," and step aboard this boat and say good-bye to my tin whistlers and the little road and the waves rocking me to sleep at night? When tourism seems to be the island's only future, will I one day return to find Bofin's heather hills scarred with glass, its old ones in the boneyard and their hearths on loan to city seekers of the quaint life?

The Great European Busking Tour

The Straats of Amsterdam

Oh, the characters you meet. When you live on the street. In wicked old Amsterdam. Sculptors who work in stolen bicycle parts...Dutch cowboys in ten-gallon hats and string ties, with English learnt off a Hank Williams record...Indonesian puppeteers and runaway organ grinder monkeys...

Now I myself did not actually live on the streets of the sinful Port where Jacques Brel's sailors ate fishheads and tails and belched and sang to the whores and pissed in the canals. But busking there for a spell came close enough. My accommodations were an Irish musician's flophouse, with whiskery bears and broken chairs and porridge spilt everywhere. Rough stuff not listed in the *Rough Guide* to Amsterdam. But when you're down and out in Paris, and there's a fortune to be made in Dutch guilders, and you've got an invite from gigging Dublin lads with mean guitars, and enough for the bus, how can you refuse?

As the bus rolled into Holland, I was stunned awake by a giant windmill with sails that slapped the sky. Flat brown canals meandered and vanished into screaming fields of tulips. And then Amsterdam and the Amstel, and bright streaks like a Van Gogh palette along the river bank. Orange, purple, firehouse red and faded army green sleeping bags and old blankets rolled into pods: The City of Free Living hadn't opened its bloodshot eyes.

For a European capital of only 714,000, A'dam has a helluva reputation. Gabriel Garcia Marquez likens this hip city smelling of flowers and spices to a steamy South American metropolis. It's always been wildly tolerant, even though its origins seem innocent enough. Two Frisian fishermen and their dog ran aground at the conflux of the Ij and the Amstel around the year 1200 and decided to open a café. Then the discovery of a holy wafer found unburned in a furnace in 1345 brought floods of religious pilgrims. The pilgrims still keep coming, looking for other things to put in their mouths. Hard drugs peddled like pink balloons, soft ones smoked in cafés like De Oude Kerk, marked with the sign of a cannabis leaf, and chocolate. One-fifth of the world's cocoa harvest passes through the Amsterdam docks.

Before hitting the *straats* with my bad-ass Irish medieval harp and tin whistles, I meandered around the *grachts*, flower and tree-lined canals with fun-house mirror reflections of tall gabled houses growing up out of the brown water. "Two towns at a single blow," mused Czech novelist Karel Capek in 1933. He marveled at the 17th century solution to the Dutch housing shortage—one townhouse on top, and another in the water.

Centuries of nicotine had stained the rich wood interiors of Amsterdam's cozy "brown" cafés, like De Schutterzolder where my host, the Dublin folk singer Kieran Halpin, sometimes performed. In the diffused Vermeer light that crept through De Schutterzolder's frosted glass, students argued Kant at its scratched oaken tables, poets scribbled sonnets on beer blotters, artists sketched studies on peeled beer labels. I sat reverently and sipped my beer, until I heard the frizzy-haired woman with the ruby in her nose.

She was noisily paying for her drinks with piles of small coins, the true mark of a busker. Margit spoke with a strange English picked up on a two-week holiday in the Scottish Shetland Islands, and made her living with only five songs.

"Aren't you bored?" I asked her.

"Noow," she replied. "I keep changing me pitches so I don'ta bore the shopkeepers. And I meetalotta guys." Margit wished me luck with the guilders and the guys as I headed out for the city's chief supplier of outrageous gear and colorful busking garb—the huge and sprawling Waterlooplein flea market.

It loomed before me like a city of rags and rust. Dented bread boxes and street sweeper's dustpans, bedsprings and bed-buggy mattresses, skis and egg beaters, bedpans and bicycle parts stretched for acres. My Waterlooplein wander led me past racks of WWII parachutes sewn into billowy pantaloons...frayed *aprés-ski habités, peau de soie negligées* with *petite* cigarette burns...grape-stained blouses left after the *vendange*, and what's this? a purple brocaded bishop's cape in a flea market? What a funky rag to solicit money in—but not for 500 guilders!

But the bicycles! The Waterlooplein was littered with the springs and innards, spokes and chains and seat stuffings of the big-boned old granddaddies with hard ornery seats I'd seen all over town. Leaning drunkenly against elm trees, teetering over canal boat riggings, doddering and rattling down the paths. Their skeletons and disembodied parts littered the town, caught on clotheslines, perched in treetops, and stuck in sandboxes.

Amsterdam had thrice as many bicycles and pieces of bicycles as human beings, Kieran told me. It had something to do with Holland's being only 37 feet above sea level, and the public transport scheme introduced by the socialist Provos in the 60's. Hundreds of free white bicycles were distributed all over the city. You could pick up a white bike and ride it anywhere, then leave it for the next person to ride anywhere, and so on. Until the white bicycles started disappearing. Dastardly capitalists were kidnapping them and painting them black, for private use. So people started stealing back the black bicycles and re-painting them white. After the dust of the Great Bike Heist settled, some people owned five bicycles and others had none. Kieran woke up after one night's drinking to find a yellow bicycle in his bedroom. How it got there, he remembered not.

Kieran warned me about busking in Amsterdam. "'Tis a fierce hard town," he said. "If it's not the freaks, thieves and addicts, it's the cops. Yer better off tryin' Alkmaar, the Gouda cheese market. Thousands of tourists—a peaceful crowd of cheese-eaters."

But I headed over to the Kalverstraat anyway. The quietest pitch I could find was in front of the Anne Frank Museum, where I'd seen a lone flute player sobbing out the notes of a sonata. But the vibes were morbid. So I began tuning up my 30 phosphor bronze strings in bricked alleyway across from a pizzeria.

When—

Uh oh, a washboard. And a guy as lean as a tiparillo wearing bubble gum colored polka dots. And a fiddler dragging a bow with limp horsehairs. And a harmonica brace with an assortment of whistles, tweeters and tooters.

"Oh, a fairy harp!" cried the leader of the shaggy band.

Harp and washboard duets? No thanks. The bubble gum-colored chap set up his barnyard box with cow-moo, duck squawk, clappers and wheezers, and I got out my penny whistle. The fiddler sawed his violin with the flabby bow, adding a wobbly turntable effect. And then the pizza-eaters lurched to the window.

Through the mélee, I could hear a merry-go-round, galloping closer and closer.

"Damn organ grinders!" Bubble Gum cried.

The carnival-colored barrel organ raced in our direction, pumping out booming polkas, while a menacing monkey rattled a decrepit tin cup.

"Crank music! Just turn a fricken' crank! Any monkey can do that!" jeered Barnyard, sounding his disgust with a duck squawk.

But our music wasn't as nice as the barrel organ music. And it made such a commotion that the owner of the pizzeria was shaking his fist at us. The motley crowd around us shrugged and dispersed, but for one curious observer.

Terry? It couldn't be the guy I'd seen playing for his daily bread and bota of vino tinto in Málaga. He couldn't possibly have made it all the way from the southern Spain with only two scratchy tunes!

But behold the busker's pluck—This Dublin lad had hitchhiked to Paris. Slept for a week on a bench on the Quai d'Orleans with a view of flying buttresses while waiting for a tent plot at the Bois de Bologne. Met up with an Armenian shepherd with whom he played tin whistle-ocarina duets at Le Place Boubourg, until he scraped together enough for a cheap fifth-hand guitar.

Now equipped with heavier artillery, he was ready to join the travelling circus of Greek pan-pipers, crooners and hairy-chested fire-eaters summering in Europe. And I was ready to leave it.

Wine for Soap

> "…and every time it comes to choosing between
> laundry soap or wine, we buy the wine!"
> —Peg's busking journal

June, 1981. Paris 1:00 a.m.

I'm curled up to sleep next to a waterfall, with my head on my harp case and camera bags tied to my legs. The cleaning staff has mopped around me and gone. Orly Airport is closed for the night. I'm the only soul left in the third floor Observation Area, the classy area of the airport that costs three francs to get into. It has an art museum and a cinema, so it attracts a higher class of people than the main area downstairs, which is free, but at this time of night is filled with homeless *clochards* and gangs of boys with bottles of cheap *vin ordinaire*. Here I have a comfortable bench near a soothing waterfall that reminds me of the Canadian North woods, where I will be safe for the night.

I'm sleeping at Orly rather than in the $10 hotel room I reserved today because Peg's flight arrives at the ungodly hour of 6 a.m. She'd better be on it, that's all I can say. This afternoon I rang her in Poughkeepsie from a phone booth on the Champs Elysée to say *bon voyage*, since it only costs one franc to call America for 8.6 seconds. She shouted, "Nan, I'm not coming! I have a prob—" and I cut her off. "Peggy Lyon! If you're not on that plane I'll never speak to you again!" I shouted back as the franc ran out. I didn't call her back to see what the problem was. I was too upset. Was she losing her nerve?

After all, this trip is for her. Peg has wanted to come to France since she was a girl. Her father had died when she was only nine years old. To help take her mind off it, her boarding school French teacher, Madame Ouimet, invited her to Marseilles for the summer. But my grandmother was afraid to let her only child make the long ocean voyage. If she had, I know I wouldn't be lying here now with a harp for headstone.

I don't know what I'll do for the summer if Peg doesn't come to Paris. In the last six months of going back and forth from Europe to New York, I've slept on so many floors and futons and train station benches, and wakened to so many cramps and kinks and visions of chair legs and baggage racks, that being a vagabond again is not the thing I most crave now. Even if the cafés and plazas of Europe are more exotic than the coffee shops and shopping malls of America. Four months and 43 different sleeping places. I counted them.

Last winter I was living in Switzerland, performing with a haphazard band called Mosaic. We did a mish-mash of Irish, Scottish, French, and American blues music. I had a fight with the guitarist in the group, and split. But at the worst time. I had the flu, it was freezing and I suddenly had to *demenager* all my clothes and gear and earn my airfare back to New York. Biel-Bienne, the little bilingual town we lived in, was too small for more than two street musicians, even though some days I'd managed to play one side of the street disguised as an accordion player in the morning and the other side disguised as a harpist in the afternoon, and solicited contributions from the same unsuspecting people. To get the money for my plane ticket, I was forced to get up at 5 a.m. for five days running to catch trains to seek my fortune in Bern, Neuchâtel, Fribourg, and Solothurn.

I returned from Switzerland with empty pockets and hit the streets again with my accordion. Peg saw me at work when I decided to busk the Poughkeepsie train station at rush hour for my fare back to Manhattan. But as soon as I sat down and unstrapped my bellows I was surrounded by cops. No musician had ever played in the Poughkeepsie Train Station before, but I was shocked by this assault. Until the cops explained that they were on a stakeout for a gunman, and they were afraid the gunman would think I was a decoy!

Peg thought it was hilarious. Over a gallon of Gallo she got me talking about my adventures as a post-war troubadour, playing on stages as diverse as a pigeon-covered fountain in Torremolinos, the Staten Island ferry, the foyer of a Reno casino, the steps of a porno shop in Amsterdam, a milk crate in a Dublin alleyway, a flower pot in a Swiss shopping arcade, and among the vegetable stands at the city market in Portland.

When I told her about playing in Reno under the neon lights of the sinful casinos, and how the glassy-eyed gamblers drifted up and down the sidewalks jangling their paper cups full of silver dollars and pitched them at me like I was a target in a game of ring toss—and how the one-armed bandit got the coins away from me in the end—she snorted. And when I told her about San Francisco's street circus of mimes and stilt-walkers and fire eaters, and the serene old Oriental man I'd seen playing a one-stringed Chinese violin in a tiny cranny of a back alley, she got that faraway look in her eyes that made me think she was only nine years old.

The last real adventure I'd had with Peg was when she drove me and my three sisters to Acapulco and left my father at home in Indianapolis. If Peg could have driven us all to Paris, she would have. Hearing about my adventures only rekindled her yearnings for a European holiday. And so, after several glasses of Chablis, I spouted "Meet me in Paris this summer. We'll make a busking tour of Europe!"

I'll show you the architectural splendors of Paris, I said to her. The canals of Amsterdam, the clocks of Switzerland. And the power you can feel on the street, making money out of thin air, with just your own confidence. We'll live like gypsies for nine weeks. It'll revive that spirit of independence. And dispel the gloom that had settled around her since the last one of her brood, my brother Robert, had left the nest, I was thinking. It would be great to have her along as my pal and business partner, mother and daughter side by side.

I wouldn't have invited my mother to Paris if I thought we'd starve. Seven years of busking had taught me something about survival. When I proposed the idea, she squealed with delight, not really knowing what busking would involve, but liking the "tour of Europe" part of it. And so for her 62nd birthday, her five offspring presented her with a fire-engine-red goose down sleeping bag and a tin cup.

My own sleeping bag is blue, and it is eleven years old this month. Its patched seams and matted goose feathers are full of many memories. It has been pawed and sniffed at by raccoons, soaked in Irish drizzles, baptized in French brandy, suffered the commotion of love under the open skies and has been flown, rowed, backpacked, trolleyed and shuttled on a hundred trips. Now it is lying expectant in a locker at Montparnasse station, where I arrived this afternoon on a train from Rennes with all my gear and my bicycle. The locker is big enough to sleep in, but it's stuffed to the keyhole with my backpack, tent, amplifier, and bódhran, the Irish goatskin drum that I'm going to teach Peg to play.

She doesn't know it yet, but part of our street act will be me playing the tin whistle, and Peg backing me on this primitive drum. After our finalé, a big flashy drum roll, she'll go around collecting money from the crowd, using it as a giant offertory plate. Or so that's how I envision it. She's never played an instrument before, except a few notes on a plastic tonette in a class for elementary school teachers. And she's never solicited money from strangers before... And I've never gone busking for a solid nine weeks before, or had to make enough money for two people... And she's counting on me to figure everything out... And so far I haven't even thought beyond tomorrow. I don't even have a map of Paris.

Peg and I sat at our wobbly table under the stars, high above the molten traffic streams on the rue de Rivoli. I raised my glass of champagne to toast her debut.

Edith Piaf couldn't have done better, I said proudly, and imagined Peg getting so good on that old goatskin drum that she'd leave me to my raggedy harp case as little Edith had left her acrobat father to pass his own hat in the smoky alleys of Le Quartier Latin.

"Oh, Nan! We're in *Par-ee!*" she cried. " Don't you feel something in the air? An elixir of romance, bohemianism, antiquity—adventure! I want to stand under the Arc de Triomphe and sing! But you said you'd show me the Louvre. I expected to see what was *inside!*"Peg laughed.

Of course I meant to show Peg the treasures of the Louvre. But today all we had seen was its métro station, the endless perimeter of its façade, and those dank mouldy underpasses where flute players vied for good acoustics and pedestrian traffic. After an hour's exhaustive exploration, we finally made our stage at the top of some stone steps flanked by majestic pillars. I tuned up my Irish harp, plugged in my amp, and started up a jig.

Our audience draped themselves on the Louvre's sunny steps, eating popcorn and hot dogs, feeding the pigeons and smiling blankly. While I attempted to rouse them with stirring battle marches and rollicking hornpipes, Peg smiled at any face and held forth the bódhran with quivering lips. She was going to pass around that Irish drum and charm the tourists into lavishing us with enough francs for dinner and a night on the town.

But when she was expecting roses and *billets-doux* for her darling daughter, and shouts of "*Encore!*" and "*Bravo!*" they gave her popcorn and centimes. I played harder, but the spectators took more interest in the tour buses disgorging the belongings of the Muncie, Indiana Bowling Team. There came a moment when Peg might have cringed and gone to eat a hot dog. But instead she narrowed her eyes, tightened her lips, and sidled up to a chic bonhomme. "*Aimez-vous la harpe?*" she said in trembling high school French. "*C'est ma petite jeune fille qui joue!*"

We didn't make enough for a dinner at La Tour d'Argent, but there was always tomorrow. Like any business, busking had its good days and its bad days. It was a gambling game with crazy odds—the public, the cops, the weather, the competition with other buskers, and your own energy and mood. One day you made lots of money and spent it; the next day the cops came or it rained or a fleet of street acts came and took over the town and you lived on baguettes. Sometimes nobody listened and you felt the fool. But sometimes it was a high-wire circus act with a cheering crowd, a pot of gold, an action-packed street drama, thrilling, joyous, even profound.

Peg took two daisies from our vase of street-corner flowers, put one behind my ear and flamboyantly tossed the other to the traffic below. As it fluttered down for eight stories, she exclaimed over the amazing ascent to our room up the dizzying, endlessly spiraling lino-covered staircase echoing with sizzling lamb and Tunisian laughter.

From a Poughkeepsie apartment to the Hotel de Paris. It sounded *très elegant*, and you might say it was. The view from our little balcony table was splendid and funny. In one direction, the illuminated column of La Place de la Bastille glowed like a firecracker, and in the other we could see the floodlit snarling gargoyles of Le Chatelet. Across Napoleon's grandest boulevard, in the windows of the gracious mansard-roofed apartments, TV sets flickered and burbled with French comedies, and knickers fluttered in the wind.

But I knew that many years would pass before Peg would ever let me forget what we'd gone through to find our hotel…

I'd gotten the name from a budget tour company called "The Magic Bus," and scribbled it on the bottom of a wooden brie box and stuck it in my handbag. After jet-lagged Peg claimed her baggage and the ripped carton with dangling strings containing her dismantled bicycle, we wrestled it on and off a city bus, dropped the bike off at a bike shop to be remantled, zoomed to Montparnasse Station before the meter on my rented locker ran out, and then hopped the métro to Hotel de Ville, the station I'd been directed to by the tour operator.

Emerging from the station, we saw a palatial edifice that looked like an Olympian version of New York's Plaza Hotel. A sign engraved in gold on the front said Hotel de Ville.

"This must be it!" I said brightly.

"Honey, it can't be," she'd said. "A room in there for $10 a day for two with breakfast? You must be joking."

"No, look at all the rooms—there must be thousands! That's why they're so cheap," I insisted. "C'mon, I'll go ask that concierge sitting at the registration desk."

We looked a sight, lugging the huge backpack, harp, dingy canvas bódhran case and Peg's lumpy bag of guidebooks. But I boldly approached the man in the small official room.

"*Pardonnez-moi*," I said. "*Nous avons reservé une chambre ici, pour deux personnes avec petite dejeuner.*"

He looked at us blankly for a moment. I thought it was my jumbled French and the Swiss inflection to some of my words. I repeated the sentence more slowly. This time the man burst into uncontrollable laughter. In perfect English he said, "*Mesdames*, this is the Hotel de Ville, the Parisian headquarters of the French government offices. And you say you have just reserved a room for two with *petite dejeuner*—in the post office!"

The "concierge" did not know of any hotel named "Hotel de Ville," but he concluded that it must not be far, because the whole area was called the Hotel de Ville.

"What's the street number of this hotel?" Peg asked me with growing exasperation.

"Oh, I have it in my bag. I have a hunch we're not far," I said. Minutes later, I spied another huge building with a metallic sign that said Hotel de Ville. Crowds of shoppers were pouring in and out of its open doors. My hunch was that our hotel was attached to this department store. I went up to the guard and asked him where we could find the entrance to the hotel. The man kept waving his metal detector and saying "*Voici, voici*" and I kept saying "*Ici? Ici?*" until Peg shouted "*Nancy!* This is ridiculous! Get out your cheese box and check that address!"

I fumbled at the bottom of my bag and pulled out the box, and read what I'd scribbled on the bottom: Hotel de Paris, 19 rue de Rivoli, métro stop Hotel de Ville.

When we finally arrived at #19 rue de Rivoli, the two lovely glass doors of the Hotel de Paris were wide open, inviting us to *Entrez*, but Peg tripped over the polished brass plating and the foot-wiping pad at the entrance and collapsed into one of the two plastic easy chairs in the small lobby. Our reservations were confirmed but our room wasn't ready. We wandered into the bar, following the drone of voices, and an "ack-ack" punctuated by an explosion. Six lanky teenage boys were taking shots at spacecraft that "shh-moomed" across a painted glass screen of the galaxies. And Peg caught the contagious hee-hee laughter of the tall man she described as having eyebrows that hung over his eyes like awnings.

The ascent up the spiraling staircase to the eighth-floor tower room #28, as far down the hall from the toilet as it possibly could be, took forever, and so did unlocking the door. The brown and yellow plaid bedspread clashed with the pink floral wallpaper and green woodwork. The mattress of the double bed was as hard as Gibraltar, the pillow was a punching-bag bolster, and the sheets were like medieval flour sacks, but as Peg said, in her condition she was not going to be particular.

Now as we sipped our champagne and gazed into our *petite chambre* from our balcony, all we saw was a comedy of backpacks, tent, battery-operated amplifier, bódhran case loaded with raincoats, thermos, notebooks and plastic plates, cups and cutlery, Peg's lumpy bag of books, my Irish harp and Peg's fire-engine-red sleeping bag and tin cup. Upon the bed was our meager first day's wages: a tiny heap of francs and centimes, pfennigs, guilders, and miscellaneous lire, less than an hour's U.S. minimum wage, between us.

I knew our act would improve when Peg learned to play that drum. She'd pound out a leathery beat to my wild tin-whistle reels, and people would fling open their shutters and mob us to see our show. But Peg had some ideas of her own.

"Remember that woman we saw today, the woman in the gumshoes?" she said.

She was referring to the thin balding tube of a woman in her 80's we'd seen at the junction of two métro corridors as we trudged home toward the Hotel de Paris. She was dressed in a faded smock that hung loosely above her bobby socks and gumshoes. She stood as still as a reed on a bed of brown cloth while people tossed coins at her feet.

Peg had been upset to see the woman making so much money with so little effort. "Look at that!" Peg had huffed. "Sure I could do that!"

"We need a gimmick," Peg said intently. "My blue jeans and tennies are just too straight. Maybe you could be a clown, and I could find some aviator goggles. Or no, wouldn't it be wild if we could dig up some flics' uniforms—go busking dressed as French police?"

"Police ? Good God—!" Clearly the champagne was having its effect.

"Nan, how often are we going to have to do this?" asked Peg, staring hungrily out at the great city glowing below.

"We should be able to make a lot of money and only play three or four times a week. If we hit the right places."

"What are the 'right places'?"

"Well, I don't know exactly. If we could get good spot in the métro at rush hour we might really clean up."

"Rush hour? *Which* rush hour?"

"Uh…7 a.m."

"*Seven aay-mmmmmm*? But honey, aren't we on vacation? They don't even serve breakfast here before eight. We're not going to face a stampede of pouting Parisians—on an empty stomach!"

"Okay, scratch that. We could play at Montmartre, or at the Centre Pompidou."

"What's that?"

"A huge modern art museum turned inside out, with pipes on the outside and a big cobbled plaza around it where the buskers fight for spectators like gladiators at a coliseum, swigging kerosene and belching mushroom clouds of fire, juggling hatchets and bowling balls, blasting punk from big bad amps."

"A circus!"

Yeah, a circus. Paris was the epicenter of the busking universe. Every busker on the European circuit started here, or ended here, and you had to be very good or very bold to take on Paris. Because getting a good busking pitch here was as hard as getting a part in a Broadway play. You had to compete with the whole European travelling circus of Greek panpipers, Romanian acrobats, French mimes, country and western crooners, opera aria singers and puppeteers, magicians and jugglers—and their entourage of drunks, addicts and pickpockets.

Like this:

On a terrace high above the roofs of Le Pigalle, in the radiance of the great basilica of Sacre Coeur, a fiddler tightens his bow, dips into a knapsack and scatters a fistful of birdseed across the sky. Within seconds the terrace is hysterical with flapping gobbling pigeons and a crowd of tourists has flown to the commotion: the musician has baited his audience. *Bad-a-boom!*

In front of a *tabac* on a lusty street of Le Quartier Latin, a swarthy man is unfolding a ladder and cajoling a goat. A crowd seethes around him, and as the man beats an old drum into a circus frenzy, the goat hobbles up the ladder and stands on all fours on a tin can. *Bad-a-boom!*

In a métro tunnel a tiny marionette mimes Stravinsky on a tiny violin and a saffron-robed sitarist sits curled in ragas against the angry tides. In another, a torrent of rock music crashes over an eight-piece band in mean leather jackets—and a droning lone accordion played by a woman with dark painted bow lips. Inside the métro cars, a strolling Japanese guitarist sings "Ret It Be" over and over, and puppeteers stage portable marionette theatre production of Le Petit Prince, red velvet curtain and all. *Bad-a-boom!*

June 30, Hotel de Paris…

Bonjour, Robert!

I love this life of wandering troubadour. Last night Nan and I played at Montmartre with the lights of Paris swimming in a mist below us. Nan says I'm getting great on that drum of hers, though the stick keeps flying out of my hand. Yesterday we met a busker who does a trained goat act—the goat climbs a ladder and stands on a tin can. He asked me to play my drum for his goat, and then to join him on the road. Of course I said no. How's P'keepsie? Wish you could see us. Tomorrow we head to the French Riviera, mobs of tourists and broiling sun. Miss you,

Ciao, Peg-Mom

Those first few days in Paris certainly tested my faith in the busking gods. I knew now what my mother must have felt all those many years ago when she awoke dizzy and breathless from nightmares in Mexico City, wondering how we would ever survive the summer and get back home again. One night Peg showed me the notebook that she was filling up with sketches of French noses and descriptions of the French confections she'd seen in shop windows—"jellied, fruited, layered, lathered and creamed; gooed, nutted, rummed, gummed, jammed and dripped; honey-glazed, frosted, marshmallowed, chiffoned, merenged, mapled and minted"—and her own impressions…

"For the sixth time today, Nan tugged her harp out of its raggedy case, to play at the Place Emile Goudeau. It was after 10 and we were both tired, but with the lights of Pigalle throbbing below, we threaded through the back streets just coming to life, heavy with the aromas of garlic and sausages and pommes frites.

The Place was jammed with American tourists. Nan set into one of her faster tunes. The crowd showered the bódhran with coins, and as Nan heard them bouncing on the skin, she revved up the music. I kept dumping the coins into her harp case, but after an hour of playing she looked pretty limp. I poured the coins into my pockets and neck purse and we packed up for the last time. If we didn't feel like rag dolls, our walk back to the Hotel de Paris from the métro could have been a dance, with the money jangling in our pockets calling the rhythm. It was so late the hotel's sidewalk café had pulled in its tables and rolled down its shutters, and there was no one around to say bonsoir to.

We trudged up the stairs to our room and like two bandits with a bunch of loot, threw all the money onto the bed in one gold and silver heap. I still didn't know the French exchange, but what a great way to get acquainted with it. It was more fun than a packet of American Express checks.

I was going down the hall to the toilet when I heard Nan yell. "Centimes!" she cried. "It's all *centimes!* Those American tourists gave us *centimes!*" And she pounded her fist on the bed and the coins jumped and crashed together. When she explained that a centime equals one-fifth of a U.S. penny I saw why she was so upset. After we counted all the coins, slugs and porno tokens—the total day's earnings came to $32, only enough money for the rent, a few groceries, and a few métro tickets. I hope tomorrow we'll find some better places to play.

July 5, Cassis

Dear Rob,

Nan and I have just arrived in Cassis on French Riviera in a hurricane with our bicycles—where it's too mountainous to ride them. And we're a week early for the tourists. I nearly committed mutiny last night, but we met a very nice widower, a fire-eater travelling with his daughter, who took a sympathetic interest in us. In his gold lamé robe, with his hairy belly slick with sweat and salve, he put his arm around me and said in a raspy voice, "You're my kind of people." But these Riviera resort towns are no place for an Irish harp.

Love, Peg-Mom

July 23, Geneva

Hi, Robert,

Nan's foot is recovering, though she still feels weak. She stepped on a broken bottle at a market in Rennes (it just missed her artery) and a doctor who happened to be passing by came to our rescue. Stitched her up, and let us stay in his château for three nights. (I practically lived in the marble bathtub). We remind him of Edith Piaf and her father, he said, and I think he wanted to adopt us. He was sorry we didn't get to do any Breton dancing. Now we're in Switzerland to strike it rich, but every other busker in Europe is here with the same idea. Yesterday two American jazz bands set up on either side of us, and when we moved to another spot in a shopping arcade, a huge mechanical clock with wind-up zoo animals clacked and chimed for half an hour, and we lost our crowd. The Swiss police harassed us this morning, and "interrogated" me for forty minutes—in German! What a way to see Europe!

All my love, Mega-Mom

August 16, Amsterdam

Dear Robert,

This sure is a funny trip. We're in Amsterdam with lovely flat bicycle paths all around, and our bikes are in Paris. Nan was afraid to busk here, but the punks really like our music, and we haven't seen a cop all week. We found costumes at the Waterloopein flea market and are thinking of dressing up like Dutch masters with accordion-pleated collars and waxy mustaches. The Dutch make great peanut butter! I can now say what a splendid variety of accommodations we've had on this trip, a Breton château, a train platform in Geneva, the floor of a karate studio, the kitchen table of a farmhouse, a muddy tent in Avignon, a Paris artist's garret, and now a houseboat in Amsterdam.

Love, Mom

Back in Paris, after our earn-as-you-go holiday in the south of France, Brittany, Switzerland, and Holland, it was a Sunday afternoon at the Place Beaubourg, the day before Peg's flight back home. I was playing sad slip jigs in front of the old cathedral, heartbroken that our summer had come to an end. Suddenly the street exploded. Everything stopped. The stunned crowd around me stood gaping. A squad of flics appeared, gesturing and shouting. Yet I could hear nothing. I had been deafened by the firecracker thrown from a window above. Peg was motioning me to go on with the tune. Was she stunned too? Why was she smiling?

For an endless moment I sat in a macabre silence. Confounded that anyone could want to harm a harp player plucking peaceful tunes. Suddenly I realized why the flics ordered Peg to keep me playing—they wanted me for a decoy. Not *again!* First Poughkeepsie, then Paris.

I knew I'd been vulnerable all these years before crowds of strangers—alone in the dark on 8th Street in Greenwich Village, in tawdry Reno and dicey Amsterdam. Perhaps it was amazing that nothing had happened before now. I thought of my busking friend Bruce who used to play Irish fiddle while walking on a tightrope strung between two trees in Central Park—an act that eventually got him a part in the Broadway play *Barnum* and a gig with the Ringling Bros. Circus. One day a drunk knocked Bruce off his rope and beat him up, sending him to the hospital.

I jumped up with my harp and folding seat, grabbed the amplifier, ragged case, and loose coins and started stumbling through the crowd. Peg took me by the sleeve and guided me to a spot some 50 yards away from where we had been playing. Then as she had done when I was only two, after I'd fallen face-first into a lake, she put me back into the water so I wouldn't be afraid of it.

"*Jouez!*" she commanded. This time I could faintly hear the words, and all the other familiar street sounds I thought I'd never hear again. I played a slow march, and she joined in with the drum. Then a shiny squad car pulled up and stopped. I nodded and smiled, thinking the cops must be glad to see us unharmed and back in business. But they gruffly ordered us to stop.

"*I-n-s-u-p-p-o-r-t-a-b-l-e!*" cried Peg with an indignation I hardly recognized. "You order us to play and then you order us to stop. Isn't this Mitterrand's France? Go pick on some real criminals!" We took our sweet time packing up, smiling smugly at the four big mustachioed men who glowered at us for a full half hour from their shiny car. And we left the streets of Paris after the bang without a whimper.

Peg and I had one last night at the Hotel de Paris. One last bottle of champagne. Then after a teary jag over our espressos the next morning, I put Peg on a bus to Orly and I boarded a train to Cherbourg to catch the ferry to Ireland. When the train arrived in Cherbourg, I had four hours to kill before the ferry departed for Rosslare. I considered busking because I'd done it here before, and gotten lots of coins from lusty sailors. But without my business partner by my side, I didn't have the heart. So I wandered into a café, where I heard the news.

Planes were grounded in Paris. The French air controllers had just gone on strike in sympathy with their U.S. counterparts. And I'd left Peg in Paris with only her airline ticket and the brie box of centimes, dinars, escudos, pfennigs, guilders and pesetas, the debris of the summer's earnings, to get her back to America. I leaped for the telephone in the café. I rang her number in Poughkeepsie. The phone rang and rang. I was imagining her destitute and alone in Paris, when at last the phone answered and her groggy voice came out of its sleep fog and mumbled "Nan, I got the *very—last—plane* out of France!"

It was unbelievable. And her cocky Air France pilot had said to the passengers over the intercom, "If we don't make it to JFK before the strike deadline, where would you like to land? Fuel is no problem." And didn't Peg, still tattered and worn from our adventures, start thinking of Cuba and Peru and Martinique? With a last stroke of busker's luck, my franc got stuck in the telephone slot, and we talked for 15 minutes, shouting our reminiscences over the cold Atlantic. Finally, I asked her: "Would you do it all over again?"

There was a long, crackling pause and then a "Ha!" laughed so loudly that the franc rattled down the slot.

Montréal–Montreal

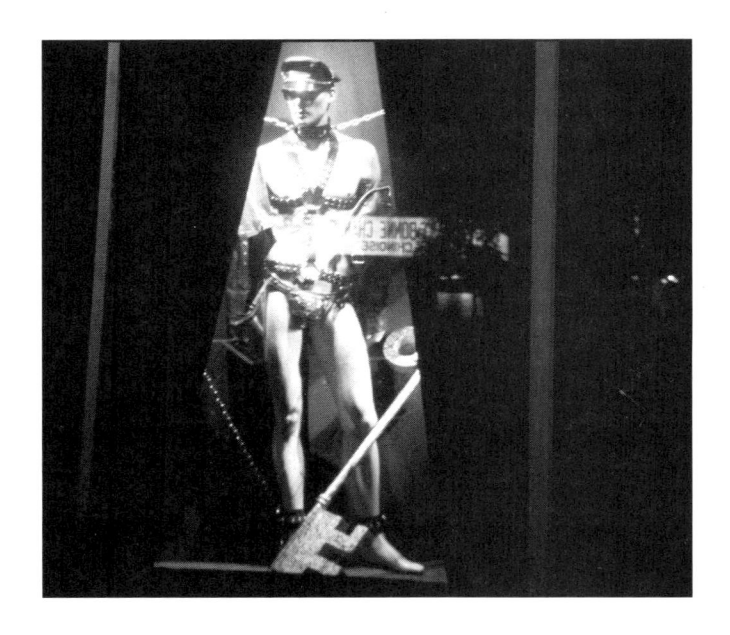

Montréal-Montreal

Bang

It's summer in Montreal. Drag the beds out onto the balconies. It's too hot to be alive. But no, no, heat makes life. Weeds blooming riot in the *ruelles* again. Beans shooting from vegetable gardens. Jungles of flowers dripping swoony nocturnal scents. Sheets crumpled on damp beds in the morning.

The sticky smell of love drifts over the city, especially pungent along rue Sainte-Catherine, where *Le Plus Grand Sex Shop en Amerique du Nord!* sells edible undies, banana nipple licker drops and all you need to get it on. And along Boulevard René Levesque billboards painted with puckered ruby lips welcome tourists to Montréal— *Ville d'Amour.*

Dreamy hot-white bloated sky darkens and bursts with Jurassic thunder. Then fire-cracking flowers explode in the sky over the Jacques Cartier Bridge. Bright shooting pistils rocketing up to burst into stamens of electric red and blue. Pop! paff! hiss *Neowww* whines the symphony of triggered car alarms. A mammoth chrysanthemum sparkles—oooh! aahh!—eclipsed by bewitching blooms of extraterrestrial turquoise.

Swoooosh! Silvery spermatozoids shoot up under the Gothic silhouette of the bridge, swimming through the dark to detonate in showers of lavender and orange and gaudy sangria! Glittering aerial waterfalls flash and fade into weeping willows. Feathery plumes of light. Dizzy visual aphrodisiacs! Then it comes—the bridge lit to its shadows with throbbing colors in a stupefying climax. You could die with the beauty of it. *Bravo! Chapeau!*

On this hot rainy rooftop night, I am high above the city watching lovers watching our city's midsummer ritual of fireworks, Caressing under umbrellas tugged by the wind, exchanging skin wet deep kisses, their billowy silhouettes move in a hypnotic ballet against the flashing pink night. Until the petals of a hundred shattered blossoms scatter and dim and fall to cinders into the St. Lawrence River. Hot reds and sassy purples pulse and die, trailing delicate smoky threads over the old spired bridge. Leaving cobwebs in the sky.

Enfin, summer is sizzling again in our voluptuous twin-souled métropole. Montréal-Montreal, the city where Chinese fortune cookies offer aphorisms in two languages, a *chien chaud* at the Jacques Cartier Hot Doggeria tastes better than a Coney Island hot dog, The Lone Ranger and Tonto converse in the language of Sartre—and even Mynah birds insult you in two tongues.

It is summer and we are hysteric. Sex-crazed. Heat-craven. Lusting until the death knell crackle of the first autumn leaf. Seasonally schizoid, we are, like our city, a doddering granny bundled in old afghans and furs from October to May, and a shameless ageless sexpot from June to September. It's a Jekyll and Hyde kind of life, dictated by a climate-driven, manic-depressive, hypo-hyper sexual psychosis, if you know what I mean.

Now the city's gone heat-wave berserk. Now there is flesh, and I am a perpetual gawking tourist, following the carnival of bared bodies—lusty, busty, lean and hungry—around the jazzy cafés on rue Saint Denis, the bistros and raunchy hideaways on The Main, and the cobbled rues of Vieux Montréal. Festival feeding frenzies of Fireworks and porno Fringe Theatre spiced with Schizo-Swing-ska music, Jazzy Jazz and Lollapalooza and bilingual street comedy, and Gay Diverse-Cité and Tango Tango Tango, day and night and all night and all day and you gotta live without sleep for three months to take it all in.

Take a midnight stroll through my *cartier*, with its doors open to the lush and ovenly summer night. Where you can hear cicadas and see stars, feel like Louisiana and act Latin. Pinch me, I'm living in a technicolor postcard.

After ten years, I'm still a tourist in my own gender-bent neighborhood, the Cartier Latin. The city's oldest and liveliest sector is now listed by Tourism Québec as a bonafide tourist attraction along with its *Village Gaie*—Gay Village. Ville de Montréal bureaucrats numbly refer to the area as *Centre Sud*—South Central Montreal. And Statistics Canada confers it the status of—*voilà!*—the poorest district in the nation.

Join me on Freak Street, *La rue des freaks*. Ah, but it don't translate. Emerging from the bowels of my local métro station Beaudry, I'm greeted with hands outstretched: The Beggar's Opera costumed in meticulously ripped, frayed, torn and shredded jeans and T's, tights and fishnets. Stomping mean Doc Marten boots or running you down with roller blades and shocking you with hair like fireworks. Red-blue-green-orange. Bursting from shaven skulls, tweaked, spiked, slick and stiff as a knife. Check this one: you think he's wearing a woolly red cap with a funny design, but his close-cropped cherry-colored hair is painted with a blue spider web.

After ten years of living in *Le Village*, I'm still a gawking spectator at its Felliniesque street scenes, with characters like the one standing at the corner of Sainte-Catherine and St-Hubert in striped T and orange shorts, holding a boa constrictor at the window of a car stopped for a red light. While the driver inside keeps screaming and screaming. There are no laws against walking your snake in the City of Montreal.

Le Centre Sud was the first district in Montreal to be settled, and some old warehouses and 300 year-old houses still stand within the shadow of the Jacques Cartier Bridge. The *arrondissement* is a patchwork of *pur laine Québécois* working class and welfare families, gays and lesbians, punks and students and genteel gentrification spiced with tattoos and angels from hell. A mélange of mansard-roofed Victorian dwellings with spiraling staircases and wrought iron balconies, cute corner cafés named Banana and L'Eléphant Blanc, Radio Canada recording studios, charity shops, magnificent spired Catholic churches and lewd leather bars.

As the summer waxes to the solstice, I watch the cartier preparing for the annual renewal of Québécois national pride—La Fête de Saint-Jean-Baptiste. First celebrated by the habitants of New France in 1638, it's been going every June 24th for the last 150 years. Out of closets come the fleur-de-lis covered T-shirts, shorts, hats and beach towels beaming

Vive le Québec Libre!
101% pur Québécois"
Fier d'être 100% Québécois
Pur 100% Sang
Pure-blooded, pure wool Québécois!!!

Balconies and spiral staircases are draped with gigantic blue-and-white flags and banners and fleurs-de-lis covered balloons. The tabloid *Le Journal de Montréal* promises a festival exploding with thunderous joy and so much commotion that *aux confins de la galaxie*—from the outer limits of the galaxie, extraterrestrials observing our planet will have proof once and for all that yes! there is life on earth!

Tell me now, Madame Lyon, how does a hillbilly girl born in Nashville and raised on Indiana summer tomatoes and sweet corn and sun-brewed iced tea end up in the east end of Montréal? What's your fascination with this expatriate game? And what exactly inspired this passion for French places? Was it that chance *rencontre* with the mime Le Monsieur Marceau? Or was it the name Two Cities In France?

Nancy is the historic 12th century French capital of the Dukes of Lorraine. It is north of Lyon, which lies at the confluence of the Saône and Rhône Rivers. I learned this in my year of French at Broad Ripple High. Madame Bévard pointed out these cities on the map in my scribbled over second-hand textbook. I proudly circled them with thick black ink. Later I was fascinated to learn that Lyon, the ancient capital of Gaul, was the city of Lugdunum founded in 43 B.C. by Lucius Muniatius Plancus, and that Emperor Augustus had named Lugdunum in honor of the Celtic god Lugh, a many-talented lad who happened to play the Irish harp.

These curious place-name connections came back to me while traipsing around Europe in the early 80's with my Celtic harp. In the south of France, the owner of the campsite in Avignon balked after he saw the name I signed on the camp register.

"Mais non! Non! your real name," he insisted. "These are two cities *en France*!"

"*Oui, je sais*," I told him. I tried to explain that it was just a quirk of fate. No conscious design on my parents' part. They'd never even been to France. My Manhattan-born Yankie mother did have a French-looking nose, but my Confederate father, of prime hillbilly stock from Bulls Gap, Tennessee, thought the French were inveterate snobs.

The owner of *Le Camping Avignon* pouted and thrashed his arms. "*Ah oui? Mais alors! Bon!—et puis moi, MOI, je m'appelle PARIS BREST!*"

It's been ten years now since I tasted my first Paris-Brest, that sinfully rich praline-almond pastry named after the French capital and the harbor town in Brittany. It was on a night in February, at the café Brioche Lyonnais on rue Saint Denis in Montréal, with clumps of wet snow falling through a neon pink sky. It was the night I plotted to flee New York's Hell's Kitchen forever and move to the Paris of the North.

Coup de Foudre

You have only to be born in Tennessee and grow up in Indian-No-Place to develop a longing for foreign faces and sounds. Or have a mother who drives you to Acapulco when you're on the cusp of adolescence. That wild Mexican summer was my first trial of learning a language under survival conditions. When we got back home to Indiana, I wanted to study Spanish, to write hot tamale letters to Armando, the handsome lawyer who saved me from the waves at Pie de la Cuesta. But I was pre-registered for French and the hierarchy at Broad Ripple High refused to change my curriculum. So I was stuck with Madame Bévard learning sentences like: "Last summer we visited France. The trip was very interesting."

That scrappy year of French came in handy 20 years later when my latent gypsy tendencies emerged. I left New York City after 13 years to live in a series of damp cottages and bed-sitters in Ireland. In Dublin I heard French again from Bretons and brushed up my conjugations with an Alsatian pastry chef. Eventually, I packed off with an Irish band to Biel-Bienne, a bilingual German-French town in Switzerland, and performed in folk clubs and in the streets all over that tiny country.

You can't go busking around Europe forever, I could hear my lawyer father saying. When I returned to New York in 1984, I was dismayed to find my hippie Irish music friends grown up into Yuppies and Manhattan more unlivable than ever. I wondered where to lay my exiled heart.

In February 1985, a weekend getaway to Washington, D.C. fell through and I found myself driving north on U.S. 87 through the Adirondack Mountains instead. I didn't expect a weekend in Montreal to change my life, but there, on Ste-Catherine Street, with glinting snowflakes drifting onto fur hats and fat mittens and mustaches and long trailing *foulards*, with lovers floating arm-in-arm over the snow, and tall jaunty boots crunching through powdery festive streets that felt like Tolstoy, I lost my heart in a snowstorm.

That weekend I saw a man with a waxed mustache drinking café au lait from a bowl, through a warm and steamy window on rue Saint-Denis. On rue Ontario near Papineau, I heard music coming out of an old barber shop. I peeked inside and saw three frosty-haired gents playing fiddles and a melodeon, and a lusty young woman perched in the barber's chair battering out the steps of a clog dance. They played every week, they said, but next week it would be at *la poissonnerie*—the fish store.

Intimate cafés, métro buskers, mansard roofs, real church bells—not pre-recorded—and snow. In Montreal I felt myself in Switzerland, Dublin and France all at once. What a handy place to be an ex-pat, just over the New York state line. And what a novel way to live: if you didn't like your daily horoscope in one language, you could consult it in another. But an adolescent wing-ding to Mexico and busking in French was one thing. Living in a foreign language for real was quite another.

That spring I got accepted to McGill, ostensibly for post-grad Irish Studies, and smuggled myself and my instruments and some lawn chair furniture over the border, seven months before my student loan and visa came through. I rented the first apartment I found, a cheap four-and-a-half on rue des Erables with front and back balconies, a *ruelle*, a view of the Jacques Cartier Bridge and some pretty garrulous neighbors.

Alain lived next door with his sister and her five kids from five different fathers. He was a lithe young man from the Gaspé peninsula. We could hardly communicate, but he painted my toenails Moulin Rouge red on the balcony, threw pebbles at my window before climbing up the spiral staircase into my kitchen, and finally showed me his collection of feather boas and platform shoes. He liked to go out dressed up as a call girl sometimes, and his greatest ambition in life was to move to Edmonton, Alberta.

Charlaine lived upstairs. She was a very pretty pop singer/songwriter whose boyfriend—*quelle coincidence!*—happened to be the leader of the Irish band Shenanigans. When I met Golo I met all the Irish musicians in Montreal, and got invited to the tiny *rencontre champêtre*—country gathering of French and Breton musicians on a farm in the village of Saint-Patrice de Beaurivages. There I met Clément Demers, accordion player and tattoo artist extraordinaire.

The day I signed the lease on my east end apartment, I eagerly called up my McGill adviser (one of two people I knew in town) to tell him. It was then I got my first baffling glimpse of Canada's Two Solitudes. "Why would you want to live out there?" he asked flatly.

I was to learn more about franco-anglo realities when I married—*en français*—Clément, a *pur laine* who spoke my language—traditional music—and played voluptuous French waltzes on a button accordion. Ten months after the wedding, when I finally got my work permit, I discovered that without fluent French, the piece of paper was worthless. I had planned to freelance travel stories about Quebec to survive. But New York editors weren't interested in stories on Quebec; it wasn't exactly a "hot" destination.

Feeling like a persona non grata, I grabbed whatever work I could find, brief stints as a mute lunchtime waitress in an Indian restaurant (I lied about having done it before), a babysitter and temp secretary. One day the temp agency mistakenly sent me to a junk mail distributor to replace their French receptionist—answering 40 phones and paging and announcing French names over the intercoms. The adrenaline-shocked minutes there dragged like hours. But they wouldn't let me go because they couldn't get anyone else. Evidently, an anglo mangling French was better than nobody at all, and must have provided a few laughs.

After that harrowing day my confidence soared—for a while. I devoured French grammar books, binged on tenses, gobbled nouns, swallowed *La Presse* whole every morning, crammed French TV, slept with the French radio on—until a sudden bout of indigestion made me want to throw up the whole mess and go back to the States.

What really pushed my French was being asked in May of 1987 to write *The Gazette* travel section's weekly "Short Hops" weekend getaway column. It didn't occur to the *Gazette* editor hiring me that I would need French for the job, because many of the reporters on staff didn't have it themselves. But in those days, none of the travel information was translated. In order to write my column, I had to decipher French press releases and guidebooks, conduct interviews, and take walking tours of Vieux Québec, archeological visits to Pointe du Buisson, go star gazing on Mont Mégantic, and learn white-water rafting and how to ride a mountain bike over a sand trap—in French. The $225 a week on-the-road column turned out to be a seven-day-and-night a week ordeal.

In the course of my travels for that column, which forced me to become a self-taught translator, I made a collection of amusing spellings and translations. I also compiled a dictionary of memories, still in progress, of how I came to learn certain French words.

Montreal's "Just for Laughs" festival comes but once a year, but misadventures in translation in a bilingual society provide comedy all year round. Quebec guidebooks and brochures are full of delightful spellings and coinings, such as delated, flee market, hereunder, homologated, iland, childreen, phenomenous, unfluence, unsular, varioux, whalesalers, and whishes. Then there is the confusion of using a word that sounds vaguely like another...a playground for the young at *hearth*...stands *has* a reminder, and the *sandpaper* that was really a sandpiper scuttering along the beach. I once discussed this tricky task of translation with a contact at the Québec Minister of Tourism who generously offered to help me in my work. "I could be a sounding bag for you," he said.

Some examples of Québécois tourism brochurese meant to be enticing are...

- "Ski without border. Through your migrations you will learn to harmonize with the inherent laws of nature."

- "This beach reaches out into a lake of fish."

- "A jewel in a rocks box, that's how appears Baie-des-Moutons."

- "Just imagine 300 kilometers of sturdy coastline." (Are we talking earthquake-proof country here?)

- "Drummondville, which currently deposit a city of gathering, is the turntable of the region."

And there is always that pesky confusion over *ancien* which means old (but not that old) in French, and ancient which means before the end of the Roman Empire, A.D. 476...

- "The town of Granby, known for its ancient fountains origination before Christ..."

- "The festival will feature a fashion show of ancient and now firetrucks."

- "Le Bateau Ivre, an ancient grounded tugboat, is a meeting place for those who want a feeling of evasion in the middle of the ocean."

In Quebec, menu items can lose their appeal when translated into English. Like this: "paw and meatballs stew" for *ragôut de pattes et boulettes*; "the crudity bunch" for *le bouquet de crudités*, and *entrées* called "entrances." The "liver pie Caroline" just ain't the same as *la Caroline de mousse de pâté foie*, and "house pie" isn't a match for *pâté maison*, while the "broccoli with bread crumbs" sounds downright silly.

Some day I may finish my dictionary of experiential French. It reads like an autobiography of my decade in Quebec.

écluse: One of my first Short Hops, someone at the Canadian Railway Museum suggested I visit *"les écluses"* at Ste-Catherine, Quebec. I drove off to find them, thinking they were monks in a monastery (the Saint Catherine recluses), and was embarrassed to find they were shipping locks.

baiser: On a white-water rafting trip on the Rivière Batiscan, my river guide André Lavoie was singing a Québécois song with the words *"baiser ma grandmère."* He explained *baiser* with a simple gesture involving two hands.

tiguidou: My friend André the hurdy-gurdy maker had a cockatoo named tiguidou, (Tziggy-do) that he let fly around the house. I tried to kill it after it gnawed through the electric cord that connected my laptop computer to the wall. Now I know the word is not a bird, but means wow—*parfait!* as in *ça va tiguidou*.

péché: I saw this word on a church marquée one night, and asked Clément why they were putting fish in Hell. The word for fish is *pêche*, but the wages of *péché*—SIN—is Hell. And the wages of learning a language is getting laughed at.

petite crotte: My Québécoise *belle-mère* (mother-in-law) used this affectionate nickname with me. One day, after I saw someone shouting at his little dog for making crotte on the sidewalk, I looked it up in Le Robert: *"excrément solide en petites boules."*

boue: La Société Québécoise de la Speléologie—the Spelunking Society—once sent me a press kit containing a smelly gray lump of mud marked *boue veritable de la grotte de Saint-Leonard*—actual mud from the Saint-Leonard caves. The envelope was decorated with a hand-drawn *chauve-souris* which I knew already was not a bald mouse, but a bat. I'd learned that while hanging upside down from a wall in a bilingual Iyengar Yoga class.

Bilingual Love in the Uh oh! Zone

"Why are you yelling at me in English?" raved Bernard.

"So Nancy can understand," Benoît shouted.

The three of us, Bernard, Benoît and I, had been walking up Boulevard St. Laurent on our way to the Jean Talon market to buy some fresh herbs for our dinner. I'd never seen these two francophone lovers arguing before. Suddenly they were hurling insults in the street, but even more passionately because one of them had attacked the other in English.

I found it odd, because my two actor friends and I always conversed in the language of Molière. But now Benoît felt compelled to rant at Bernard in English—for my benefit, to let me in on the imbroglio. As if I wanted to be included!

"Why are you yelling at me in English?" Bernard demanded again, seeming more outraged at the choice of language than the choice of words, and raising the altercation a few more decibels.

I was terribly embarrassed to be caught in their crossfire, yet I found this whole language twist fascinating and hilarious. Benoît's cursing and swearing in English was too hesitant to be deeply insulting. His barbs didn't fly, but wobbled like arrows stuck in jam.

My friends were fighting in English for my benefit. But what language do you fight in—and make love in, negotiate in or break up in if you're part of a francophone-anglophone couple, as so many of my friends are? And what about the elusive and fragile emotional nuances that make communicating in two languages a delightful challenge, or a dangerous ordeal?

I didn't have a fighting chance to fight with my husband in French, which would have been fun for me. Whenever he used French-Canadian "*sacres*" (swear words) I just grinned, finding them charmingly innocent compared to the scatological English words that carried a lifetime of emotional baggage.

Québécois swear words based on sacred objects used in the Catholic mass don't even make me flinch. *Tabernacle!* is considered so obscene that most good people swear in a variant of it such as *taberouette* or *tabernouche* (like darn for damn, and shucks for shit). And the way of intensifying a curse like *hosti*, the holy communion wafer, is simply to burn it—*hosti toastée!*

Clément didn't have the patience to *chicaner* (argue) with me in French because he knew I wouldn't understand half the words he was using. And having to express his anger in English made him even angrier. I was always surprised at this, because he was so fluent in English. But when emotions run high, the effort that it takes to communicate in another language can push one over the edge. Anyway, it doesn't take a translator to know when someone's angry. Body language says it all.

Early on in the relationship I can remember the strange sensation of hearing angrily spoken words that I could not understand. The emotional part of me was ducking for cover, while the intellectual part of me was grabbing the dictionary—an oddly contradictory response. I remember how I learned the word *theière*. One morning I was jolted out of my slumber with the words jangling from the kitchen "*Ou est-ce que t'as mis la theière?*" (Where did you put the *theière*?) I felt too timid to ask what a *theière* was. I knew it was supposed to be in the kitchen, because that's where Clément was looking for it. So I stumbled out of bed and joined him there and we looked for it together.

It wasn't the coffee filter. No sir, that was hanging on the rack in full view. And it wasn't the coffee grinder, still plugged in where it always was. It wasn't the egg beater or the salad spinner or the frying pan. Finally, Clément spotted the ceramic white teapot hidden under a stack of washed dishes.

How does one fall in bilingual love? Montréal-Montreal needs a *Chère* Abby /Dear Abby columnist to help us to tread the tricky, exciting waters of a budding two-tongued love affair.

Dear Abby,
I am an American who has just landed in Montreal. I'm enthralled with these French men with their aquiline noses and frothy foulards, and just the very sound of French sends sensual quivers down my spine. But what does it mean when a man I've just met says "*je t'aime?*" Does he love me, or just like me? Does it mean swell or sweltering? And when he leaves a phone message ending with "*Je t'embrasse*" does it mean he hugs me (like a bear), embraces me (tenderly, like in the French movies), or kisses me? And dear Abby, how do I find out without having to ask him?

I got married in French. It seemed the most exotic thing to do. Ravel's Bolero was playing through the sound system in the little room at the Hotel de Ville. The music was so corny—high school music to neck by—I wanted to laugh in between faltering pronouncements of "*Oui, je le veux.*"

Three years later, when my lawyer left a message on my answering machine, asking me whether I wanted to be divorced in French or in English—I wanted to laugh again. Only in Montreal! I chose French, of course. Signing divorce papers I couldn't decipher seemed *un petit peu* less painful.

Busking To Death
1986

Making a spectacle of yourself is never easy, especially if the audience is only an inch from your face or your toes. For the last few years I've thought of myself as a retired street musician, a veteran of Paris cafés, Swiss trains stations, and Irish vegetable markets. But while undergoing the humbling ordeal of immigrating to Quebec from the U.S., the only means of survival I have is playing my Irish penny whistle in the Montreal métro. It's the only job I've found that doesn't require any French, any connections—or any working papers.

Some people imagine busking to be easy work, bohemian and well-paid. And others that it's not even work at all. Few people have any idea of what it's really like.

It's like this. Seven days a week, for two to four hours a day, I toot out jigs and reels at the foot of métro escalators all over town. In order to play those few hours, I spend the whole day sprinting through 40 miles of tunnels and 65 stations, hopping in and out of métro cars, running up and down escalators, around and around turnstiles and back and forth in the tunnels, to snag a 7 a.m. pitch at Place Bonaventure or a 9 p.m. gig at Place des Arts, or anything I can grab. But by month's end, my pile of coins never amounts to more than $300.

If I were to list the qualifications for this job, I would say busking in the Montreal métro requires agility, endurance and clairvoyance. The ability to leap into and out of closing métro cars in a single bound. And when the doors open at each station, the aural acuity to distinguish instantly between métro Muzak and the music of a rival busker. (It helps to know the Muzak repertoire of each station.)

It takes a gambler's instinct to know which station will be lucky—or even available. It takes a love of escalator noise, the ability to smile for endless hours and not get dizzy staring into rushing mobs. And it takes a gimmick, or a crowd-stopping routine—walking on stilts while juggling pineapples will do.

Another requirement of this job is courage, particularly if you're a woman. I've tangled for busking pitches in Paris with the travelling circus of three-chord guitarists, Greek panpipers, Romanian acrobats, opera singers and fire eaters. I've battled rock guitarists with big bad amps, put up with cops and Muzak, foul weather and fatigue, and I've stared down punks and drunks on Eighth Street in Greenwich Village on late and lonely Saturday nights. But the Montreal métro beats them all for spooky busking.

In July it had been exhilarating on rue Prince Arthur with the lads—"Shenanigans"—tin whistling reels and dancing pert jigs in my sun dress and jelly sandals to a feisty backup of banjo, bódhran and fiddle. In August at night on cobbled rue Saint Paul in Old Montreal, I'd marveled at feeling like a gypsy-tourist in my own town, as I sat there with the moon rising over the Marché Bonsecours beside the Old Port, coaxing melodious slip jigs from my brass strings, while the $2 and $10 bills fluttered into my case. In the harbor below, I could see twinkling blue lights among the paddle boats and the floodlit lakers asleep for the night. Some jazz notes floated around the corner from the Place Jacques Cartier, followed by a man from Massachusetts who came over and talked in rhapsodies about how he loved Montreal and had travelled all of Quebec. He'd been coming every year since Expo '67, and was all for Quebec independence.

With Clement, playing in the cobbled streets of old Quebec City had been "très romantique." At the bottom of the *casse-cou* steps in the Quartier Petit-Champlain, wearing colorful bandannas, I played my Irish harp and he played his sweet accordion, and backed up my whistle tunes with the dancing limberjack he'd hand-carved and painted to look like an 19th century salty French sailor. We plied the tourists with saucy French gavottes and bourées, Breton sea chanteys, spicy Cajun tunes and melodic Parisian waltzes. Our handpainted sign sprinkled with shamrocks, triskells and *fleurs des lis* announced our trade:
MUSIQUE IRLANDAISE, BRETONNE ET FRANCAIS
petite flute irlandaise, harpe celtique, accordeon diatonique

I love the serendipity of street performing, making stages out of sidewalks and vegetable stands, and the candid-camera view of passing humanity. Sometimes nobody listens and you feel like a fool. Sometimes it's a high-wire circus act with a cheering crowd. You never know whom you might meet, or what you might win—silver dollars, white roses or gingerbread men. All of these I'd won while playing my Irish harp on corners near and far. But after busking alone in the

Montreal métro, after haunting the cold drafty tunnels from September through March, out of the Christmas hysteria and into the existential winter doldrums, I had won scars.

When I married Clément Wilfred Francis Demers, I thought I'd get my working papers and a job—or at least permission to freelance—right off the bat. And so did he—or he wouldn't have sold his tattoo machines, inks and designs in a fit of disgust after tattooing a rally of greasy bikers in Granby one weekend. With my being an American, we expected that my immigration to Canada would be a cinch. After all, what was a little border between friendly next-door neighbors?

While my new husband returned to school and worked on his career change from a tattoo artist to a *je ne sais quoi*, I braced myself for the six-month wait for my working papers and scoured the want ads for clandestine jobs. Montreal's linguistic reality hit me the day I found an ad in *La Presse* that announced:
> Pour vendre: oiseau mynah bilingue (francais-anglais);
> age de cinq ans; grande vocabulaire—50 phrases

In a society where even five-year-old Mynah birds were bilingual, what chance did I stand for a job? Even menial positions required French, as an ad in the Montreal *Gazette* made all too clear. I didn't even qualify for a job as a humble *plongeur*...

"Bilingual dishwasher wanted. Experienced only."

In Paris nobody gave a damn if you knew the difference between an *assiette* and a plate, only whether it was clean or dirty. In Paris you didn't have to speak anything to torture your arms with scalding water and catch greasy plates for 10 hours a day. The only requirements for such a post were being desperate for work.

I knew this from Jeremy, a brawny Viking from Detroit whom I met while busking with my harp on Saint Stephen's Green in Dublin. Jeremy had gone and done the whole Hemingway writer-in-Paris-garret bit, working as a *plongeur* in a greasy *cuillère* while writing a novel about hitchhiking through Afghanistan during the Soviet invasion of '79. He scrambled for extra francs with his jazz flute in the Paris métro, between tangling with the thugs of the Paris Métro Mafia for a busking pitch, and flicking off the bedbugs parading down his arms. According to Jeremy, being a *plongeur* in Paris had a certain *je ne sais quoi*, a grubby literary dignity that dishwashers in North America were never accorded. In Europe, it was assumed that washing dishes was only a *rite du passage* to a great and famous end. Like George Orwell. Like *Down and Out in Paris and London—1933*.

Well this wasn't Paris, and at age 38, after my achievements in magazine writing in New York City, it was odd to find myself groveling for menial work. All because I had only a monkey's grasp of the language of the country to which I had immigrated.

Forget what you know of the grubby New York subway, with its ghoulishly-lit, cop-patrolled anti-mugging zones, its colonies of rats, its leprous walls and chewing-gummed floors, ambient ammoniac aroma, and grime-caked ornamental tiles left over the Golden 1930's. Montreal's elegant Underground City is a true *musée d'art*, linked by designer stations serviced by sleek, clean, quiet rubber-wheeled graffiti-free cars. Each métro station has been designed by a different architect to reflect the ambiance of its *cartier*—its neighborhood. Stations are grandly named after historic French-Canadian patriots and heroes, like Louis-Joseph Papineau, leader of the 1837 French-Canadian patriot rebellion; explorers and coureurs de bois, like Louis Joliette and Pierre-Esprit Radisson; writers, like Octave Crémazie and Henri Bourassa, and pious Catholic saints. Stations shimmer with vibrant colors, murals, mosaics, stained glass, rose quartz, clay tiles, enameled steel frescoes, and displays of art, sculpture, photography and even archaeological treasures dating from the first days of the French colony, dug up during métro excavations.

Most of downtown Montreal and its métro stations are linked by pedestrian passageways, so you can float from one experience to another in the Underground City, never having to brave a snowflake. You could take in a documentary at the National Film Board, then go swim 50 laps and get a shiatsu massage, have your teeth pulled or capped, check out an exhibition of Robert Doisneau photographs at the Musée d'Art Contemporain, get your shoes re-heeled while you wait, sip an espresso in an elegant café, eat Chinese or Armenian—or go busking, and then challenge your pile of quarters to a one-armed bandit at the Montreal Casino. With 30 film theatres, 150 bars and restaurants and 1,400 boutiques, it's possible to live in the métro, as many buskers seem to do. But with so many places to blow your dough, even the most successful busker can leave the métro penniless.

Montreal is known all over Canada as a year-round busker's town. From 7a.m. to 11p.m., a brigade of roving entertainers enlivens the métro, belting out razzmatazz jazz, blues, baroque or folk, and juggling, miming, clowning and stilt walking. You might find a sax player in the Bonaventure tunnel, or a classical violinist in a tux at McGill, or a female drummer dressed like Sergeant Pepper at Peel, Mexican horns and brass at Place d'Armes, or a plaid-shirted band of Country & Western crooners—*maman, papa, oncle et fils*—spread out in summer lawn chairs, bellowing and strumming into portable mikes, at the Métro Berri. Certainly an Irish harp was not the instrument to tug around Montreal's métro system, to heft into and out of stuffed cars. No, the tin whistle was yer only man. Pocket-sized, high-pitched and handy. So one frosty morning in mid-September I slipped it into my pocket and set off to seek my fortune in the belly of the beast.

I was hoping to play in the tunnel at Place des Arts, but there was a musician already there, an old man crying into his harmonica. He would sigh back and forth over two notes, then beat the harmonica against the floor, then sing a ragged phrase. He sat slumped under a torn hat with his legs crossed, under the glaring neon, with two shopping bags and one battered suitcase by his side.

I zipped to Métro McGill—baroque quartet. Métro Lionel Groulx—cellist. Métro Mont-Royal—guitar player. I finally landed at Métro Peel and found it free.

Standing under the blue lyre sign, where musicians are permitted to play, I shyly took out my tin whistle and blew out a hornpipe. But after 15 minutes and no customers, I got bolder. I set up my show where every métro rider was obliged to pass me by—in the three-foot space between the up and down escalators.

As if to encourage me on my first day on the job, a man in a flight technician jumpsuit wearing a what-the-heck expression and a toupée that looked like a muskrat poised to leap off his head tossed me a $5 bill. Then a flock of ruddy schoolboys in Catholic school uniforms vied to impress me with their donations. A nickel. Two nickels. A quarter. One little guy paused, put down a man-sized leather briefcase, got out a wallet with slots for credit cards—and slipped me a dollar! Oh, the sweetness of it—to be subsidized for my performing art by a freckled, spectacled eight year old.

After two hours of playing, my lips felt swollen and parched, and I was breathless. I noticed that people responded more to polkas than to hornpipes. I made $6 for playing "Mickey Chewing Bubblegum" but only $2 for "The Boys of Blue Hill." In two hours, 15 minutes of playing, and 2 hours of looking for a busking pitch—4 hours and 15 minutes, I'd earned $26—an unheroic $6 an hour.

Before heading back to our four-and-a-half apartment on rue Champlain, I stopped at Métro Papineau to see if I could make a few more dollars. But the school kids there, street brats swarming like rats, grabbed my carton of apple juice, threw it high up on the escalator, and it slid down and sprayed sticky juice all over me. The piped Muzak was so loud I had to toot furiously and jump around to get people's attention, and the punks in torn black leather and spiked green hair gave me funny looks.

I decided to hang in for a few more tunes, until a crumpled old man in a shredded sweater with a decrepit cardboard box strapped around his belly hobbled up to me. The shadowy young man with him asked me how long I was going to play. "*Trente minutes*," I said, and added, "*pour manger.*"

The younger man muttered something at his charge. They walked away, but ten minutes later the old man was back beside me breathing oniony smoke at my face. And his talent agent—pimp—was leaning over by the railing smoking a fag. Suddenly, I got it.

People began giving me indignant looks, and the money suddenly stopped. The moral quandary was obvious: did they give their donations to me, the musician playing her heart out, or to the pathetic drooling man with his chin cocked to the ceiling and a cig stuck on his lip? To protest my upstaging him, three riders in a row looked straight at me while giving him money, and it was curtains for me.

As I packed up my whistle and turned to go, I ran into Greg, a curly gray-haired flute player I'd seen busking at the Papineau escalators with a flute case brimming with coins.

"How's it going?" he asked.

"So-so. But it's my first day," I replied. "Gotta crank up my nerves. It's tough out there."

"Get yourself a regular gig, and regular customers, and you'll be okay," he coached. He made it sound so simple, but as the months wore on, I wondered just how Greg did it. A woman who'd known him for years told me how he had Métro busking down to a science, with regular times and places to play, and customers who gave him $20 Christmas bonuses and even sent him Christmas cards. He made enough to keep himself and his young son, who wanted to join the Cirque de Soleil, Montreal's uniquely offbeat circus, in chocolate croissants and juggling balls. And he had just bought a house.

A regular pitch, and regular customers. Great if you could arrange it. My other busking coach, Willie Drennan from county Antrim in Northern Ireland, had found it profitable enough. With what he earned from busking, this fellow tin whistler had left Montreal to go into organic farming in Nova Scotia. Like a real *spalpeen fanacht*, a wandering laborer out of an Irish folk song, he still came back in winter on the bus all the way from Halifax for periodic métro busking binges.

I met Willie while changing trains at Métro Lionel Groulx. I thought I was dreaming when I heard that old jig "The Geese in the Bog" floating from a penny whistle one blustery morning, and saw a slip of a young man dressed in a green felt cap and pointy-toed slippers, with a quiver of tin whistles hanging off his shoulder.

Over a schtrong cuppa tay Willie described métro busking as a crazy kind of roulette. There were 65 stations, but only a dozen were good for busking, and once the cold weather hit, every guitar scratcher in eastern Canada made a bee-line for them. To vie for a slot on the daily lists, you had to be a night owl or an early bird— or a bully.

The system of "lists" was created by the buskers of the Métro Musicians Association to divide up playing hours and places fairly. Each morning when the métro opened at 5:30, the first musician to get to a station started a list (usually scribbled on the back of a pack of Player's), and taped it over the blue-and-white lyre sign at that station.

The Métro Musicians Association code of ethics required each busker to show up in person to reserve a two-hour playing a slot for the day. No musician could sign another's name on the list. Handwriting and inks were checked. So It Was Said. My second day on the job I got to the Métro Bonaventure at 9a.m., and noticed that the list was written in the same handwriting—and with the same pen.

"This list is not valid," I complained to the dozey-eyed guitarist strumming there.

"I never look at those things," he said coolly.

I ripped it down and walked away.

Guessing like a gambler which station might be lucky, I sped to Villa Maria. Good hunch. It was free. I set up my money box. I remembered to park my apple juice on the UP side of the escalators (even at the risk of someone taking a sip or taking off with it), because on the other side, kids sliding down the ramp would knock it off. I jabbed a straw into my apple juice box and got up a breezy jig. I hated faking smiles at the crowds coming at me, but this was show biz. Better to look like I was having the time of my life than look like a loser.

But what was happening? Métro technicians seemed to have reversed the direction of the escalators. I watched in amazement as one person after another stumbled UP the DOWN escalator. To and from work on automatic pilot, métro riders were like mice rushing blindly to the cheese.

While whistling up some jigs, I tried to play traffic cop. I stuck my leg out and waved it around to warn them about the escalator. But all I got were baffled looks—until they set foot on the escalator, got thrown off, or collided with the people coming down, and turned wild shades of red. A kid tried to warn his mother—"Mummy—it's backwards!" but did she listen? Then a husky man in a leather bomber jacket plastered with Canadian badges asked me in broken English—was I the dancer-fluter he saw last Saddyday? Sunnyday? For the next hour I watched him aimlessly going up and down and up and down on the escalators.

By early October I was bored with my two-and-a-half hour repertoire of jigs, reels, hornpipes, slides, polkas, set dances and harp tunes. I decided to pep up my act, and conjured up a gimmick. I bought a plump pumpkin. I scraped out the inside so it was good and dry. And then I carved a jolly face on one side and "MERCI" on the other.

At Mont Royal station, I plopped the pumpkin on the metal surface between the escalators, put on a day-glo green Halloween mask, and started cranking out the tunes. I felt embarrassed to be exploiting the holiday so prematurely, but the good people of Plateau Mont Royal, partially employed actors, artists, writers and musicians and their like, loved the novelty and put their money right in. After two hours I had $30 in slimy change and limp bills.

After all these years of busking, I've never gotten over my stage fright about those awkward moments of "setting up," getting out my instruments, putting out the hat, claiming my stage and setting the scene. The vulnerability in that long transitional moment from bag lady to performer always felt excruciating.

At Métro Jean Talon the atmosphere was conservative—somber Eastern European immigrant women in head scarves, with baby strollers—and it felt too frivolous to wear the Halloween mask. People crept up to my pumpkin and peered inside, making faces when they saw a soggy $2 bill, my own, put there as bait. Revolted by the idea of putting their hands inside a gooey pumpkin, they walked away. I didn't blame them. I packed up and walked away too.

A week later, my pumpkin was much the worse for being squinched into and out of my knapsack several times a day, and my back full of aches from the odd-shaped burden pressed against it. By mid-October my jack-o'-lantern was rotting and near collapse. I pitched it out with a pang of pathos like you'd feel for a dead pet. And when Halloween finally came, I didn't have the heart to carve another one.

As Christmas loomed, an idea came to me in a dream for the Busking Receptacle Par Excellence: a delicate Chinese paper parasol—painted with a big MERCI! It was portable, eye-catching and coin-catching. (If a kid slid a quarter down the escalator ramp, it was a sure hit.) The wooden latticework made a perfect little cage to capture dollar bills and secure them against a sudden métro tunnel updraft, and I could put my leaflets announcing tin whistle lessons between the spokes. The tip of the parasol balanced nicely in a Twinings Irish Breakfast tea tin, and the handle was topped with a tin whistle to sell.

I started out busking with the biggest parasol they sold, but that looked too greedy and tripped people as they walked past. And despite my weighing it down with coins, rocks and tin whistles, it picked up and flew every time an in-coming train launched a gust of air. Every night I patched the rips and holes with masking tape, and I finally threw it away. Just before Christmas, I bought a new petite and discreet parasol, lacquered up in glossy green, and a spiffy pair of fingerless gloves, every digit a day-glo color.

A few days after that, I was lying in a warm bed, snuggled up to my husband's tattooed back and the red-and-green inked parrot I had come to love so well. It was 4 a.m. and I was trying to psyche myself into leaping out into the snow-drifty wicked cold, to go claim a pitch at Place des Arts. Thinking, Oh Lordy, what I wouldn't give for a busker's computer-operated reservation service.

You'd telephone ahead—from your bed—to the little mustachioed man in the métro box, and he'd check each station to see where musicians were and weren't playing. Infra-red sensors would detect body heat under each Lyre at each station. Via an intercom set into the Lyre, the musician could announce his intended playing hours—*et voilà!*—you'd make a guaranteed reservation. Of course this might lead to graft among the métro guichet men, who might be tempted to take bribes from richer buskers. Nobody in this busking racket was honest.

After a jolt of coffee I bolted out the door into a blizzard. I trudged to Métro Berri to catch the first train. I made it to Place des Arts by 5:40 a.m. and no musicians were in sight, but there was a list already up. All slots were filled except 9-11 a.m. and 5-7 p.m. I scribbled my name in the 5-7 p.m. space and caught the next train back to bed, relieved at having reserved a good place for late Saturday afternoon peak busking.

At 4:50 that afternoon. I was back in the passageway of the Place des Arts. I signaled to the flute player there that I was playing after him.

"Uh oh," he said. "It seems there are two different lists," and he handed me a list with a man's name in the 5-7 p.m. slot.

"This isn't the list that was here at 5:40 a.m.!" I complained. "I'm playing here anyway!"

I grabbed my things and marched 50 feet down the passageway to set up in front of the Lyre, the official place to play. Twenty minutes later my parasol was nicely filling up with coins. As I was tootling a fast reel to a small crowd, I looked up to see a dark man with shiny black Western boots and a pearly guitar scowling at me. He kept glaring, but I was not unnerved, feeling protected by the crowd and the simple goodness of my music.

Then, his eyes like razors, the guitarist backed up in a deliberate slow motion and, with a wild animal force, kicked my parasol to smithereens. It flapped through the air like a wounded goose, and the coins rained and rolled over the station. The crowd was stunned. The busker strolled off with a petulant look. People quietly bent to pick up the coins. They dropped them gently onto my coat. With a squeaky nervous laugh I called out my next tune—"Comb Your hair and Curl It."

Thirty minutes later the guitarist was back—this time with the Places des Arts security guard. He ordered me to move, to let the guitarist play, but I refused. They could call the métro police, arrest me if they dare. The bully guitarist claimed I was discriminating against him, and the security guard regarded him with obvious sympathy. Until I displayed Exhibit A: the smashed umbrella.

Abruptly, the guard dropped his insistence that I leave, and he turned to offer the guitarist a concession. What it was I realized a few minutes later, when the miserable strummer was back playing where he started. While I could still hear him banging on his guitar down the passageway, I stuffed the shattered parasol into my whistle box and quit the pitch. Luck was something you didn't press too far. And I'd need lots of it to play the Montreal métro again.

My first married Christmas came and went with no grand tra-la. Clem and I tied together some spruce branches rummaged at a tree lot to make a Christmas tree, and decorated it with popcorn balls, travel magazine cutouts of the Fiji islands and other tropical destinations, and at the top, he tied a bright new silver tin whistle. The pre-holiday busking had been good enough to celebrate the new year with a Chinese dinner and champagne, and to buy métro passes for both of us. No more pass-swapping or stile-hopping to ride the métro together. After the dead umbrella episode, I didn't bother getting up early anymore to claim a busking pitch. I relied on Clem to scratch my name in wherever he found a place, or I just winged it to one of the stations in the hinterland, like Angrignon, Plamondon, or Beaubien…

The newsstand shop at Beaubien sold Sprite instead of apple juice, which meant that I kept burping into the tin whistle in the middle of my tunes. I wondered if people could hear the burps. The creepy saxophonist who played Place des Arts and waffled the bottom note like a fart showed up, and came over to the escalators to ask me when I would finish. And a few minutes later, an old blind man waddled up to me and muttered "*Tabernacle!*" the most offending swear word in the Québécois language. It made me laugh. But the sound of his wheezy accordion did not.

"*Excusez-moi, je vais jouer ici jusqu'a quatre heures,*" I explained politely.

He grumbled away, but not far. Under the Lyre sign he opened his accordion case to accept coins, not intending to play a single note. People looked at us both and started giving him money. He was, after all, blind. I packed up and just as I was riding up the escalator, I looked down to see him grab a peek at his watch.

I headed toward Métro Crémazie, a station I'd never tried. There I found a bleak atmosphere and mournful mushroom-colored tiles. After $4.23 for one hour of hard playing, I squeezed my eyes tight against the despair welling up, and that question that haunted holes in me "How did I get here—into this life?" Again, I cursed that perverse urge that drove me to live these strange survival adventures, and pushed me to brink of sanity…

When I opened my eyes, a cherub face was smiling up at me. A tiny boy so bundled in fur he could barely stand. He didn't blink, he didn't budge. After a few bars of a set dance, his mother tried to drag him away, but he was fairy-fixed to the spot. His mother lifted him up and spirited him away. He stared at me all the way down the corridor, and just as the train was pounding into the station, I grabbed the tiniest F whistle out of my box, leaped down the platform, and put it into his little hands. I saw the old magic of the music in its power over the boy. I felt grateful to be reminded.

Bon, ça va, ça va. The tunes were catching. The coins were showering in, when a shabby pre-teen with a baroque recorder came up to me.

"*Quand toe fini?*" he shouted. I held up four fingers. He frowned and started playing a fractured version of "Doe, a Deer."

"*Aie—arrêt-toe!*" I cried good-naturedly, in my best East Montreal slang.

Holy Horrors! He was blowing loud shrieking sounds that stabbed my ears like glassy shards. I tagged a passing métro officer and complained, but he only shrugged. People were getting agitated, and giving me dirty looks, like he was my kid. And I knew if I were a big bag guy with a Fender bass guitar, this would not be happening...

He's shrieking the notes at my ear now, and I go berserk. I jump at the kid. He falls to the ground, hugging the recorder tight to his body. I clench the recorder, and his whole body comes with it, and when I let go, his body lands on the concrete. I'm scared to hurt him, he could crack his head. I look imploringly at the dizzy rush of métro riders. "Non, non, non! Il n'est pas mon fils!" I scream.

The recorder's end-piece falls off and I grab it. The kid is rabid to get it back, and now I'm staring into the eyes of a werewolf in a plaid shirt. A low inhuman growl issues from deep in his throat, then a hiss. He grabs my arm and tries to sink his teeth into my skinny exposed wrist. His eyes are bulging with nightmarish fire, and he is hissing and growling, hissing and growling. His barred teeth graze my veiny wrist. With my free hand clenched to my flute case, I hold off his teeth from my skin. With eyes drawn to slits, he spits and spits.

Around and around we swing in a hellish circle and people are passing, staring, passive. In a delirium I drop my flute case, and fumble for the mouthpiece in my pocket and push it at his teeth. Then it flies out of my hand and rattles down the métro steps. Instead of my veins, he goes for the mouthpiece, and while he chases after it, I take a running leap up the down escalator, and run and run, through a blur of shocked faces, and run and run, forgetting my coat in the fright, and run and run down the street into a hardware store, where I stand jittering among the mops and the brooms.

That experience left me depressed for weeks, crying every time I looked at my tin whistle or thought about my lost winter coat. Had my dream of immigrating to Quebec—writing in cafés, making love in French, ice-skating in the moonlight, swathed in furs, serenaded by musette waltzes—come to this? To fight with a dirty brat in a dingy métro with everybody watching? I swore I'd never go busking again. My working papers would come through, and we could keep on charging our coffee and croissants at the local café until then.

After all my vows of never never, one snowy afternoon on my way to the immigration office, I was seduced by the acoustics in the underground passageway from Atwater Métro station to Westmount Square. They were perfect for strings, and the wily lady strumming there told me the pitch was free between 4-6 p.m. My harp and amplifier were cumbersome to lug around, but the acoustics begged me to try it, just once. So after stripping to my panties for a beluga-shaped Russian immigration doctor who made me sit there in the cold "like a good soldier" while she frisked me for alien germs, I sped home and grabbed my harp and amplifier, and ran for the gig.

The coast was clear on arrival, so I set up my show. Instead of the usual embarrassment, I felt excitement as I anticipated my harp strings ringing off the walls of mirrors. I plugged my pick-up mike into the amplifier, set up my sign, propped my harp case to welcome shower of coins, and tuned up my good old harp that looked like a medieval relic, made in a night school in Brooklyn.

The acoustics were *exquis*. The strings tingled and rang with a thrilling resonance. I worked myself into a happy trance with the hypnotic "Exile's Jig" and the coins clinked in. As I was plucking out "O'Neill's March," transfixed by my image reflected into the infinity of mirrors, a real coureur-de-bois of a tall man streaked past me—in the mirrors and in life—hugging a six-foot inflated Godzilla.

Zut! and *tonnere de Brest!* Was this for real, or some sit-com being filmed for the CBC? In hot pursuit of the man were two huffing cops. I couldn't believe that anyone would be so stupid to shoplift something that huge and ridiculous, conspicuous and useless. With the cops gaining on him, the thief dropped the Godzilla and it sailed in my direction. It bounced and toddled and nearly fell over, and landed on its feet right in front of me. And the creature's scaly vinyl claws pressed together looked exactly like hands clapping.

People stopped in their tracks, not to give me money, but rude looks—as if Godzilla and I were a perverse busking team. I tried to pluck my harp with a straight face. But what was more hilarious than this applauding Godzilla were the people who passed by and glanced at us and didn't even bat an eye—as if a lady harper with a dinosaur by her side were an everyday thing in the Westmount Tunnel.

An hour later the rookie cops were back. To the lilting notes of "The Bag of Spuds," they came right up and grabbed Godzilla by the scruff of the neck and hefted it over a shoulder as routinely as a lady's stolen handbag. I laughed to split my sides, but they looked away, embarrassed to be two tough cops dragging not a thief to his justice, but a dusty shoplifted Godzilla back to Toyland.

Spooked!

My Friend the Witch Doctor

You'll laugh if I tell you that the very first person I asked about voodoo in Guadeloupe turned out to be a *houngan*—a witch doctor! But this is exactly what happened…

    One morning, after climbing down the smoldering La Soufrière volcano with the smell of rotten eggs still in my nostrils, I stopped in the tin-roofed village of L'Habitée and bought some bananas. The skinny little boy selling them by the side of the mountain road was dancing and waving bunches at passing cars. When there were no cars, he stood behind his shabby table under the banana tree and waited.
    On the other side of the road another boy was standing behind another shabby table, peddling bottles filled with cloudy amber liquids. His mother's potions weren't the zingy rum punches I'd seen at beachside bars on Grande-Terre, the wilder wing of this lush butterfly-shaped Caribbean island of the French Antilles. The big glass jars of dark rums lined up on the mahogany counters of those trendy watering holes were floating with fleshy chunks of cherries, mangos, and pineapples. But these village home brews selling for 150 French francs were spiked with branches of the *Richeria grandis* tree.
    Bois bandé. Hard wood. Wood that gives you a hard on.
    Bois bandé is the island aphrodisiac. A botanist in Saint-Claude had told me all about it, and I didn't think it'd make such a smart souvenir to take to the boys back home—even if it might slip through customs.

Bois bandé was such a powerful vasodilator that a certain dose of it could leave a male with permanent priapism. An erection that wouldn't wilt even after dozens of orgasms. The botanist had shown me a Richeria grandis tree by the side of the road. The bark of it had been scraped away. Monsieur Maré said without a smirk that there were men on Guadeloupe who, after too greedy a dose, had chosen surgical amputation over permanent torture.

Bois bandé was easy to find. At the outdoor market in the bustling port of Pointe-à-Pitre, I'd seen buxom women in colorful madras plaid headdresses hawking little vials of it, along with their vegetables and the waxy phallus-shaped bars of ground compressed cocoa beans. I almost bought a vial as a conversation piece, but out of embarrassment opted for the chocolate rod instead.

Continuing my meander through L'Habitée, I decided to look for a café. I wanted to rest my legs from the 1,467-meter ascent up La Soufrière and to ponder the experience before returning to my noisy marina bungalow in Saint-François on Grande-Terre. Its tra-la of nightclubs, topless sunbathers, and Parisian girls modeling lacy white Créole dresses on the beach was starting to get to me. But in this corrugated tin village crowing with cocks (wherever you go on Guadeloupe— with 18 cockfights a day—there's a crowing cock on the loose) not much was open on Sunday. A three-table Créole restaurant dripping with primitive charm looked inviting. But the mere sight of the word *"boudin"*—squishy, spongy, intestinally pink blood pudding—sent me bolting in the opposite direction. The night before I had endured an island family dinner featuring boudin followed by *huitres*, slimy raw oysters, a mountain of gooey, garlicky *escargôts* and greasy pork and gray-brown beans. My soul for a green vegetable!

Farther down the road I spied an outdoor cantina where loud men gulped strong rum in the midday sun. Uh...*oui*, a warm Coca Cola without ice will be just fine, *merci*.

From my wobbly table I sat staring up at La Soufrière, which was now swirling with fog. The volcano is the magnificent centerpiece of the 17,300-hectare Parc Nationale, a rarefied cathedral of blooming orchids and flamboyants, tangling lianas and towering tree ferns and redwoods. The Park covers the central portion of Basse-Terre, the most mountainous island of this archipelago which is officially an Overseas *département* of France.

I'd never smelled a live volcano before. La Soufrière has been sizzling for 13,000 years. It erupted disastrously in 1976, but its temper is supposedly under control, or at least predictable. The area for miles around is planted with devices that monitor its seismic activity.

The hike up the uneven rocky path had been quite steep, but the excitement of climbing a live volcano had fired me on. Thick green walls of spongy sphagnum moss had risen up on all sides. The strange smell of sulphur got more intense as I huffed to the top. A light whiff of it was okay, but a full nose of it was nasty. At first it smelled like a beauty parlor. Then like a struck match. Then like really rotten eggs. Then as I climbed closer to the steaming fumeroles, it became a stink bomb.

A sulphurous stench that got more nauseating as scalding vapors hissed from the molten maelstrom, and an angry roaring churned in the earth's bowels.

One of those marvelous Raw Elemental Experiences.

Now why had I been thinking about voodoo on Guadeloupe, when the real action was on Haiti? This animistic religion woven with black magic originated in the French Antilles with the African slaves working the sugar plantations. ("voodoo" means god or spirit in the languages of Dahomey and Togo.) Haiti is the home of voodoo, but I had just read in Gallimard's *Guadeloupe* that it was still practiced here. And then I noticed on my map that a certain pond near L'Habitée bore the name Étang Zombie—Pond of the Zombies! Zombies were no black and white B movie joke. They were for real, as the botanist in Saint-Claude had reminded me. Harvard University ethnobotanist Wade Davis had explored the zombification phenomenon in Haiti in 1982, for the sake of medical science, and it was rigorously complex and unspeakably frightening.

Guadeloupe reeks of tradition and superstition. Beyond the beaches at Gosier and Sainte-Anne, and casinos in Saint-François, there's real folklore going on, in villages where the severed head of a black cock means death, and any black dog can be a lurking evil spirit. Take the town of Morne-à-l'eau. You're driving into it, and you look up to see strange village of—outdoor shower stalls?—covering a whole hillside. A checkerboard city of black and white and pink and baby blue bathroom tiles gleaming in the sun, vaguely clownesque. What is it?

You stomp on the brakes for a good look. Drive your rental car into a ditch. Get out, poke around. Gawk at the acropolis of wrought iron-gated mini-mausoleums, hung with old sepia photos of black grandpères and grandmères in Créole headdress. The residences of the dead in this Guadeloupean graveyard are fabulous, freshly painted, cost more than a house. And among them them, much humbler burial mounds of sand ringed by conch shells and covered thick with years of candles melted into macabre puddles of wax. Vaguely voodooesque.

Fascinating. My imagination was stoked up by Guadeloupe. By the tropical heat, by my nocturnal readings of *Interview With The Vampire*, by visions of bloody boudin, and the banana-sized cockroaches haunting my bungalow. Now it was the Devil's perfume, the smell of sulphur, that got me going…

Maybe he read my thoughts, the man sitting alone at the next table of the cantina. His jaunty smile invited me to *jasser en français*…about the weather in Canada…about the volcano…about the village and the little boy selling those bottles of potions…and then, well…did he, *par hasard*, happen to know anything about…voodoo?

Thin Toussaint in a neat white shirt. Spoke now in mutters. About being a *quimboiseur* with many international clients. What did I want? Love potions? Revenge? Personal power? A hex on the boss? An antidote for jealousy? Jealousy was a big problem on Guadeloupe, he said.

He got up from the café table. Some beastly curiosity made me follow him down a dusty side road. To a windowless concrete shack smelling of damp earth and smoke. Where a ragged bed darkened one corner, and a low table draped in blood-red satin occupied another.

Toussaint squatted behind his voodoo altar cluttered with objects. He lit a black candle. Then a cheeping sound, like the coqui tree frogs that sang through the Guadeloupean nights, came from under the table. Grinning, the youthful *sorcier* grabbed the thin plastic bag pulsing with life, and shook out the black-feathered baby chickadee fighting to escape. He would soon mash it live into a mortar with other ingredients for a *medicament*, he explained. If I wanted, he would brew me up a medicine too, for only 300FF.

I didn't have 300FF, I said. And I wasn't sick, although I was now feeling quite anxious. It was one thing to read about Wade Davis' harrowing quest for the ingredients of the Haitian voodoo zombie medicine, in his brilliant and spellbinding book *The Serpent and the Rainbow*—while I was snug in a bed in a Québécois winter. And another to be in the presence of a voodoo master who just might be a *bokor* and who just might have a deadly blowfish around the house. It was the blowfish, the puffer fish, Davis explained, that produced the paralyzing neurotoxin teterodoxin, which was 160,000 times more potent than cocaine and 500 times stronger than cyanide. (A lethal dose could rest on the head of a pin—which is why Japanese gourmands of *fugu*—puffer fish—sometimes drop paralyzed in a death-like trance—or stone dead—at their chopsticks.) But teterodoxin may one day provide modern medicine with a safer alternative to general anesthesia. This is what Davis and his colleagues are hoping. The blowfish looks like a balloon from hell, with spikes like vampire fangs and a mouth curled into a nasty sneer. I'd seen a one for sale in a shop at Pointe-à-Pitre—with a light bulb shining through its translucent skin and an electric cord hanging out of its tail.

Toussaint had been flipping through a stained and musty book of 19th century Tarot. Now he was playing with the rubber doll and chunks of human bones on the table. He offered me a sip from a bottle of thick cloudy liquid suspended with bits of organic debris. It was a "tonic," he said. And I said No. *Non, non, non, merci.*

Sensing my nerves, Toussaint turned chatty. "*Ka fé nwé?—Comment ça va?*" he asked, as the cheeping black chickadee hopped onto the table and Toussaint stuffed it back into the sack. Then he took out his Haitian passport and asked "*On parle le français au Québec? On mange bien?*"—already knowing the answers. He always wanted to immigrate to Canada, he said. I said I didn't think "*Sorcier en Voodoo*" would exactly fly as a profession, forcing a laugh. Then as the candle dripped, he chanted on in French mixed with musical Créole—the *bouillon* of French words, African syntax and Caribbean rhythms. He talked about the "craft" he had inherited from his parents...

They taught him magical incantations in Créole and French, and from an early age they could see he had the gift. He participated in their magic ceremonies. He chanted, went into trances, held seances with spirits, knew all the magic symbols and rituals, and how to concoct all the potions, powders and philters from ingredients procured in Haiti.

"*La magie noire* or *la magie blanche?*" I asked bluntly.

"*Les deux,*" he replied.

"Do you kill people?"

"*Mes parents sont encore en vie.* My parents are still alive. I have to be very careful. Avoid revenge. *Mais, oui, il faut tuer les gens des fois.*"

Yes, sometimes he did have to kill people, he said. But most of his work—mundane as it sounded—was with marriage problems. Spells for potency, desire and boredom. Spells for jealousy. And he could even break up marriages, he said. If I wanted a man who belonged to someone else, he could prepare me a *boulot*. It only took 21 days and $6,000 and it came with a guarantee.

Toussaint offered to concoct me a perfume with special powers. Wearing it would make men my slaves. The ingredients were complicated to obtain. He turned his back and brought out a little black bottle. When he opened it a vile death-like stink burst forth. I gagged at the odor, which was revolting and impossible to describe. Toussaint found my disgust amusing. He laughed and explained that he would disguise the magic mix with a rich knock-em-dead perfume. For only 300FFs.

Gotta go, I said. Gotta work on my sun tan. Try my luck at the casino, or betting at a cockfight. Maybe I'll win 300FFs and maybe I'll be back. And as I got up from the table, said my quick adieu and rather bolted for the stable door wondering if he'd even let me out, Toussaint reached over his head and with a smile that could have lit up the dark side of the moon, offered me "*un souvenir de la Guadeloupe*"—the funnel-shaped straw basket hanging over his voodoo altar.

Now the odd-smelling basket is hanging on the wall of my music room in Montreal. If straw could talk, I wonder what it would tell. And I wonder... should I have bought the voodoo perfume, and a dose of bois bandé to go with it? It's winter in Montreal, the best time for sex.

Excavating Arthur

It is historically inevitable that there should appear, in the town of Tintagel on the stormy coast of Cornwall, a car park named King Arthur, a launderette named Launcelot, and a lottery draw machine named Merlin. After all, Celtic mythology and Tintagel tourism have it that the heroic chieftain who saved Britain from barbarians in 12 great battles was brought forth into the world from Merlin the Enchanter's sea cave at the base of Tintagel Castle.

And it is inevitable that County Somerset, which claims Camelot and Arthur's burial place, should engage County Cornwall in endless blathering about which is "the real King Arthur Country," thus provoking a plethora of Arthurian theories, archaeological disputes, pretenders to the reincarnated King, and various Knights of the Round Table restos and bars.

But let's back up a minute—to Stonehenge—to Celtic bards and harps, and *Excalibur*, the movie, not the sword—and to what has brought me here, back to the 4,000-year-old stone circle on the Salisbury Plain and to Glastonbury, King Arthur's enchanted Isle of Avalon.

It was a peculiar initiation into Celtic matters, but I was a teenage Druid. In June of 1968 I came to London to spend the summer interviewing West End drama critics for a university thesis on English theatre criticism. I landed at Heathrow on the morning of June 21st, and for some reason thought of the crotchety old English lit prof named Decon I'd had, who had a thing for the old "Oak-Knowers," the Druids. I hardly expected to find any Druids in London, but I looked under "D" in the London phone directory anyway. The next thing I knew, I was on my way to the Salisbury Plain with a busload of urban Druids, to celebrate the annual Midsummer's Solstice rites at Stonehenge. By 2 a.m., jet lagged out of my mind, they had me dressed in a long white gown, groping slowly through the fog in a long chilly procession to the giant stone circle. I did my duty, bearing a bowl of soggy sacrificial bread crumbs past the Heel Stone and the Slaughter Stone, and around the North Barrow to the Station Stone, where I waited to greet the dawn of the Midsummer Solstice.

    I'm glad I have my photos of the Druid rites, because Stonehenge is roped off to visitors now. In the late 70's those Midsummer's rites got to be a free-for-all, with tents and teepees littering the Salisbury Plain, mobs of unclad hippies scampering over the stones, graffiti artists scribbling obscene petroglyphs, and vandals chipping away bits of souvenir monolith. Today the A303 Motorway flies by the old stones without a blink, but they make a startling vision by the side of the road. And their presence still evokes an aura of Celtic mystery and the legendary persona of King Arthur.

It is mid-afternoon when I arrive at Stonehenge. I have never seen these megaliths in broad daylight. They seem smaller than they've loomed in my imagination these 27 years. The play of dark cloud and flashing sun on the old sarcen stones and lintels makes them appear to move, drifting me back to that Midsummer's Eve of 1968 when the spell was cast.

I came here on a teenage lark, but seven years after my Druidic "initiation," I discovered Irish music and was inspired to build a medieval harp and pack off to Ireland, where, in an old Druid forest, I was to meet up with King Arthur.

The forest was an hour's drive from Dublin's Fair City. I met King Arthur—the actor Nigel Terry—as a lady-in-waiting movie extra in the film *Excalibur*, John Boorman's 1981 answer to Sir Thomas Malory's 1485 *Le Morte d'Arthur*. I had been busking with my harp on St. Stephen's Green one May morning when I met Jeremy Johnston, a brawny Saxon lad from Detroit. He had discovered that foreigners could survive in Dublin with a 50-pence Woolworth's photo and an Actor's Equity card, easily procurable for a £5 membership fee. He was earning about £18 for a 15-hour day as one of Arthur's Knights of the Round Table (good work when you could get it), and suggested I might, with my harp, get into the production as well.

I went straight to Woolworth's, then to the offices of Actor's Equity and the man in charge told me to show up the next morning at 6:00 a.m.—no harp necessary—to meet the bus which would take all of us extras to a forest deep in the Wicklow Mountains.

The first day on the set, the costumers spent hours dressing me as a court lady-in-waiting in a long medieval trailing gown. The next day I was a peasant in rude burlap sackcloth. (I knew what it was like to go from riches to rags, but extras had to changes lives and costumes in a flash.) It was a great week. We were fed well and often, and most of the time just hung around the forest and gabbed. Being in on the making of *Merlin* (as the film *Excalibur* was originally called) was like watching *Monty Python and the Holy Grail*. It was hilarious to hear the medieval monk standing next to me (who was really a used tire salesman from Ballyfermot) cursing and swearing in broad Dublinese, and to watch the antics of the knights, who, when the cameras weren't rolling, amused themselves by trying to stand on their heads in full suits of stage armor.

One day the tech crew brought in several buckets of "Kensington Gore" to prepare the scene for a bloody joust in the forest. As the camera rolled, the stunt men playing King Arthur and the Black Knight galloped full speed toward one another, when Arthur's lance caught in a tree branch and nearly yanked him off his steed. They shot the scene at least five times. That lance just kept getting stuck in that tree, until someone came and chopped off the offending branch.

Excalibur was the name of King Arthur's magical sword, of course. It was the Lady of the Lake, clothed in white samite, who rose up out of the magical waters on the Isle of Avalon, held aloft the flashing sword, and bestowed it upon him. (In the Monty Python version, it was some watery tart who threw a sword at him.) Avalon was the island of sacred apple orchards inhabited by a race of female enchantresses. After Arthur's death at the gruesome Battle of Camlann in 539 AD, his body was taken to Avalon, *Ynis Witrin*, the "Isle of Glass" where no hail, rain or snow have ever fallen. And where his soul was housed in a glass castle.

Did Avalon ever really exist? In Arthur's day the Glastonbury Tor was actually an island in the sea of the Bristol Channel. In a ten-mile wide circle around it, features in the landscape appear to form a zodiac, which some say was the original "Round Table." And excavations in 1190 at the Glastonbury Abbey unearthed a stone slab buried seven feet down, and a lead cross engraved with the inscription:

Hic Jacet Sepultus Inclytus Rex Arturius in Insula Avallonia—

Here lies buried the renowned King Arthur in the Isle of Avalon.
In a hollowed-out tree trunk the Abbey grave diggers found the bones of a tall man with a bashed-in skull, and smaller female bones and locks of yellow hair. On the tree trunk was scratched the name Guinevere…

Hailstones! The brooding sky over Stonehenge has suddenly erupted in an icy pelting shower. Nothing like nasty nails of ice to punch holes in a reverie. I run for cover into the gift shop, warming myself among the Stonehenge sweatshirts and baseball caps. Then I'm back on the A303 headed for Glastonbury, where, if it is really Avalon, it should not hail.

From a distance, the Glastonbury Tor and its ruined tower look like a lone breast popping out of the horizon. It is a conical hill rising 520 feet straight up from the Somerset Levels, over a small market town of 9,000 colorful inhabitants. It is a small hill with a giant mythology. It is threaded with earthen ridges in a circular maze pattern which may date from 3,000 B.C. It has been called many things: a Druid initiation center; *Caer Sidi*, the Celtic fairy king's glass mountain's secret passage to the underworld; a 5th century hill fort where King Melwas of Somerset held Queen Guinevere prisoner; a convergence point of earth ley lines, (energy lines running through the earth like acupuncture meridians in a human body), the Castle of the Holy Grail; and a hot spot for flying saucers.

Climb to the top of The Tor, where the wind screams through the ruins of the 14th century monastery tower of St. Michael the Dragon Slayer, and you feel why it has drawn pilgrims through the ages. The views of the Mendip Hills and the Vale of Avalon, which were once part of the Kingdom of Dumnonia, are exhilarating. But the summit of this bald mound has an eerie presence. After the Dissolution of the Glastonbury Abbey by King Henry VIII in 1539, the old Abbot Richard Whiting and two of his monks were dragged to the top of the Tor by Cromwell's men. Whiting was drawn and quartered, and his head lopped off and stuck on the Abbey gate.

The town of Glastonbury has been a magnet for pilgrims and seekers for long ages before the bones of "Arthur" were uncovered here. But since that day, Glastonbury and the George and Pilgrims Hotel (circa 1475 and still good for a pint) have been flooded with visitors to Arthur's grave and other sacred sites. According to the legends contained in the apocryphal *Evangelium Nicodemi*, Jesus came to Glastonbury as a boy with his great-uncle Joseph of Arimethea, who was a sea-faring merchant on a tin-trading expedition. After the Crucifixion, Joseph was imprisoned for many years, until finally released by Emperor Vespasian. In the year A.D. 63 Joseph of Arimethea returned to Britain, bringing with him the Holy Grail of the Last Supper and the spear with which Longinus had wounded Jesus. Joseph founded the world's first Christian church at Glastonbury, and buried the Holy Grail at Chalice Hill, the "Cauldron of Cerridwen" of ancient Celtic myth. The researcher David Young goes even farther, to say that Jesus lived in Glastonbury as a boy, and that the Virgin Mary came as well, and was buried in A.D. 48, in St. Joseph's Church. And at least one Arthurian theory contends that Arthur and his father Uther Pendragon are direct descendants of Joseph of Arimethea.

As for New Age pilgrims and Merlins, Glastonbury is full of them. Dowsers and healers, witches and Druids, geomancers and necromancers, mediums, monks and meditation masters—they come and go in this town with as many layers of beliefs as an archaeological dig, where it's more usual to wonder about your past lives than the one you're in. The buzz in the air is about sacred egg stones, horoscopes and healing wells, magical swords and crystals, and inexplicable shafts of light. Rainbow-colored shops sell New Age doodads like divining rods, amethyst massage wands and crystal balls, and copper pyramids to meditate in; aromatic oils and herbs to sniff and smear over your body, and tomes covering Arthur to Zarathustra. A sign in a café begs:

Please don't bring in sticky lollies, drippy drinks, or other droppy things

—and shop notice boards are tacked full of announcements:

Used Kirlian camera to photograph auras, only £790...

Teletherapy machine for sale, like new...

Spiritual healing for animals—send a snapshot of your pet, or a snippet of fur, or whisker, or feather, and a self-addressed stamped envelope...

Please help—50 homing pigeons need a retirement home, no racing...

Chakra ceremony—tools for personal and planetary ascension...

A haze of incense hangs over the town, and every week another New Age pagan arrives, claiming to be the reincarnated King Arthur, or Uther Pendragon, or Merlin or Guinevere. Wandering through The Glastonbury Experience, a small mall of hallucinogenic boutiques, I poke my head inside Wildwood Gems, a lapidary shop perhaps designed by an elf. A tall booted man with tidal waves of red hair is eyeing an emerald. Sensing my curiosity, he turns to me with a knowing air. "There are jewels and gold buried around here that are much more valuable than this," he says, "—along with the 17,000 ounces of gold that were removed from the Glastonbury Abbey before the Dissolution." And then he introduces himself as "Lifus."

"Lifus? Is that a Norwegian name?"

"No, it was given to me by three different ghosts that I helped. It means 'Life Anew' or 'Flight of the Eagle.' As well as being a speleologist, songwriter and musician, I'm a ghostbuster," he says casually. "Sometimes the spirits I contact help me with information. I have an sword at home that I dug up. It's about 2,000 years old, and is encrusted with enough jewels and yellow and pink gold to buy two houses."

"But shouldn't you take it to a museum?" I ask, challenging the verity of this claim.

"The police have been wondering about it, but they've got to prove that I've got it. It's not in my interest to part with it now, because it will lead me to more treasure. I also have a 2,000-year-old Caduceus, the magical air wand with the wing at the top of two coiled snakes, that helps me with my work as well."

"Which is what, exactly?"

Lifus meanders into a monologue on the mystical significance of swords. "Swords are what it's all about," he says. "I'm a member of the Essenes, a secret order that only broke cover in 1928," he explains. "There are only 70 of us actually initiated, and I have the great honor of being the Sword Bearer in that society. Prince [Unpronounceable], the heir-apparent to the throne of Qatar, is a very good friend of mine. He has just ordered us to make a set of swords for him. He wants me to research his ancestors' most famous swords and reproduce the originals... After a grave pause, he adds, "There are very serious things afoot in Glastonbury. Avalon is coming back to life. That movie *Highlander*—reincarnated lives, histories, past and present colliding—is what it's all about. It's so to the point it is unreal. My musical agent in London, Her Highness, the Princess of Pakistan, is helping me with my album *Angel Isle*, the story of spiritual activity in Avalon since Jesus. In it I release two secrets of the Church, and woe betide me when they realize what I've done."

Lifus offers to show me his excavated treasure, but I have a rendezvous at the Abbey. After thanking him for his esoterica, he says, "Well, I like to help people. Two women from Minnesota have been visiting me the past few days. I've given them lots of information. And they've taken one of my songs back to the States, to try to get it released in Indianapolis."

Walking back down High Street, wondering if Lifus is brilliant or crazy or both, I stop in the Gothic Image Bookshop to have a browse. The Gothic Image, which publishes guides and histories of the area, also organizes tours of Glastonbury's hallowed places, including The Tor and Wearyall Hill, Chalice Well, Gog and Magog, two old ancient Druid oaks, and the Glastonbury Zodiac. Jamie George, who leads many of the tours, is shelving some new books. I joke that Glastonbury seems like a New Age Zoo.

"No—" he says with a mischievous arch of the eyebrows "—it's like living in a pack of Tarot cards."

Glastonbury Abbey, "grandly constructed to entice the dullest minds to prayer" was once the largest in Europe, if not the world. According to the ancient science of gematria, the study of the earth's energy currents, the Romanesque Abbey is linked to the center of Stonehenge by a ley line. The custodian of Glastonbury Abbey, Brigadier David Morgan, is delighted to give me a tour through the magnificent ruins. They cover an area of 36 acres. We tromp through the misting rain, over the distance of 580 feet between the ruined nave and the bell tower, and then retreat to the shelter of the 14th century Abbot's Kitchen. Its vaulted dome roof, designed for ventilation, is now exploited for its acoustics.

Brigadier Morgan tells me about the night some New Age monks snuck inside it, locked the door, and proceeded to bang on drums and make awful wailing noises. "It happens quite often," he says with mild exasperation. "One night we caught some weird Buddhist sect from across the road meditating inside a copper-tubing pyramid they'd smuggled inside." (Probably the same pyramid I'd seen in the shop window at #13 Market Street.) "It looked like something from outer space. We like to maintain the Abbey as a sacred Christian site. But it's not a prison camp, and anyone who's reasonably athletic can get inside."

We stop for a contemplative moment at the simple plaque commemorating the excavation of the said bones of King Arthur. (The original spot where the grave was discovered lies 50 feet from the south door of the Lady Chapel.) David likes to believe in the Arthur-Guinevere story, although some Arthurians contend that the bones were a hoax perpetrated to attract pilgrims and rebuild the Abbey's coffers after its destruction by fire in 1184. On April 12, 1278, King Edward I and his young Queen Eleanor made a pilgrimage to see the bones wrapped in silken cloth and placed in a marble tomb in front of the High Altar. But the tomb has since been destroyed, and the current mayor of Glastonbury Brian Henderson calls the Arthur and Guinevere bones discovery "a load of rubbish—a great con story."

Nancy Hollinrake, known locally as the "town archaeologist," believes in the mythical Arthur, not the man. "Anyone who tries to nail Arthur down to the time span of an active man's adult life is doing the whole body of Arthurian material a terrific disservice," she says ardently. "A myth is a story of the gods and demi-gods and it is far more important than any one individual." Nancy, who obtained her degree in archaeology from the University of York, adds, "How can there be *bones*? Arthur didn't die, did he? He sleeps in the hollow hills, wounded in battle then taken to Avalon and put to sleep in a glass house—so why would there be bones?"

Nancy Hollinrake is a down-to-earth sort of woman keen on presenting Glastonbury as a town of museums rather than New Age flakes. We met in the old 15th century Tribunal at No. 9 High Street where Glastonbury's Tourist Information Center is housed (and serviced by an information officer named Arthur...Garfitt). Nancy led me upstairs for a tour of the Glastonbury Lake Village Museum. Its artifacts date from the era around 400 B.C. when Glastonbury was only a lake settlement of mud and wattle huts on stilts, and the area was known as *Sumersaeta*— Land of the Summer People. It is the best preserved Iron Age site in the whole of Europe, Nancy says. "Its inhabitants were remarkably skillful. Look at this Iron Age safety pin. A young monk on his way from Asia to visit his family in the States, saw it and cried, "Oh my God! My family became terrifically wealthy by patenting the safety pin!"

Later, Nancy invites me for a drink to meet her husband Charles, a consultant archaeologist who believes in Arthur, the man. We start with ales at the Who'd 'A' Thought It on Northload Street. This cheery pub/restaurant/hotel at the end of the town, warmed by a piano, a coal fire and lively chatter, is a whimsical memorabilia museum. The ceiling is papered with old commercial signs and hung with antique tennis and squash rackets, cricket knee pads, old cross-country skis, fishing poles, and harpoons. But in its last incarnation, it was something else. Only hours before, I had stopped in at the music shop, and owner Gary Crowley from County Cork had been inspired to describe the pub as it existed *before*. With the ferocity of a long-winded Gaelic curse, he called it the roughest, meanest, nastiest, dirtiest, scruffiest, horriblest, uncouth, vulgar, male, chauvinist, piggish, noisiest, smuttiest, grottiest pub you could possibly find. Then quickly said that since Bill Knight (as in shining armor) bought it and completely renovated the place, its "ethos" had changed.

After listening to Nancy and Charlie's friendly bickering over mythical and manly Arthurs, we carry on to The Rifleman's Arms on Chilkwell Street for bracing pints of cider. (Glastonbury is prime cider-making country—another hint at Avalon's "Isle of Apples.") The Rifleman's is the very pub I've been told to avoid— "a rough crowd of warring bike gangs and scruffy New Age travellers." But it's the Hollinrakes' local cider house and Nancy effuses over the rich bouquets of the various "designer ciders" made from apples specially planted for the cider's tastes— from dry to sweet—and each taken from a different orchard.

It's a rowdy zany night. Nancy introduces me to members of The Reapers and The Necromancers bike clubs as a journalist who's come looking for Avalon and Arthur. Then it's a free-for-all of jokes, puns, slams and jibes. Poor Arthur is laid out on the bar counter and disemboweled by public autopsy. New Age wand-wielders who shop at The Glastonbury Experience battle it out for conversational preeminence with New Age sword-wielders who call it The Ghastly Experience. Last week someone pointing a crystal wand walked into a shop and the owner screamed "No—don't shoot! I don't have any money and my children need me!" Glastonbury is godly. Glastonbury is goofy. And Avalon is really Babylon.

Babble on…Avalon really existed, yes, but now it's just a shoe store…a tire works…a car park…a rugby team. I can hardly hear myself think in this shouting match of cynics and mythologisers. But Will Vaughan is sitting close enough to hear me shout for a "Kalibur"—the non-alcoholic beer made by Guinness—and then I end up telling this blonde frizzy-haired young poet about my screen debut in the Boorman film. "Look for me at the joust in the forest," I say. And he says, "Oh, *you're* the one I've been dreaming about all these years!"

Will really believes the story about the bones of Arthur and Guinevere, and tells me that they unearthed the actual bodies of the lovers, perfectly preserved until a monk touched them and they turned to dust. While Will is waxing romantic, some of the bikers are trying to show me the old English game of shove-ha'penny, a kind of hockey played with half-pence on a slate board. The ha'pennies are the hockey pucks, made slippy-slidey with arrowroot powder, and you use your finger as a hockey stick. Neat. But I can't help noticing that these bikers I've been warned about don't look that tough. Nancy says it's a club of guys who ride bicycles and make long-distance trips with them. "Oh, where do you go?" I ask. "Well, nowhere, really," says a thin chap with thick spectacles. "You see, we don't actually go anywhere, because we don't own bicycles."

I do not see. But it is no more confounding than anything else I have heard this night. Perhaps these men pretend to go on long bicycle expeditions just to fool their wives, so they can go binging in the pub. I do not care to ask. I'm thinking that it's probably time to leave the bones of Arthur in peace and head for Tintagel on the moody coast of Cornwall.

On my way to Tintagel, I stop in the tiny village of South Cadbury to explore some more Arthurian geography. Cadbury Castle, 11 miles from Glastonbury, isn't a castle at all but an astounding 500-foot high Iron Age hill fort, which many believe to be the site of King Arthur's Camelot. Excavations on the site in the 1960's revealed the remains of a gatehouse, a cobbled road and the foundations of a large timber hall dating from 475 to 550 A.D., the Arthurian epoch. I hike up to the crest for a view. On a clear day you can see the Glastonbury Tor, but today is foggy and I pace slowly around and around the steep grassy cliff edge, with my ear cocked for the lost echo of thundering hooves and clashing armor.

The Bodmin Moor is the wildest stretch of moorland in Cornwall. Legend has it that the Dozmary Pool was the bottomless lake into which the sword Excalibur was plunged upon Arthur's death. In the movie *Excalibur*, the Lady of the Lake floats up out of shimmering waters to take the sword as it is falling. But this pond overgrown with rushes is disappointingly brown and bleak, more like *Wuthering Heights* than *Le Morte d'Arthur*. And if it ever was bottomless, it was very, very long ago.

Beyond the King Arthur Car Park and the leprechaun statues in the Fairy Grotto of The Dragon's Breath crystal shop, there is real coastal drama around the cliffs of Tintagel. Whether King Arthur lived, and when, the Cornish coast is spectacularly Celtic and evocative. It helps to have a hearty rugged old Arthurian like Roy Standring showing you around.

The ruins of Tintagel Castle crown a headland which hangs 270 feet over the lashing Atlantic. It was the 12th century Welsh Bishop Geoffrey of Monmouth who planted the idea that Tintagel Castle, the seat of Gorlois, Duke of Cornwall, was King Arthur's birthplace. But the castle was not built until the 12th century. In his *History of the Kings of Britain* published in 1145, the bishop simply bumped Arthur's lifetime up six centuries. Another legend has the Celtic chieftain being brought forth into the world by Merlin the Sorcerer, from a sea cave below the castle. Roy Standring leads me to the beach in front of Merlin's Cave, but at rising tide its huge black mouth is crammed with rushing water and foam.

It's a long steep climb to the ruins of the Norman fortress that was Tintagel Castle. The slippery rock-cut steps wind around and around the exposed cliff side to the windswept top, where the brooding castle spreads over 27 acres. We roam around the rubble of the castle's inner ward and hike up to the top of the headland for a panoramic view. Beyond the foaming breakers Roy points out to sea in the direction of the Scilly Islands. "Have you heard of the lost kingdom of fair Lyonesse?" he asks me. "Lyonesse was the legendary land that existed between Land's End and the Scilly Islands, before it was swallowed by a tidal wave. Seers claim to see it still in visions, its ancient towns old hills deep beneath the waves..."

Lyonesse! So that's why Lifus the sword-finder was so struck by my name.

The headlines in the local *North Cornwall Advertiser* are announcing that King Arthur's Great Hall in Tintagel will be the venue for the live broadcast of Camelot,

England's National Lottery Draw. And the draw machines are named Arthur, Guinevere and Merlin. From the outside, King Arthur's Great Halls looks like a Tintagelian restaurant, but Roy assures me that there are no Cornish pasties to eat inside. I decide to give it my parting shot, and am astounded at what is within. Majestic oil paintings by William Hatherall and 72 cathedral-quality stained glass windows depicting the life of King Arthur and the quest for the Holy Grail, and granite and wooden thrones and round tables, and 50 kinds of Cornish stone—all representing the obsession of the Arthurian who built it in 1933. It was the dream of the late, eccentric custard-maker millionaire Frederick T. Glasscock, who died in 1933.

Director Mike Godwin shows me around while telling me about Glasscock's Fellowship of the Order of the Knights of the Round Table. A teenager could become a "pilgrim" for a small fee, and then progress to becoming a "knight" if he were proposed and seconded, and paid another fee. (Sounds a bit crass, but what harm.) Glasscock was open-minded, or business-minded, enough to let females become knights. He played the role of King Arthur and did all the knighting himself, in a ceremony with robes, oaths, prayers and a sword named, what else? Excalibur. Godwin let me sit in the throne and pose with Excalibur, so heavy to lift that he who could should be king.

After all the myths and theories and commercial hype about Arthur, I'm Arthured out. Yet I am moved by the source of it all—the noble chivalry of another day, and Will Vaughan's words to me as I was leaving The Rifleman's—"For all these ages they've been looking for Arthur... In England, in Scotland, in Wales, in Ireland, in France and even in Germany. But nobody's ever figured it out. The real King Arthur is in you."

The Ultimate Adventure Travel

It's been many summers since I've visited the southern Indiana of my teen years, but on these potent August nights sizzling with crickets, I think about how I'd sit out on the old farmhouse porch under zillions of stars and scour the big glittering sky for flying saucers.

Travel by UFO—the ultimate adventure travel. Must be something about it in the air these days. I thought it would make a cockamamie travel story, and began looking for an abductee who had travelled with aliens. "How were the in-flight movies? Interesting scenery? Bring back any souvenirs?" I'd ask the abductee, in the spirit of an inquisitive travel journalist. But is it politically correct to call beings from foreign spheres *aliens?* Should we not refer to them as intergalactic visitors or extra-terrestrial tourists?

I was abducted once. It wasn't on a summer's night on a farm in Indiana, but on a winter's dawn, in front of my apartment in Hell's Kitchen, New York City, a few blocks from Jimmy Rigberg's Flying Saucer News Bookstore. I knew it was a dream because there's no place to land in midtown Manhattan, and they never abduct you in the dead of winter.

My abduction nightmare was a sort of spiritual chastisement for an extended bout of misanthropy. The alien spacecraft landed near the bus stop in the middle of Tenth Avenue right in front of Sonny's Delicatessen. When I got inside the big white ship, I felt an unspeakable sadness at the thought of never, ever seeing a fellow human being again—no matter what kind! The dream's effect has stuck to this day, and flashes back whenever I'm feeling ornery and belligerent.

To begin my search for a suitable abductee, I dug out the six-page handwritten letter dated June 4, 1989, that I received after the Montreal *Gazette* published a story I'd written on Quebec's Lac Mégantic Observatory. The letter writer, a former British Royal Air Force medic and UFO buff for 48 years, implied that Quebec astronomers knew more about UFO's than they would admit.

Five years after I received the letter, I answered it. I called up Ronald W. J. Anstee, who was still at the same address, and got an invitation to come over and watch some UFO videos. Maybe he could help me find an abductee, he said. On a stormy night in June, I drove to his home in Rosemont to meet with him. Driving east on Sherbrooke in the lashing rain and lightning, Montreal's arched Olympic Tower glowed like a thing landed from the Pleiades 500 light years away...

The evening was as casual as a bowl of potato chips. We all sat around munching—Anstee, his son and me and the whole family of in-laws and visiting grandchildren, while *UFOs: The Secret Evidence* and what was said to be censored NATO Cosmic Top-Secret footage rolled across the screen. Stuff like UFO's filmed by astronauts orbiting the moon, testimonies of Puerto Rican abductees, and a UFO crash in Durango, Colorado in 1978 in which five extra-terrestrial tourists were rescued and supposedly kept alive in a special Atomic Energy Commission "alien habitat."

National Enquirer meets B movie sci-fi and *The X-Files*. Hangars housing UFO's being test-flown by U.S. Air Force pilots, anti-gravity research, alien autopsies, and UFO's hovering over the Place Ville-Marie in downtown Montreal. Some of the stuff seemed pretty extraordinary, but some of it seemed too goofy to be true.

After all, most UFO photos turn out to be hoaxes. (A friend of mine faked a good UFO picture while lying on a beach, by throwing a soda cap bottle into the air and snapping it with a Polaroid). One of the most famous and funniest pictures that inadvertently became a hoax was that of the elfin-faced alien in a silver suit photographed in Montreal in 1967 at Terre des Hommes (Man and His World). Christian R. Page, a Montreal journalist specializing in the paranormal, took the photo of the plastic model ET as a personal souvenir of the exhibition. But it fell into the hands of a British UFOlogist who peddled it as authentic to sensationalist newspapers around the world.

At Montreal's first UFO Conference sponsored by SOS OVNI/Québec, Page, its president, offered dramatic proof that the "alien face" photograph, which he'd taken in 1967 and which had subsequently circled the globe, was indeed a fake. The conference ended with a screening of the controversial footage supposedly made in 1947 of a medical autopsy of an alien crashed at Roswell, New Mexico on July 2, 1947. Before the black and white movie started rolling—reel by gory reel—dry ice smoked over the stage and a "doctor" in a surgical mask wheeled out an operating table with an alien just waiting to be disemboweled—the very same silver-suited ET tourist from Terre des Hommes—miraculously retrieved from an auction.

Anstee loaded me down with books, including D. Scott Rogo's *Alien Abductions* and Timothy Good's *Alien Liaison*. Then he showed me an odd metallic fragment found 30 miles north of Montreal on a farm in Saint-Alexis-de-Montcalm. He also sketched the strange face with button eyes he'd seen on the #64 bus a few days later. Then he gave me the phone number of a French count who might "know someone."

Lucky for me, The Count happened to be in town rather than at his ancestral château in Brittany. Philippe de la Messuzière is a seemingly modest man, a retired electronics engineer with a quirky sense of humor and a passionate interest in UFOlogy. He has some highly-placed friends in the Canadian aerospace industry who are investigating UFO activity around Montreal. Apparently Laval, perhaps because of the Cosmodôme's Space Science Centre, is a real traffic jam of UFO's.

I met The Count at his apartment on a quiet street on the Plateau. A short, delicate man in his fifties, he greeted me with a wide-mouthed smile that was dolphin-like, sweet yet enigmatic. Over a *tisane vervaine* he showed me his albums of fabulous news clippings and filled my ears with stories about local UFO activity—mass abductions in Saint-Jovite, strange lights over Laval, and the work of Dr. Jean-Roch Laurence, Professor of Psychology at Concordia University. Dr. Laurence directs the Quebec Institute of Clinical and Experimental Hypnosis and publishes the Institute's findings in the *Journal of Abnormal Psychology* and other prestigious medical revues.

One of the Institute's projects is to study cases of claimed abduction. Professor Laurence is the first to point out that hypnosis does not produce accurate, undistorted recall of an event. Hypnosis may serve to open the doors of memory, but what comes out is from inner, not outer space. Hypnosis is only one of the tools the Concordia team is using to study the experiences of those claiming to be suffering the after-effects of alien abductions. One of the cases that particularly interested The Count was that of a young mother of two who lives in the Laurentians in the ski-resort town of Saint-Jovite...

It's Sunday morning and I'm on my way to the Laurentians, not to make the Perrier umbrella scene or go boutiquing or canoeing. I'm navigating route #117 north in a thunderstorm with a rather skeptical journalist friend Jean Bianchi. We are going to Saint-Jovite to meet Lyne M., who, upon arrangement with The Count has agreed to talk about her "trip."

The suburban bungalow is light and cheery. Lyne welcomes us in to the living room, and as Jean and I sit drinking sodas, she tells us about her experience *en français* in animated detail.

"*Il y a trois ans...*" she begins. Three years ago, on a Sunday night in late August, she was at her desk doing some bookkeeping for the family business, a restaurant and billiard hall. Her two children and husband were fast asleep, but she was wide awake and deep into her figures.

Without warning, Lyne felt groggy, then stuporous. She was used staying up until 1 a.m. and felt annoyed at this sudden urge to fall into bed. She stumbled into the bedroom, and the last thing she saw, the clock read 10:30 p.m…

"Lying on the bed, I was still conscious, when I had the weird sensation of feeling myself shrinking and becoming very tiny, and being sucked up into a long tube. Then I became my normal size again. I was in a long hallway, feeling my way along a concave white wall made of some shiny material which was neither metal nor plastic."

(In print this looks preposterous, I know. Like *Honey, I Shrunk the Kids*. But let's go on…)

A small grayish humanoid about three feet tall silently beckoned Lyne to follow him into a chamber. There, she says, she underwent a kind of examination to see if she was fit for the voyage. (Voyage to where, she never found out precisely, but it must have been awfully darn far away.)

Lyne describes the tall blonde human-like beings—two males and a female—who monitored the machines during the examination as "Wow! *Quelle beauté!* They were gorgeous! They belong in Hollywood!" She didn't feel scared, she says, because she was so fascinated with how incredibly beautiful these beings were.

Fit for the trip, Lyne was strapped in alongside blonde Hunk and Fabian and they took off. Lyne compared the G-force of the take-off to the wildest roller coasters at Montreal's La Ronde amusement park—*mais cent fois plus intense*—a hundred times more intense.

"The pressure felt awful," she says. "I don't know how long it lasted. I kind of blanked out. The next thing I remember, I was on another planet with strange scenery. I was looking out through a giant window onto a strange-colored city with no water, no trees. Just fantastic buildings I can't describe. But no water anywhere. It was dry and looking at it I felt very felt sad."

Why did they choose to take her, Lyne wonders. And why go all that distance to just turn around and come back? After feeling the G-force pressure on the return trip, Lyne was back in her bed. When she looked at the clock, it was 4:30 a.m.

Since her experience, Lyne complains of severe sinus problems, neck and back pain, and is sometimes afraid to go to sleep at night. And she says that now she's obsessed with conserving water and recycling everything in sight. And she's bugging her family and neighbors in Saint-Jovite to do the same.

Was Madame M. really an Innocent Abroad on the Planet X? She can hardly believe it herself. But who cares if it makes a good travel read and keeps you on the edge of your seat like it did Jean and me for two hours.

No need for an If-You-Go travel tip box. Unlike The Count, who'd love to meet some ET's and plans to booby-trap his apartment to kidnap them if they ever do visit, I prefer to be an armchair UFO traveller. Give me a good book like *The Monuments of Mars: A City on the Edge of Forever* by Richard C. Hoagland, and I'm gone.

Alien (Vac)ation

Hey, this is supposed to be Florida, and the town with "the most astounding multiple sightings of UFO's in U.S. history" witnessed by thousands of people. So where are the flying saucer fast-food joints and the "I Was Abducted By Aliens" T-shirts and all that jazz?

Admittedly, I'm arriving in Gulf Breeze after the amazing "Skywatch Era" of 1987-88, when crowds of locals gathered nightly for "UFO picnics" along Soundside Drive, bringing shrimp and strawberries and saucer-shaped "UFO cookies," a locally-inspired treat. With video cams pointed at the sky, there'd be silence, and then a rush of excited shouts and screams. "There she is, oh my god! What is that baby doin'?" I see two of 'em. *Three* of 'em! Moving to the west, slowly, oh whoa whoa whoa *whoa!* Y'all see that green halo? Go, baby, go!"

These were the days when every kid in town carried a camera, and ABC, FOX, and Nippon and Fuji Japanese TV cameras were rolling at marathon vigils in Skyline Park; when busloads of UFO "tourists"—five at a time—came from all over to see the landmarks—the circle of fried grass on the Gulf Breeze High School playing field, the lonely stretch of the "Miracle Strip Parkway" where the photo of the hovering UFO was shot, and the picnic table at Skyline Park where Ed Walters was "zapped."

You'd think a beach community on the Gulf of Mexico, where aliens were reported to have buzzed Hardees, Food World, and the Naval Live Oaks Visitor's Centre, would have cashed in on that media circus, with simulated abductions ("The UFO Experience"), rides in saucer-shaped hot air balloons ("The Gulf

Breeze Experience") and Emerald Coast tourist kiosks serviced by little green men. At the very least, a museum documenting the Gulf Breeze drama (witnesses vs. debunkers) and hands-on computer exhibits which let you hoax your own UFO photos, and virtual aliens to go with them.

But Gulf Breeze, nine miles from Pensacola on the Florida Panhandle, with its K-Mart Country "downtown" and Leave-It-To-Beaver suburban backyards, looks rather normal. The sugary white sand beaches of the Gulf Island National Seashore offer spectacular swimming and surfing. And should you want to go hunting with muzzleloaders for skunk or armadillo (yes, Florida cuisine can be weird), Eglin Air Force Base, the largest in the world, is nearby. There's a territory consecrated just for weapons development, and another devoted to outdoor recreation and nature preservation, i.e. kill the humans and save the manatees. (Eglin P.R. calls this schizoid mandate "Enhancing Environmental Quality while Maintaining National Defense Capability"—and if I remember my UFO lore, rumor has it that crashed saucers are stored in Eglin's hangars.)

Gulf Breeze looks normal. But there's a twilight zone feel about it, as if what was happening above ground went underground…

It started when the weekly *Gulf Breeze Sentinel* published the light-blasted, laboratory-analyzed Polaroids of a UFO (taken November 11, 1987, 5 p.m.) by a local building contractor. (Hundreds of other witnesses reported sighting similar crafts.) The contractor eventually revealed that his family life was being turned topsy-turvy by very close repeated contacts with a UFO and its occupants. He described strange voices and humming noises in his head, abduction attempts, and being zapped with a blue beam by the craft that buzzed his house. Ed Walters and Frances Walters finally broke their silence and anonymity and "came out" with the meticulously documented story and photos in *The Gulf Breeze Sightings*, a disturbing page-turner that gave me a migraine headache.

These days, Gulf Breeze UFO sightings have died down to a mere two a week, but sky watchers still gather at Skyline Park, and the Chamber of Commerce still gets calls from tourists asking about the UFO's. Boots Eckert, a retired high school teacher who is now Abductee Support Group Chairman for MUFON (Mutual UFO Network), once gave free informal tours of Gulf Breeze, and still enjoys showing people around. Boots is as spunky and likable as her name. She's committed to her work with MUFON, but she does not go sky-watching every night ("Honey, I got a life!"), nor does she talk about her counseling work with those suffering from apparent abduction syndrome. It's not her concern to substantiate abduction stories—as if anyone could—but to facilitate meetings for those who feel the need to share their experiences.

First off, Boots cruises by Gulf Breeze High to show me her old classroom and the house where Ed Walters used to live. Between the classroom and the nice suburban house with swimming pool is the school playing field where the 12-foot circle of dead Bermuda grass appeared one May morning in 1988. From that day on, her pupils talked about nothing but UFO's that they or their parents or friends of friends had been seeing—in the sky or zipping up out of the Pensacola Bay.

"Shark Zapped by Unidentified Diving Object!" I joke, with a touch of irreverence.

Boots tells me about how the University of Florida's nematode assays of soil samples taken from the circle of grass showed no trace of disease, chemicals or burning. "It was a year and a half before anything grew back there—even with fertilizers. The debunkers argued that a hoaxer made the circle by jumping up and down all night on a trampoline!"

Call me an open-minded skeptic when it comes to UFO stuff—"seein' is believin'"—but the trampoline theory is positively zooey.

Next stop on Boots' tour is the isolated stretch on Route 191-B, where on January 12, 1988 at 5:45 p.m. Walters snapped a photo after his truck was "stopped" by a hovering craft that "lit up the road and shot down blue beams." As a special souvenir, Boots gives me some first generation copies of the Polaroids made in 1988 by Ed Walters, of the crown-shaped UFO in the sky over the road, beaming down a bluish light, and then hovering only a few feet over the yellow dividing line. Whether they are real or not, I feel a certain amazement at having the photos in my hands.

Boots and I get out of the car and walk over to the blue spiral painted in the middle of the road to mark the spot where the UFO supposedly hovered. The blue spiral looks eerie, yet oddly mundane, as if someday it could figure in our repertoire of road symbols along with bicycles and wheelchairs. I step inside the spiral, and Boots takes a souvenir snap of me, chuckling about the landing pad for UFO's that somebody has built in Elmhurst, Illinois. But as we get back into her car she says, "I never, ever drive by here at night."

Driving back from the most beautiful place to go sky-watching that Boots knows of—Santa Rosa Island (45 miles of white quartz sand beach and emerald green breakers) my eyes pop out at strangest dwelling I've ever seen. It's straight out of *Plan Nine From Outer Space*, Ed Wood's 1959 black and white cult sci-fi flick featuring alien UFO's hoaxed with paper plates—a house shaped like a flying saucer!

The weird thing is that this house was built in the 1950's, before all the multiple sightings began. As if ET energies had been floating around Gulf Breeze even back then… The porthole curtains are flapping in the breeze. I walk up the strange launch pad ramp, and look for a door. Round and round and round I go, until I finally spot a keyhole, and a hatch. (What a weird door to come home to every night. What furniture goes with round walls?) I knock on the metal hull. No answer.

An hour later, Boots and I meet some of her MUFON friends for dinner at Chris' Seafood Grille. Over coleslaw, French fried sweet potatoes, alligator tails and iced tea, Art Hufford, a chemical engineer, is showing me his photo album of Gulf Breeze UFO's. The talk is about sky quakes and hyperjump phenomena—a sort of pre-briefing before heading out for a sky watch at Skyline Park.

Skyline Park is on the waterfront, at the edge of a creepy forest of live oaks hung with Spanish moss, frequented by snakes and alligators. The gathering this chilly night is congenial, and I'm happy to meet Ann, Mary, Ginny, Carol, Ken, Tom, and Hi-I'm-Ray-I'm-New. I ask what they do for a living, and get answers like "servicing UFO's when they land," "UFO traffic controller" and "alien spy." I'm regaled with stories of UFO's and flashing lights sighted—yikes!—only 50 feet away. But all I have to describe, I say, is the bright red thing I saw today flying high over a kid on the beach on Santa Rosa Island, tied to a string.

Boots is driving me to my hotel at Fort Walton Beach. Suddenly, she throws caution to the wind and heads for the lonely road and the blue-painted spiral, so I can see it at night. I know that nothing will be there, but my heart is pounding anyway. Just as we approach the long dark stretch of the blind bend, a bright yellow light flashes out at us through the trees and we scream—at the YIELD sign.

After saying our reluctant good-byes, I take a restless midnight walk on the beach to ponder it all. The March moon is full. With the crunchy squeak of crystal sands under my feet, I walk down to the water's edge. I pace for a while, then looking up from the softly lapping waves, I see reflected in the moonlight what I didn't see on the way down: hundreds of silvery luminous discs landed on the sands. And I scream again—at the jellyfish.

A Jaunt Around The Lakes

If you know nothing of Ireland—how to drive there, muttering Hail Mary's with your elbow on the wheel and your hands fumbling a Saint Anthony medal and rosary beads; how to drink there, in stupendous marathon rounds; how to chat there, filibustering gossip, boasting and harmless lies—you end up on a prepackaged bus tour bound for Killarney.

Oh, you should see it! When the tourist tide washes into Ireland's tourist capital, the whole town scrambles for the jetsam. Jaunting car jarveys quit the pubs, shave their faces, rouse their horses. Lakes of Killarney boatmen dredge up leprechaun tales. And merchants chanting *Cead Mille Failtes*—a Hundred Thousand Welcomes—tout their plastic leprechauns and T-shirts beaming "I Have Irish Roots!" Hustle, bustle, charm, inveigle, for the flood of tourists will ebb in a few hours, rolling away to the Blarney Stone and Bunratty Castle and back to the shores of Amerikay.

I didn't come to Killarney in a package. I came to see if it really was, like the Kerry joke says, a stage-Irish movie set that smells like a stable. The town does have this rich fecund aroma, a mélange of smoking turf, horse dung, and spilt Guinness, and its doo-dad shamrock shops are an embarrassment to the Irish race, and its pubs are jammed with sentimental Yanks crooning "Danny Boy." But the town of Killarney is only a stage-Irish façade for deeper things in the Irish psyche, and a cheery Celtic camouflage for the transcendental wonders in the countryside beyond, where a bosky light descends into ancient yew forests, and ghostly tangles of vegetation hide silent ruined farms.

Every traveller to Ireland loves to hear fairy stories, and Irish people love to tell them. But ask a Kerryman if he believes in fairies and you'll hear shouts and protests of "God, no!" And then the solemn aside "...but they're there."

In the dense woods around Killarney's lakes, you expect strange things. Here, the balmy wet has sprouted a shadowy Druid fantasia of stumps, moss, vines, bracken; trees towering, tangling, gnarled. Rivers of maidenhair ferns flow between moss-covered thrones, and giant lichenous stones hatch furry green beasts of trees. A grey oak hag with withered limbs reproaches a willow sipping daintily from the lake. A holly bends in an arabesque toward an owl-faced oak split by lightning, wearing ears of fungus and a belly full of birds.

You can tramp for hours, lost in the fantastic green zoo, and see no one. But sooner or later you feel presences that hint at Irish superstition. It drones under the garrulity of the Kerry people like a dark note under a hearty jig. For lush, mountainy Munster, merrily sacred and profane, is the Irish province of the supernatural. Indeed, the very breasts of the pagan Irish mother goddess, Anann, rise over the countryside east of Killarney, at Rathmore. These twin mounds over 2,200 feet high are odd even in a land of odd geology, and shapely even by *Playboy* standards.

A few years ago two lads climbed "the Paps" and toppled the ten-foot high stone cairns that for millennia had served as Anann's nipples. Locals said bad luck haunted the vandals for weeks, until they climbed back up and rebuilt the cairns.

Four thousand years ago, beneath the enchanted slopes of the Paps, the mythical race of the Tuatha de Danann, people of the goddess Anann, built *Cathair Crob Dearg*, their "City of the Red Claw." The DeDananns, renowned seers and necromancers throughout the Sumerian, Mycenaen and Egyptian worlds, raised magical mists with their chants, and changed their shapes at will. They settled at Rathmore in 1981 B.C. It's said that they were never conquered by the Milesians who came 200 years after them, but that they melted underground, into the raths—the prehistoric hill forts—to become Irish fairies—the "good people," the *Sidhe*.

In those mystical ages, all Ireland was a forest and an Irish squirrel could hop from Kerry to Derry without ever touching the ground. But Ireland was stripped of its great stands of oak and yew, hazel, wych elm and alder when trees were felled to smelt pig iron for England, to build ships for the Royal Navy, to tan hides for new English saddles, and to clear land for farms.

A balding Irishman says of his head, "Sure the waves are gone, but the beach is still there," hoping you'll admire the beach. You admire the forest remaining in Killarney's 19,955-acre National Park because it's grand compared to the treeless terrain around it. But the Earls of Kenmare preserved the Killarney forest as a playground for their royal sport—the hunt. The trophy heads of the native red deer hang in the stately rooms of Muckross House. A scattered few of their descendants roam the Derricunnihy and Tomies Woods, where the battered cottages of evicted farmers lie in ruins.

The Derricunnihy oak woods, perhaps the finest in western Europe, have stood for over 4,000 years. To tramp them you need good Wellington boots, a walking stick, and some bug stuff. Paddy MacMonagle, who runs the Killarney Printing Works when he's not poking under rotten logs or meeting up with badgers, lectures me on choosing Wellington boots—"make sure they're properly sprung, with spongy soles, thick cleats, and mudguards to protect the bunions!"—on finding oak branches for walking sticks, and on meeting up with creatures.

"You can scuffle and snort, sniffle and poke with your stick—these are natural sounds. But the moment you open your mouth—they're gone!"

With Paddy's scrawled map and blessing, I take off on the track behind the old Derricunnihy Church to look for the wooden bridge, old sheep pen, mushy spot, path through the rushes, and the old Kenmare Road.

A *pook* of a day just sits on top of you, Paddy says, and a *glaub* of a day is a mess. But this day is cloudless. The brittle light fires the sessile oaks into a brassy blaze, and the veils of old moss hang on them like yellowed Cambric lace. The mountain road to Kenmare has grown back to nature. The wheel tracks of the Derricunnihy crofters who rumbled over it a century ago are sprouted with tussocks. The lazy beds where their potatoes once grew are green ripples on the hills. Stubborn tenants weren't always driven out with the battering ram, they say around here. Some landlords had a tidier means of eviction: they sent a bagpiper out around the cottages at night to play one long wailing note. If that didn't put the fear of the banshee in the tenants, a melodeon player with a screechy wheeze box was certain to do the job.

Yanks are easy to spot around Killarney in their new Aran fisherman sweaters and leprechaun golf caps. I'm not wearing either of these, but Pat O'Callaghan takes me for a Yank anyway, from what I buy at his fruit and vegetable stand. "Bananas. Yanks always buys bananas," he announces when I buy a banana, and he grins as if concealing a deeper insight.

The next evening, I am on Loch Leane in Pat's rowboat with him, his son, his brother and his hairy sheepdog, on the way to see O'Sullivan's Cascade. Loch Leane has many moods, Pat warns, and sudden squalls keep sailboats off the Killarney lakes. But it is purple satin as we row along in the fading light, passing tiny lumps of islands named Mouse, Rabbit, Lamb and Cow, and odd-shaped rocks said to be enchanted.

We row past Library Point, where some god or another hurled stones like encyclopedic tomes in a rude stack on the shore. As the Killarney boatmen like to tell, the stones are the enchanted books that flew after the great Irish Chieftain O'Donoghue Mór when he leaped out of Ross Castle to escape Cromwell's men. One day soon, the last castle in all of Ireland to fall to Cromwell will be another tourist restaurant.

O'Sullivan's Cascade is startling, godly. A green cathedral pouring silver from its heights, thundering hymns on the rocks. A misty sanctuary of oak and arbutus, lush with the incense of decay. We sit on big rocks, faces to the spray, for a long quiet while. Then after a hike in Tomies Woods we row on to Glena, a gloomy spot fit for ghosts. Pat reckons they do be around. Hidden under a tangle of vines are the ruins of Glena Cottage, built by the Herberts of Muckross House for the visit of Queen Victoria.

The Visitor's Cottage slumbers deep in a cocoon of rhododendrons, and beside it are the remains of a once grand ballroom. In Pat's grandparents' day, people rowed over from Ross Castle to click their heels on its famous timbered floor. Now broken mossy stones ascend to rotted timber blown with holly leaves, and a nettle-wild graveyard lies beyond.

To escape from the taunts of the jarveys—"A jaunt around the lakes?—'tis too far to walk!"—you need a bicycle or your own horse. One misty morning I cycle away from the line-up of jaunting cars along Killarney's main street, and into the Muckross Demesne. I wander into the melancholy peace of Muckross Abbey to see the graves of the hallowed Munster poets, and the fabled yew tree growing inside. It is over 600 years old, and the largest in the world.

"If you touch it, it bleeds," swears a wrinkled jarvey.

I want to touch it just to see, but its trunk is caged inside a spiked iron fence, and from no point on any gloomy parapet is it possible to touch any of its branches or leaves.

The Abbey has a peculiar live presence. In Jimmy O'Brien's Pub they tell stories—about how this one's car broke down at the Abbey's graveyard one night, and how that one heard bones scraping together…"Well of course…they might have been deer antlers." But in the pub, Life is a ee-jit, everyone tells tales, and it signifies nothing.

One sodden afternoon a big man with hawk-winged eyebrows turns on his bar stool and asks me if I've ever heard of Jackie the Scratch. He looks me dead in the eye, and a hush falls over the circle of drinkers.

"Jackie the Scratch, the King of the Fairies, was last sighted in 1951 wearing a green waistcoat and cravat, gold buckled boots and a conical hat…"

"That's right," chimes in another.

"…and if you hear a scratch like this in the night," says he, scraping his nicotined fingernail against a CARA matchbox, "that's Jackie calling the fairies to a big meeting."

Pints are laid on and the bar burlesque begins. Enter and exeunt leprechauns and banshees and *foidini meara*—stray sods of turf that make you lose your way when you step on them; three-legged horses and blue hounds in silver chains and things that leave cobwebs on pillows and shriek in the night. Pints and actors come and go. I am regaled with details, down to the scores of various fairy hurling matches and the sound of the rustle of the silver gossamer robes of the banshee, and I am told I will die a mermaid. They swear by all the goats in Kerry it's the truth.

Down in Kerry they joke about fairies, but rare is the Kerry farmer who will disturb a primitive earthwork—fort, *lios* or *rath*—or a tree growing there. Neither will he build a house on a fairy path or in any other "*sheoguey* place." Bad luck comes to those who dare it, they say. Sure wasn't a planned airstrip at Shannon Airport re-routed when they discovered it lay on a fairy path?

At Lissyvigeen, two miles east of Killarney, a Bronze Age stone circle is marked on the Irish Ordinance Survey map. One morning I cycle up and down the Cork Road, off side roads and into mucky booreens for hours looking for it. I nearly give up the chase when something draws me to an old farmhouse to ask directions.

"Ah, begob!" the farmer brays. "If 'tis fairy circles yer after, the Irish Tourist Board won't allow you to write about them. 'Twould keep the tourists from Killarney."

The farmer is leering at me from out of a sunken stubbly face. Greasy tatters of ripe old sweaters hang on his bones and dangle from his arms in shreds. The cowl-neck collar of one has rotted away from the sweater itself and circles his neck like a grotesque parody of a Celtic warrior's gold torc.

"But if ye just want a look at the stone circle, 'tis over there beyant, in the circle of oak trees. What it was built for I wouldn't say. Maybe a spot for the Druids to do their dancing or maybe some actual people turned to stone. Sure those stones must be enchanted, for a man came all the way from the City of Rome just to look at them. "'Twas, as he said, that he saw the stone circle all the ways from the top of some church there, in a vision. But I don't go around that place meself."

"Why not?" I challenged.

"Ah…yer as well off not knowing. Good day now!"

I expect to find a circle of standing stones smothered by briars, or ignobled beside new corporation houses. But a venture through a rusty gate and muddy field, and across a windy gap brings me to two tall sentinel stones inscribed with ancient Ogham script. They guard a path down into a dark glade, where, in a peaceful nest of seven oaks, a circle of seven stones glows like opals in the tarnishing light.

That night nobody in O'Brien's pub can tell me much about the stone circle of "Seven Sisters" but that they are old, yes, very, and could lay on a fairy path. But when I describe meeting up with the wild-looking farmer in rags, a local fixture on a stool spouts up: "Sure, I know that farmer well. He's a millionaire. A genius. Owns hundreds of acres of valuable forests, plays the stock market, he does, and races horses. Though he never goes to the races. Never goes out at all, since the wife died 25 years ago. Plays the organ day and night, and the bagpipes, and any other instrument you can name. Sure he's the Boris Karloff of Irish music."

The only paean to Midsummer's Eve going in Killarney is a fake medieval banquet in a cardboard castle erected in a conference room of the Three Lakes Hotel, hosted by a chattering representative of the Knights of Inishfallen. I decide to take my tent and pack off to the stone circle. But not without a thermos of strong tea, and Irish superstition be damned, two red-haired women.

My red-haired friends, who've spent the last weeks destroying themselves in music and dancing pubs around Sliabh Luachra, are Jan Callaghan, a genealogist from Lethbridge, Alberta, and Jane Kelton, a Ph.D. candidate in Semiotics at New York University, who divides her time between the East Village and one Irish bog or another.

We pitch my orange domed tent inside the stone circle, joking about how it looks a fairy-sized haycock. Jan decides to inspect the crystal-flecked stones for white blotches of "fairy blood" and the trunks of the oaks for "access holes." Her father always told her that the holes were made by the beings who live in the earth, nourishing themselves with the blood of slaughtered heroes. They are big holes, and for one night you might believe anything.

Jane is waiting for signs. And I am pouring tea. Then we are babbling…about ley lines as conduits of energy…fairies and elementals…magnetometers…stone circles as time-space warps…veins of Chi dragon energy racing through the earth…geomancy…crystals and altered states of consciousness…

Then purple twilight turns to starless black and a soughing wind circles the tops of the oaks. It circles, and stops, and we slither into the tent and fumble with sleeping bags and cough to hide our nerves. My attention rivets on the wind circling in mad spirals, and becomes wildly alert. The skin of the tent is an amplifier. Raindrops tap and splat out of time. Each drop taps to get in. The zipper scratches the flap. A singing current races through the earth, gluing me to the ground. Then I feel as if I'm being pulled out the top of my head…

"Jesus, Mary and Joseph!" cries Jane like an Irishwoman from the bogs. "Did you hear that?"

A piercing shriek jolts me back into my body. For endless hours after, we lay awake in electric silence, until the spiraling wind stops and the earth feels still again. By dawn, a streak of Jane's hair has turned white. Jan's sleeping bag is soaked with sweat, and I am primed for weeks of nightmares.

Our bones creak back into town for soothing cups of tea. The next day, curiosity lures me to pay another visit to "Karloff."

"God almighty!" he says when I proclaim our deed. "That was a foolish chance to take. "Some German campers came screamin' out of there one night. I didn't want to frighten ye the other time we met. You, being a Yank, would be green to certain things. But don't be fond of fairy forts or any thing like them, because God, they are bad… One evening, 'tis a few years ago now, I went to fetch my pony for to take her to the creamery the next morning. The pony had wandered down to the stone circle, and I followed her in anyway. But then she just disappeared, and I couldn't escape out of there till 5 o'clock in the morning!"

"Were you lost?"

"Lost?" he says agitatedly. "Begod no I wasn't lost. A big wall 20 feet high was all around me, shining in me eyes and blinding me. And it covered the whole field—the whole field! I couldn't find a gate, I couldn't find nothing!"

"But there's no wall there, only trees. Were you…drinking?"

"Begod I know that and sure I wasn't drinking, you understand me?" he says with a strange stare. "I reckon 'twas some kind of vision come over a man. Them stones should all be bulldozed, but no one will put a hand to it. No, no, NO. No one will touch it…. But thanks be to God ye came out all right. Because ye could a had a—what ye call it—a ring of fairies dancing around you, tippin' the tent and there'd be nothing there in the morning. And if they rattled you with their bloody fairy music, ye'd go dim and dreary for years. I am telling you, never make bold with fairy forts. Yer as well off going back to Amerikay not knowin' any more. Ye had, I'd say, foolish courage. And I'm damn glad the thing came out all right for ye. Now good day!"

"Are you really a millionaire?"

"Sure we're all millionaires. And why wouldn't we be?"

Homecoming

Gotham, My Ex-beloved

Oh New York! Fueled to a frenzy by rivers of caffeine! You're as filthy rich and filthy poor, picaresque and prurient, rude and chaotic, glamorous and grimy, lunatic and lovable as ever. After all these years away from you, Big Rotten Apple, you, I'm hungry to pound your teeming streets, gawk at your characters, din my ears with your cacophony, smell your skin, and dig through the layers of my personal archaeology, from Harlem, where it started in a dorm room at Columbia, to Coney, where I nearly lost it on the beach.

The Manhattoes paddled around this island in a canoe. What would they think now, to see their oyster beds replaced by the ventilating towers of the Lincoln Tunnel and their hunting grounds covered over with garbage chutes through which the city's waste zips along at 30 mph, to be turned into landfill—to make more Manhattan? The Circle Line Sightseeing Cruise around Manhattan Island, "America's Favorite Boat Ride Since 1945," reveals all—New York's fancy dress clothes—the Fifth Avenue skyline…Wall Street and the World Trade Towers…the Statue of Liberty…the United Nations, the Gracie Mansion, Cher's condo at the Promenade, smug yuppie Yorkville—and its smoggy smelly underwear—garbage dumps, police pounds, empty railroad yards and junk yards, ventilating towers, and the grimy underbellies of 19 of New York City's 20 bridges. Good old Circle Line. It's the same old boat with the same old scuffed hard wooden folding chairs, the same old 1969 hot dogs. Glory be! It's bringing it all back to me…

Take The A Train...

When the boo level gets loud enough, and the screamers in the $5 seats start hissing and pounding the railings, a siren goes off and a clown in a white frizzy wig drags you off the stage. And it's not funny. Not if you're a black kid who's taken the Greyhound from Selma and spent his last greenback on new duds, just to test his rap routine on the Apollo Theater's Amateur Night crowd. And not if you're a young Miss from Mississip who breaks her piggy bank to buy a taffeta dress covered with bows to sing "Summertime."

You get one chance. One dance. One song. One joke. It's either please the applause meter or get laughed out of Harlem. Tonight, like every Wednesday night at the Apollo, there's an eager crowd milling around the old foyer of the theatre on 125th Street which opened as a burlesque house in 1913 and went vaudeville in 1934. They've come for the four-hour-long talent show where greats like James Brown, The Jackson Five, Gladys Knight and the Pips, the Ink Spots, Billie Holiday and Sarah Vaughan have been discovered since 1935. But the Apollo's Amateur Night audience is one of the toughest in the world, tough enough to scare Sammy Davis Jr. mute even after he became a star, and to spook Ella Fitzgerald into singing when her knees started knocking too hard to dance.

Five bucks buys me a high-altitude seat in the balcony behind a tall dude with a mean beehive. The band trumpets. The pink curtain rises. Then a tornado of break dancers whirls across the stage, shooting megavolts of energy through the excited crowd. Yellow satin jiving devils. Then it's a seven-man group with drums, flute, sax, trumpet, electric guitars, keyboards, white felt hats and white sunglasses. There's hoots from below and grunts in the balcony. Teenage girls scream when the crooner's hand clutches his bulging...

This carnival crowd of catcallers rivals a night at the Coliseum with gladiators and lions. Gospel singers, reggae and rap artists, stand-up comics come and go. Then a lone jokester cracks a flat one-liner, and a kid named Ralphie gets booed back to Birmingham with his jazzercise act. A plump teenage girl comes on. She shyly takes the mike and people turn to butter and drip down the seats as she sings "Somewhere Over the Rainbow" like Judy Garland never could.

Harlem is New York City's exotic new tourist attraction. Tour buses chug up Broadway, the road built over an Indian trail by the black slaves of the Dutch West India Company...past the Wishy Washy Laundromat, Dixie Drifter Variety & Grocery, Trumbo's Funeral Chapel, the Nubian Gro-Deli, and Chewy's Café...and on to Duke Ellington's old home, the Ansonia House where Caruso, Mahler, and Toscanini lived, the Teresa Hotel where Joe Louis celebrated his victories, and the 1884 mansion of James A. Bailey of Barnum & Bailey Circus fame. They stop for some history at the Morris Jumel Mansion, which served as George Washington's headquarters during the Battle of Harlem Heights in 1776, and Hamilton Grange, built in 1882 as Alexander Hamilton's summer home. Then they head on to Sylvia's for Soul Food, the Showman's for Jazz, and the Mount Nebo Baptist Church to hear big-mama gospel singers open throttle with "Jacob's Ladder." And God bless 'em.

Hell's Hot Kitchen

"Come visit the Big Apple—if you dare!" the sign on the Times Square Visitors Information Center seems to say. "Closed Saturday and Sunday. No guides. NO MAPS." But look—there is a perpetual welcome committee gathered on the Visitor's Bureau front steps—a crew of bums waving empty bottles.

Mad-hattan! Up go your luxury condos, and out go your homeless. But even they are going upscale, no longer living out of measly grocery carts. They now have giant canvas carts snatched from construction sites—yah! they hold more stuff—and alfresco living rooms under the stars. And look—New York's jobless have turned West Side sidewalks into bizarre recycling bazaars lined with last year's diet books, last season's designer jeans, last month's *Condé Nast Traveler*, and last week's computer keyboards—upscale icons ironically far from the reality of the Great Unwashed desperately peddling them. Here's a drab older gent sitting on a crate, hawking $5 massages to relieve urban tension—five minutes for the neck, three for the shoulders, temples or "subway whiplash."

My old mid-Manhattan neighborhood, Hell's Kitchen, was named after a dive near Corlears Hook and a street gang organized in 1868. It runs from West 35th to West 56th between the Broadway theatre district and the Hudson River, and is still predominantly Irish and Puerto Rican. (Corner *bodegas* still sell sugar-shock homemade candy, voodoo candles and charms, and coffee strong enough to raise a zombie.) In 1939 the Works Progress Administration Guide to New York City described Hell's Kitchen as "A district that bears one of the most lurid reputations in America." With its freight yards, factories, garages, warehouses, slaughterhouses and tenements, it was the haunt of hoodlums, gangsters, pimps and prostitutes.

Prostitutes! Oh where is Rosie the transvestite 'tute who lived upstairs from us, clopping up and down the stairs all night in her platform shoes? Boy could s/he look you up and down to make your flesh hop and wonder, were you being cruised woman-to-woman? man-to-woman? or man-to-man? It was all so gender-bent and confusing. And where is Melva, the hop-in-the-car blow job mistress who serviced our corner of 46th and Tenth? Friends who came to visit me and Bill Ochs would try to be discreet, but bolt for the corner window in our living room, where if the sun were at the right angle, they could see…

Gentrification has peppered my old haunt with snazzy sidewalk cafés and off-off-Broadway bistros, gourmet pie shops and expensive thrift shops. Fancy developers insist on calling it Clinton to give it a presidential air, but the rawness of *West Side Story* and *Slaughter on Tenth Avenue* remains. At midday on Ninth Avenue, a squat Latino woman with fuschia lips and ample hips is doing a sinuous sidewalk samba to salsa blasting from her radio, with a beer can balanced on her head, and a smirk and a taunt for all who pass. And while strolling down Ninth between 56th and 57th on a balmy September evening, my foot catches in the cord of a color TV set rigged into the open innards of a towering street lamp. Before me is a sidewalk colony stretched out on fleabag mattresses, arms propped under pillows—engrossed in a National Audubon Society TV special. I want to salute the electrical wizard who tapped the city's energy supply, and the others for making the best of a wretched situation. But I feel like an intruder who has just barged into a private living room with invisible walls.

SoHo Sass

Down Wooster and Greene Streets art gallery banners glow like stained glass in the afternoon sun. Everyone here looks like Yoko Ono. Black leather, big black sunglasses, and lots of hair. That peacock stroll. That impudent artsy smirk. That flaunt-it look. Hip. Wacky. Grimy. Decrepit. Decadent. Dazzling. That's SoHo. New York City's historic industrial district of cast-iron buildings SOuth of HOuston St. (*How*-ston, not *Hew*-ston, please).

Oh, the cast-iron Venetian palaces! Oh, the cornices, architraves and acanthus leaves! They're as grand as the heroic stone work of the Roman Coliseum. But they're F-A-K-E, fake! These pretties were all cast in New York iron foundries and bolted into place. In 1848 the American watchmaker James Bogardus discovered a way to have the Sansovino Library in Venice for pennies, with a cast-iron modular construction. Just add sand to the stone-colored paint and it would pass for real, unless you banged it with a hammer.

SoHo is the impudent epicenter of the contemporary American art world, as vibrant and visceral as the Paris of the 1920s and '30s. And its grubby warehousey underpinnings—sidewalk vault covers and yowling freight elevators, and rusty loading bays for twine jobbers and corrugated box makers, and shadowy side streets and alleys give it an irresistible allure of danger.

Cherchez-vous la bizarre? Your portrait as a hologram? Some alligator pants? Feather neckties? A hand-made stuffed gorilla? Or a dressing table slab of prehistoric bluestone, with antelope-horn legs for your stone-age boudoir? Salmon sausage over seaweed? Squid-ink linguini? Buffalo mozzarella? Designer jelly beans in 40 flavors…bubble gum, cantaloupe, jalapeño, peanut butter, piña colada, A&W root beer, and toasted marshmallow?

Wandering into a clothing emporium called Studio la Rue, a busty mannequin in a pink ballet tutu, wearing an elephant head with one of the ears missing, seems to say Boo! In "The Temple" a jungle green parrot squawks in a big rattan cage. And in "Rome" (a plaster column erected among the threads) a perky salesgirl tries to sell me a skimpy velvet medieval page's costume. Just the thing I'm going to wear to Cave Canem to dance in a renovated bathhouse deconstructed to look like the ruined Roman Forum, or the bar called Mars, hideously lit with psychedelic lava lamps and Jesus statuettes.

Preposterous cuisine. Unwearable apparel. Furniture to torture your body by. Art galleries trumpeting the fabulous and far-fetched. And performance artists dealing in neo-neon and nouveau mime.

Roving art magnates are cruising down West Broadway in their stretch limos. But will they take a second glance at these colorful pigs and yaks flapping like circus flags in the breeze? I'm standing on West Broadway talking to Matthew Brzstofski about his Animal Art. It's like being inside a Stan Mack "Real Life Funnies" cartoon in *The Village Voice*.

"I used to be a construction worker. I started painting this stuff after I broke up with my girlfriend. At first it was slap-dashy. Then when I got happier I started painting my pigs and my horse. Then I started checking out other animals."

"Uh…I like the bull."

"That's actually a Tibetan yak. It's quite popular. But the pigs are the most popular. They're all acrylic paints on high quality watercolor paper."

"And how much are they?"

"It depends. I ask for $40 but the price is negotiable so everyone can afford it. I believe everyone should be able to own great art."

Life's a Knish

By the end of the 19th century, New York City's newly arrived "huddled masses yearning to breathe free" all lived on the Lower East Side. The area rivaled Bombay for urban density, with streets packed with horses and carts and hawker's pushcarts, and the hand-washed shirts and dresses and knickers of new immigrants from Prussia to China fluttering on clotheslines in the breeze.

One of the oldest tenement buildings in the city, which was sealed off in 1935, graffiti, cockroaches and all, is now The New York Tenement Museum. This five-floor, 15-apartment building at 97 Orchard Street was built in 1863, before housing laws were even heard of. Now it's a fascinating window on 19th century New York immigrant life in those cold-water sweatshops and flats where a kid could be tenth in line to take a Saturday bath in the kitchen, and the fire escape was the only escape from a 10' x 10' crowded bedroom on a hot summer's night.

The wonder of this museum is that is doesn't even look like a museum. Its old tenement rooms look as they must have the day they were vacated by the last occupants—fruit sellers, mustard factory workers, seamstresses, barbers, cigar makers and tailors. Look on the wall, you'll see the tailor's list of orders scratched in pencil: 18 suits, 100 dresses, 11 jackets, overcoats, vests, 118 shirts, and pants, $1.50. Walking through the old tenements, whose walls are yellowed by years of cooking, brings back the aromas of gefilte fish and onions and matzo ball soup, and hot summer nights on Eldridge Street…

The Lower East Side had seemed so exotically Eastern European to me when I first came to New York. While working at *New York Magazine* and claiming an doorman address on the Sniffy Upper East Side, I was mostly living in a crummy walk-up on Eldridge Street with my lover Charlie the film critic. We met on the beach at Coney Island the day I went there with some magazine interns to see the Atlantic Ocean. Charlie took me to an Israeli folk dancing at Co-Op City and taught me the grapevine step. He showed me his neighborhood synagogue, with dour bearded men in black with black leather prayer phylacteries wrapped around their arms.

Charlie and I used to go to Ratner's for blintzes with sour cream and Yona's for knishes, those heavyweight Jewish egg rolls stuffed with vegetables, cheese or fruit, that hit the gut like Québécois poutine. Vulgar versions of the knish are fried, but at Yona Shimmel's on East Houston they're handmade one at a time and baked in old brick ovens, as Yona Shimmel, the l9th century rabbi and Talmudic scholar from Eastern Europe made them and sold them from his pushcarts. What a place is Yona's. A petrified bagel (one of the 19th century rabbi's first?) hangs on a string from the white enameled tin ceiling over the counter. The walls are plastered with old photos of New York politicians knoshing bagels. And coat hooks painted a jaunty red invite you to sit down at the worn red Formica-covered wooden tables that have known a million dirty plates.

And Charlie took me to Orchard Street, as zany, loud, and pushy a shopping adventure as the Tijuana border. Years ago it had been even wilder. Bill Ochs (alias "Hornpipe") told me about going there with his Uncle Max when he was a mere lad of ten, to haggle for underwear.

"He forced you to haggle for your own underwear?" I laughed in disbelief. Hornpipe swears it wasn't child abuse, but fun and exciting to push and shove your way through Lower East Side streets steaming with hot dogs and sauerkraut and clogged with hawkers chanting in Yiddish or Italian.

"The schleppers, or 'pullers-in'—or was it puller inners?" (Hornpipe hesitates over terminology here)—"they'd stand out on the sidewalk and say 'Hey, c'mon we got some great *under* wear here, c'mon in and take a *look* at it!"

"And you and Max would—"

"Haggle. He'd pretend not to want it. That the boxer shorts were too baggy or the wrong color. He'd turn to go, then the guy would knock a buck off the price."

Under the Boardwalk

The Circle Line Boat floats under the Brooklyn Bridge, the most talked about and written about bridge in the whole world. In 1933 Hart Crane rhapsodized over its silvery cables, stone towers and neo-gothic arches…

"O harp and altar, of the fury fused/
How could mere toil align thy choiring strings!"

This aerial masterpiece linking Lower Manhattan to Brooklyn Heights was built for pedestrians, horses and buggies. On the day it opened in 1883, 150,000 people crossed over it, exhilarated by the views of the Manhattan skyline through the silvery filigree of cables. Billions of feet have tramped its weathered planks since, including mine. I strolled over it one soft September Sunday with a happy traffic of joggers, cyclists, tourists and strolling lovers, then wandered over to the Brooklyn Heights Esplanade and Brooklyn's History Museum.

Brooklyn has been the home of Walt Whitman, Woody Allen, Isaac Asimov, Truman Capote, Beverly Sills, Mae West, Woody Guthrie, Al Capone and Harry Houdini, but the personages greeting me that morning were Jackie Gleason and Art Carney—in life-size cardboard. I enjoyed the exhibit on the 1950's TV series *The Honeymooners*, but what grabbed me more was the stink of hot dogs and mustard. I could almost smell it coming from the memorabilia display on Coney Island, where two grandmothers were cooing over a handbill advertising Coney Island's tin-skinned "Lucy"—the hotel, dance hall and shopping bazaar built in 1884 in the shape of a 130 foot high elephant….and the famous aerial photos of that beach—completely black with tiny human dots as thick as poppy seeds on a loaf of Jewish rye.

"My grandpa took me to Steeplechase Park for the carousel and the Dodg'ems. Luna Park burned down in '44, when I was only ten," said one to the other.

After inspecting the Brooklyn History Museum's ventriloquist dummy left over from some sideshow, I took a long look at myself in the carnival mirror. I was a squat fat troll strung with melted cameras, setting out to take the D train to Brooklyn all the rickety way to West 8th Street, to give my regards to Coney Island.

Oh, Coney—with its shooting galleries, switchback railways, tintype artists, cockroach races, slot machines, freak shows, and honky tonks, and Luna Park, glittering with over a million electric bulbs—its blazing towers rivaling Oz! Did the world ever see such tawdry, hilarious decadence? Oh, Coney. You just gotta go there. Smell it with your own nose. That good salt air and grease. They say the water's cleaner than it's been in a decade, and the sands get a daily sifting with nifty combines to remove the nibs of Nathan's hot dogs and bits of syringes.

Lonely old New York Aquarium octopus, how did you celebrate the summer of '95, the 100th anniversary of Konijn Eiland? With your giant suckers and your shriveled scrotal head and beak and dazed monster eye squashed against the glass of America's oldest aquarium, like last time I saw you? Did crowds gasp at your fetal ugliness and run away laughing to the cute hogfish with the porcine snout? Or did they shun the dim fish tanks altogether for the sun, fun, and fire-eaters of Coney?

A lumpy old octopus can't compete with the sword swallowers and glass-eaters at Sideshows by the Seashore, or the screaming 60 mph Cyclone at Astroland, and they know it. So to celebrate the 100th anniversary comeback of Coney's old "Sodom by the Sea," the New York Aquarium revamped its premises to the tune of $36 million. Bringing on a few more sharks and rays for thrills, and a 400-gallon tidal wave that crashes over visitors—under a Plexiglas hood—every 30 seconds.

I wish I had been there to see it all! The carnival barkers, freak shows, shooting galleries and gypsy palm readers, and the cruising and knoshing along the three-mile boardwalk. What have we now, on this dying September day, besides the cigarette butts and sticky strands of cotton candy left from summer, tired-out merry-go-round horses, and billboard clowns? Some wacky winter Polar Bears Club swimmers grasping at September sunbeams under the boardwalk. Two grey-haired lovers wrapped together on a bench staring out to sea. And a tireless lone figure with a metal detector sweeping the beach. Perhaps he'll pass over the patch of sand where I met Charlie that first summer of 1969. It wasn't a beautiful beach, but for a Midwestern girl from Indiana, it was the Atlantic Ocean!

Tennessee Gothic
Mountain English

My daddy's daddy, Emet Earl Lyon, didn't never get interviewed by any'ore them there folk-tale doctors. And hits a shore thang he warn't never discovered by the Smithalonian Institooshun. But like Ray Hicks, the granddaddy of Appalachian storytellers, whom I met on a trip to northeast Tennessee, he spoke pretty good Mountain English.

Mountain English, spoken in the Appalachian and Ozark Mountain regions of the U.S., is characterized by archaic words, 18th-century pronunciations preserved through oral tradition, malapropisms, odd grammar and wildly colorful figures of speech.

Its particular linguistic features include the use of perfectives (I done told you); double-modal and multiple-modal constructions ("might could" and "may can") regularized verbs (I knowed), double negatives (hain't nobody), and frequent use of the prefix "a" with gerunds (a-talkin'). Which is a pretty fancy way of describing the speech of a hillbilly farmer from East Tennessee.

When my granddaddy would call me to shuck the corn, he'd holler: "Nain-cee! I declare—hits a-gettin' to supper tahm for them chickens. I reckon you better go dreckly over yonder and fetch us some feed corn." I didn't dare argy with my granddaddy cause he was big and I might get a whuppin'—or worse, miss out on a piece of granny's mouth-waterin' punkin' pah.

Lordy, how Emet Lyon would have laughed to hear his Appalachian mountain speech being examined by "doctors of philosophy"—linguists, folklorists and ethnologists. It was certainly remarkable for me, on my first trip back to Tennessee since my teen years, to again hear this "Lizabeethan English" as the locals call it, and to recognize its true worth.

Ray Hicks pulled up a chair and put on his story telling cap, and with tummies full of cornbread and soup beans, our small group of travellers from Pennsylvania, Utah, New York and Washington, D.C. gathered around the lanky, twinkle-eyed farmer from western North Carolina to hear some traditional Appalachian "Jack" tales.

While other listeners strained to grasp the oddities of Hicks' speech, it fell on my ears like a forgotten lullaby, stirring pangs of nostalgia, affection and regret. My granddaddy wore bib overalls, was tall as a treed bear and told stories, and yet I never knew just how special he was.

Seventy-something Hicks was the star at the annual National Storytelling Festival in Jonesborough, Tennessee, which featured more than 85 world-class raconteurs. Yet when he told me he'd won prizes at the Smithalonian Institooshun, and had been written up in *Gerry Gravity Magazine* and in the *New Yorker Time*, it was with a childlike delight that must have bewitched the reporters for the *National Geographic* and *The New Yorker* magazines.

I was charmed by the marvelous malapropisms! Hicks spoke of "splashing" pieces of a rope together and Indians "whitewashed" (brainwashed) by sneaky white men. A library was a "libary"; a train engineer, an "engenary"; bears, "bars"; potatoes, "taters"; things, "thangs"; American, "Uhmurrikin"; and freezing was "phrasin." There were made-up words—we'uns for us—and laudy, the renegade grammar! There was beautifullest, onliest, broughten up, everhoo (for whoever), "et" for ate, clum for climbed, she done and they was. Amen!

The border between Hicks' own speech and that in his stories was so blurred that when he began telling us about how he had "larnt his false teeth," I thought it was another tale.

If I understood correctly (and I wasn't sure I did), Hicks first tried to make his false teeth stick in his mouth with a "tube of bananas." (Can you buy banana paste in a tube in the south? I don't know).

Then a dentist in Mountain City told him he'd have to sleep with the teeth in to get used to them. "I tried hit but woke up chokin', dreamin' I'd swallered a 10-penny nail. The next night I haddem in, I woke up dreamin' I'd swallered a black widow spidy...Then anutherin tole me to chew tobaccy, and that got me a-wearin 'em. Now if you have any trouble and can chew baccur, 'ats the way to larn yer false teeth."

My childhood idol was Davy Crockett (actually Fess Parker, who played him on TV). Before re-visiting Crockett's birthplace near Greeneville, Tennessee, I bought a copy of *Davy Crockett: The Man, the Legend, the Legacy, 1786-1986*, edited by Michael Lofaro. Apparently, the King of the Wild Frontier was quite a storyteller himself.

In his "fumbling backwoods attempts at grandiloquence" Crockett vouched for the accuracy of his 1841 almanac by explaining that he'd hired "a very great gastronomer" to do the work. "Whether I shall go down to posteriors," he writes, "is another question."

The reader is amused to read "sighed saddle" for side saddle; "intermined" for determined; "spontinaciously" for spontaneously; "obstropolous" for obstreperous; "corfed" for coughed; "rankantankerous" for cantankerous; and snapping "turkles" for turtles.

And some of the best of Crockett's frontierese is just plain old made-up stuff, à la Mary Poppins and Lewis Carroll: slandicular, tetotaciously, exflunctified, blusteriferous, monstratious and graniverous. Tennessee backwoods dialect may be the butt of northern jokes, but at Sotheby's, original editions of Crockett's Almanac, treasured as relics of mountain English, have fetched a grandilawfulous $10,000.

Nashville Brash

I felt like singing the phone book propped on my Opryland Hotel bed. It read like the cast of a giant country ballad, with names like Earl and Bertalee, Clydie, Flossie and Fannie-Mai—names I heard back when I was an eight-year-old Tennessee cowgirl in a fake buckskin jacket. Heft it into the shower—and why not? Everybody in Nashville was singing and songwriting in everyday places—taxicabs, laundromats, bus stations and Burger Kings. The waitresses who served up my biscuits and red-eye gravy, and the cabbies and cowboy boot sellers who proffered their homemade demos—they were all talkin' cuts, charts, flacks, hair acts, pitches and pluggers; trades, spec deals, skins, bullets and singles and looking for a lucky break in MUSIC CITY, USA—Capital of the State of Whiskey, on the Buckle of the Bible Belt, where women ain't afraid to spell out their first names in the phone directory.

You could sing the Nashville phone directory and it would sound just dandy if you gave it the proper twang. That's one thing I've never lost—the ability to reproduce from childhood memory the twangiest east Tennessee hillbilly drawl, and to pronounce my name: Nain-cee Lahhnn! But I was feeling very disoriented coming back to see the city of my birth after a coon's age.

Outside, the leaves were flamey reds and oranges but November was as balmy and zingy with cricket song as July. In my room was a promotional Easter basket stuffed with chocolate bunnies, jelly beans and tulip bulbs (which I took for chestnuts), and literature about the 3 day/2 night "Easter in Song and Story" spring package. Inside the atrium of the 1,891-room Edmonton-Mallesque Opryland Hotel, where I should have requested roller blades with my room key, I was in a tropical rain forest and it was Christmas already. Santa's sun-bleached plastic reindeer were littered around the banana trees, and fallen elves were floating in the reflecting pools of the four-acre, six-storey jungle sprouting more flora than the Montreal Biodome; while tourists with New Joy-zee accents strolled around in ten-gallon hats and snakeskin cowboy boots singin' the Whitey Shafer hit "All My Exes Live in Texas."

Where was Elvis? Where was Davy Crockett? The house where I'd lived on Gale Lane was still in one piece, but my childhood idols had kicked the bucket and now haunted the fridge magnet shops. Oh god, was Nashville brash.

Nashville was brash, with its hip now Grand Ole Opry, its Opryland USA Theme Park, and glitzy T-shirt temples to local deities. There was Conway's "Twitty City," the House of Cash (Johnny's), the Jim Reeves Museum, the Elvis Presley Museum, Roy Acuff's Museum and Minney Pearl's Museum, Barbara Mandrell Country, Marty Robbins' Gift Emporium, the Hank Williams Jr. Museum, Music Village, U.S.A., and all those worshipful wax museums. "*Les Royaumes de bebelles!*—Tinker Toy Kingdoms" jokes my friend Louise Dugas, a Montreal pop music critic born again to Country after three days in Nashville. But that was the fun of being in Nashville—watching country fans at the glittering altars of their idols, and catching the song-writing hysteria in the air.

You gotta sing your way around this town of one million when 25,000 are in the music biz and the rest are breakin' their necks tryin'. Singing for tips at Gilley's Bar eight hours a day, busking around Music Row in a cowboy hat, hanging out at Shoney's Hotel, the crashpad of the stars and wannabe-stars. And dodging scam artists and recording sharks promising overnight Fame 'n Fortune.

How many country songwriters does it take to change a light bulb?

Three: one to change the bulb and two to write songs about how much we're gonna miss the old one.

Only three? The figure in that local joke is out of date, if I'm to believe James Breedwell, who peddled me his demo one night at the Silver Dollar Saloon. This was the old whorehouse which distiller George Dickle of Tennessee sippin' whiskey—"ain't nothin' better" fame—had paved with silver dollars before the turn of the century. It's now one of eight Nashville venues, like Tootsie's Orchid Lounge and the Bluebird Café, where songwriters strut their stuff every week.

James, who auditions the Saloon's singers, came to Nashville from "Cincy" (...natti) with only $30 in his pocket, "ready to duck knives to write songs." I thought he meant ducking knives at a local carnival booth, but he meant muggers' knives—Nashville muggers mug for hot new lyrics!

"You gotta earn trust in this town, 'cause lottsa people are scared their songs're gonna be stolen," James informed me in a gravely whisper.

"Everybody here wants to have a cut. With Garth. With Travis. With Reba. The way to get your name known is to write with everybody in town, so I write with 75 to 80 different co-writers, sometimes four to a song."

"Sounds promiscuous," I say. "What do you use for protection?"

"Numbers...safety in numbers. Somethin's gotta hit. Listen, we got country music fanatics comin' here from Oklahoma to Florida to 'laska to Russia to Paris to Zabway..."

"...you mean Zimbabwe?"

"...Yeah, whatever it's called. You have people who can't even speak English trying to sing Country. One of the guys I write with is from Czechoslovakia."

Will Breedwell sell? He had a nice Elvisque kinda voice, but his $8 demo had only three songs, including "When the bottle's dry, you're gone." Go figure.

Let's face it, nobody will ever replace The King. How many Elvis impersonators does it take...to prove this?

Most of the Elvis memorabilia is stashed at Graceland, his gold-plated estate in Memphis. But at the Nashville Country Music Hall of Fame on Music Row, I paid homage to Elvis' 24K gold-plate trimmed 1960 Caddy with 24k gold-plated black-and-white TV, and gold-plated ice cube trays. And on a tour of RCA's legendary Studio B, a songwriter named Doak Sneed showed me where Elvis recorded Christmas songs in July by turning the air conditioning up to "crop kill' to put him in a frosty snowman mood.

I can hardly believe it now, but I became an Elvis impersonator at the age of 12. At a ceremonious dinner for 50 tax attorneys and their wives, where Elmer Lyon was guest of honor, I slicked on some pomade and sang, "You ain't nothin' but a hound dog," with hip gyrations and a Sears Roebuck guitar. For my father.

The Gospel According to East Tennessee

November is balmy in Tennessee. Tobacco leaves are curling to a toasty brown in old red barns. I'm heading back to East Tennessee, driving over a lonely stretch on Clinch Mountain where the only beacon in the blackness is a roadside tavern where bib-overalled men are cussin' and sippin' and wishin' they were rich.

East Tennessee, where my Daddy's people, the Harmons, Lyons, Beals and Bibles come from, seems wildly exotic to me now. With its hoary fiddlers and storytellers, antiquated Mountain English, back roads spooky with haints and witches, graveyards still flying Confederate flags, and gas station billboards selling GAS-FOOD-GUNS. East Tennessee, with its worm races and catfish suppers and restorationist Pentecostal faith-testing snake and fire-handling, and strychnine-drinking religions; and towns named Grinder's Switch, Finger, Soddy-Daisy, Parrottsville and Bull's Gap, the railroad town where the little boy who became my father sold a pair of billy goats for $10 to open up his very first bank account.

East Tennessee, where a runaway circus elephant was once hoisted and hanged like a criminal in a small town square, is just the kind of place where you expect devil-charmed canoes to fly. That's what I was saying to my friend Lucy Freeman, a Nashville-born Irish fiddler who lived in Quebec for a spell. We were having homemade biscuits and red-eye gravy at the Loveless Café. I'd been going on about that ole-time East Tennessee religion that would kill you and food that would sink you.

"These Pentecostal Holiness rattlesnake-handling sects, they actually originated around Greenville, where my daddy grew up," I told her. "Around 1909, some preacher named George Went Hensley got it into his head to interpret that verse of Mark 16:17-18 'They shall take up serpents'—literally! If you're bitten it's cause you're weak of faith, and if you die, it's cause you've forsaken the Holy Ghost!"

I'd never been to one of these churches where they dump a box of copperheads and rattlers—diamondback and timber—onto the floor and let them slither all over the place under the pews, I said. But at a Christmas party in Tusculum, the

President of Tusculum College had told me about his experience. He had escaped the fangs of the serpents by standing on a pew, and watched open-mouthed as people put the snakes up to their faces, trod on them, wrapped them around their necks and tossed them around the room! That night anyway, nobody got bitten. But there is the story of the 28-year-old mother of five kids from Parrotsville, Melinda Brown, who died of cardiac arrest after being bitten by a four-foot long black timber rattler...

Lucy hadn't gotten wind of it in Nashville, so I gave her some details. The minister of Full Gospel Tabernacle in Jesus Name at Middlesboro, Kentucky near the Cumberland Gap was only 23. Even though a 1942 law makes it illegal to handle or display snakes at religious services, the law's a joke because the fine is only $50 or $100—how cheap can you get for a human life?—and nobody ever presses charges—especially the victims.

This young preacher named Jamie Coots just said that he answered to a higher law than that of the state of Kentucky or Tennessee, and it was the Lord's will for her to die, and that it was only a misdemeanor. "It wouldn't bother me none if it was a felony. It's still the Word," were his final words.

"East Tennessee is really weird," Lucy said. "That's why I love it."

Yeah, me too, I said. But then I started complaining about all the fried-greasy-sugary-fat food they eat down here. And with the last bit of sausage stabbed onto her fork, she asked me if I'd ever tried that East Tennessee specialty, fried ice cream.

Now laudy, missy, I've heard tell of squirrel pies and grizzly mountain funnel cakes, pickled watermelon rinds and Coca-Cola glazed ham, smoked crawdads, and even fried pickles—but fried ice cream?

"Yeah, said Lucy. "You take balls of rock-hard vanilla and roll 'em in corn flakes and dump 'em in boiling fat for a few seconds and eat 'em. The outside's crunchy and the inside's cold."

I have one very important pilgrimage to make in East Tennessee: my return to Davy Crockett's birthplace at Limestone in Greene County. I went there with my dad and sisters while nursing a girlish crush on Fess Parker, the King of the Wild Frontier on the Walt Disney TV series which ran in the late 1950's. I had stared reverently at the stone marker, then took a handful of dirt from around Davy's log cabin and sewed it into the lining of my coonskin cap.

Going back there will be different now. Now I know now that Davy wasn't really Fess. And that the idea of a Dashing Davy was just a Disneyfied myth. The real Colonel Crockett was a wild buckaroo backwoods braggart politician who spun tales in his own invented frontierese language, fought "injuns," wrestled "bars" and was killed at the Alamo in 1836. But Crockett was probably also, as research by Tennessee historians like Michael A. Lofaro suggests, arrogant, racist and violent.

The Davy Crockett Birthplace State Park is a tourist attraction now. Tourism, like Hollywood, has a funny way of reinventing history. Sometimes the results are quietly treacherous. But with Fess, I think it was all okay. We need heroes to believe in, and so I'll grab another fistful of Tennessee dirt. For the sake of innocence.

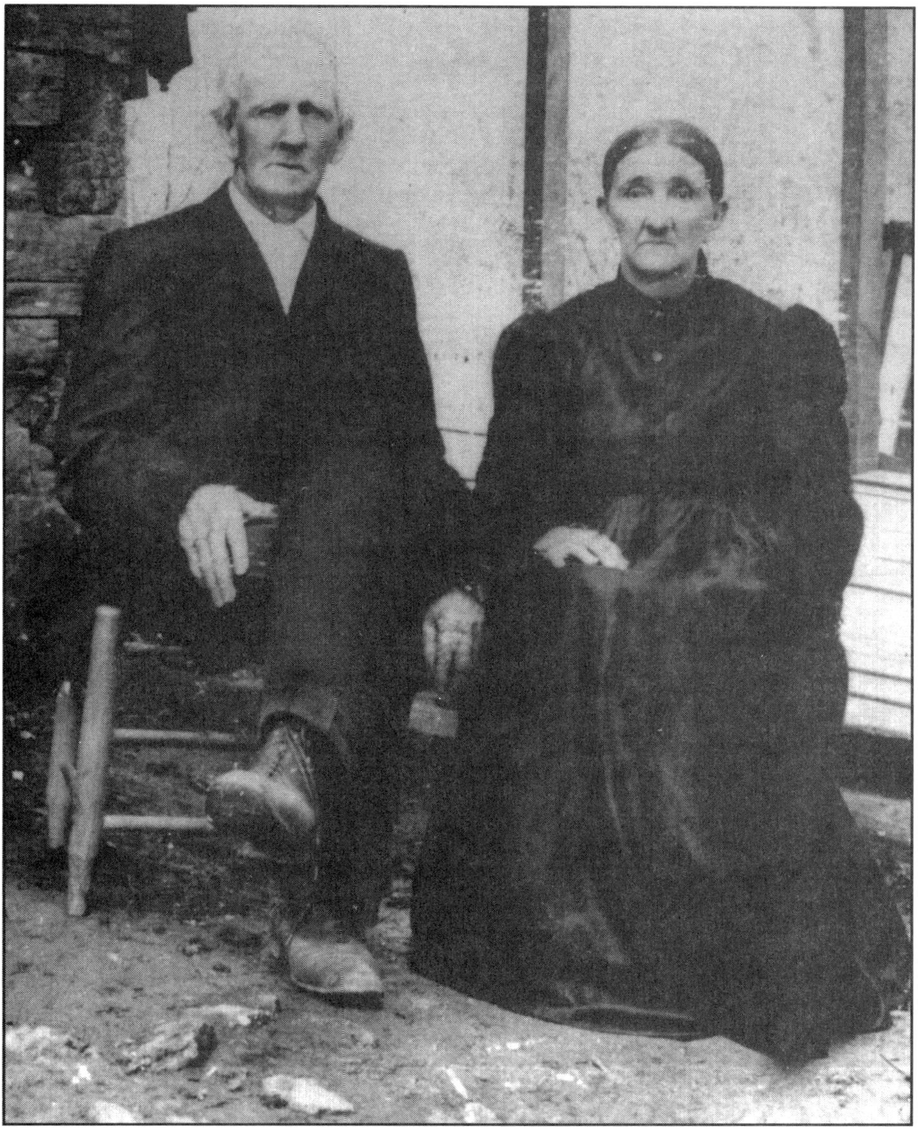

Back to School:
David Letterman Country, Indianapolis

I remember Dave. I especially remember Dave sprawled on the living room floor of my parents' house on North Delaware Street in Indianapolis in 1962 with blood oozing from a gash in his head, after it hit the antique wheelbarrow my mom had turned into a glass-topped coffee table. Now the last thing you want when you're a high school freshman having a wild party while your parents are away for the weekend—and you're supposed to be babysitting—is to leave evidence. The beer cans and cigarette butts were easy to get rid of. But Dave Letterman's blood did not want to come out of that rug.

Dave's blood made a kidney-shaped puddle on the pale brown rug, just like in the Perry Mason murder mysteries. My sisters ran for some towels and I remember thinking maybe we should call an ambulance. And I remember thinking holy cow! the guy I passed notes about in Room 219 Study Hall, and walked over to the Atlas Supermarket hoping to see bagging groceries, and lolled about in my two-piece bathing suit on a particular sundeck at the Riviera Club swimming pool—the guy whose weird antics, crooked grin and gap teeth made my heart flutter—had just fallen and knocked himself even sillier than he already was.

Other freshmen girls at Broad Ripple High School chased after varsity football studs like Wild Bill Holton, and sexy guys like Randy Sexson, and honor students like Steve Goldsmith, who's now the mayor of Indianapolis. I doted on dorky Dave and his skinny sidekick Fritz (Fred) Stark, who played clarinet in the 75-piece B.R.H.S. marching band, and whom I kissed once. They were my uncool anti-heroes, square pegs who stood up against phoniness and superficiality and mocked round hole values of scholastic achievement, good looks, popularity, Bass Weejuns, English Leather cologne and Roderick St. John madras plaid dinner jackets and watch bands. Dave and Fritz revelled in loopy school stunts like lunchroom Jello fights (ping-pong with spoons and Jello-cubes), stool races in the library, sulphur bombs in the hall, and booing Ann Landers during her auditorium address; and in extra-curricular activities like egging girls' houses and wrapping nice front lawn trees in toilet paper right before a thunderstorm. Stuff that was a lot easier to get away with if you were a guy.

I had to settle for tamer escapades like driving my parents' car around the block before I had a license; sneaking out of my bedroom on summer nights by climbing down the itchy-prickly holly tree; cruising Borky's Drive-in and the Tee Pee, White Castle and Steak n' Shake on Friday and Saturday nights; smoking borrowed fags, and inviting friends over to wreck my parents' house. But rereading some of my sophomore *Riparian* yearbook autographs makes me wonder if I've forgotten a few things…

> Nancy, you're a great girl and a good MOONER from what I hear. Lots of luck next year—"Redbird" Mike

(Mooning was the 60's equivalent of drive-by shooting: while someone drove a car, someone else pulled down their pants and shot their bare ass out the window.)

and…

> To Super, You're a great guy who can smoke like a son-of-a-bitch. Some day I'll be able to burn people down like you do—Dave Dunnington

At Ripple I never felt like I fit into any organization or with any of the cliques—the rich kids with their private telephone lines, the fast girls who dated greasy duck-tailed hoods who knew about condoms, the cheerleaders who went steady with varsity Ripple Rockets football champs. I tried out for cheerleading and didn't make it. I didn't make it onto the editorial staff of the *The Riparian* newspaper either. As a booby prize, the Publications Director Mrs. Griggs let me compile and write the one-page mimeographed sheet called *The Little Rip*—"Esoteric Information for Riparian Staffers Only." But maybe that wasn't a bad thing. It was my first crack at writing a "column." In between boring news snippets about where to find the rubber cement and paper clips in the Riparian office, and vital news flashes about Riparian staffers—

NOT HOGWASH
Paul Mannweiler's mother won $1,000
worth of meat from the Hy-Grade Meat Company.

I inserted typewriter doodles …
>Get down and help us hunt, Joe. They're *your* contact lenses.
>nnnnnnnlnnnnnnnn

interesting facts…
>Camel's hair brushes are made from squirrel hair.
>Sauerkraut was originally a Chinese dish.

stupid jokes…
>Overheard at an Eskimo trial:
>"Where were you the night of October 11th to April 3rd?"

one-line definitions…
>Archaeologist: Man whose career leads to ruin.
>Mummy: An Egyptian pressed for time.

and suggested resolutions for the new semester…
>I will not snore openly at my desk in study hall.
>I will bring a sleeping bag.

I tried to keep up with teenage fashion trends by streaking my hair with bleach and tinting it with Nestle's rinse, but it turned green. I wore a padded bra to amplify my small breasts. These beauty treatments prompted yearbook autographs like:

>Nancy, Good luck in the future (Watch those rinses)—Penny Gilbert

and

>I like your hair—when did you cut it (off)?—Love ya, Linda

and

>To the most well-padded girl I know—Bill Sellery

and

>I'm glad you finally got a date to the prom—John

Dave Letterman didn't look like he fit in with any high school group either, not even The Lettermen's Club of athletes who'd won their B.R.H.S. letter sweaters. Check that dorky expression in the freshman basketball photo on page 57 of the 1962 Riparian yearbook, and the freshman track photo on page 64 of 1963's—All the other guys are wearing Broad Ripple Rocket phys-ed shirts and beaming like chumps. David Michael Letterman is wearing a plain white T-shirt and looking like a chimp, making a monkey mouth with his tongue stuck into his lower lip. But Dave always seemed like he didn't care whether he fit in. Out of all 467 Ripplites in our class of '65, he acted like he knew something the others didn't. But I couldn't figure out what it was.

After we ran out of beer and the party fell apart at around 3 a.m., I scrubbed and scrubbed like Lady Macbeth, but that bloodstain under the coffee table wouldn't budge. That spring, Dave autographed my Riparian freshman yearbook, in big writing that scrawled across the top of the back cover—

To Nancy, thanks for letting me bleed all over your rug and furniture and brothers and sister. Love, David Letterman

Love! I knew it! None of the other guys who signed my yearbook wrote "Love." It was "Good luck" or "Lots of luck" or "Best of luck" or nothing at all, just their names. I knew Dave secretly liked me, but was just too shy or stubborn to show it, except by "burning me down"—making fun of me, smirking and making prank phone calls. It was hard to imagine Dave kissing a girl anyway, that he could stop joking long enough to keep a pucker on his lips. He was even cracking jokes while I danced slow with him at a sock hop party in one of those neighborhood basements made into a rec room. I always wilted like old lettuce under Dave's gleeful mockery.

Oh, the Midwest! Oh, those days of hairspray, pimples, garter belts and hoses. Those stupidly carefree days our parents told us we'd one day miss. And yessiree Bob, now we do. As so many Midwesterners who've moved away to escape the blandness of the Heartland and for career reasons, Dave talks about the town we called Indian-No-Place, Naptown, "the largest U.S. city not on a navigable waterway," and the "Crossroads of America" with nostalgia now. He says how he misses the early springtime, and seeing the first buds on the trees. And how when he comes back for the Indy 500, and to visit his mother, he always goes for a burger and some greasy fries at the Steak 'n Shake in Nora. "Same hamburgers since 1934—we put 'em on a 385° grill and quick-sear each and every patty!"

Since my parents split up and moved away from Indiana, I've been reluctant to go back to Indianapolis, scared I might be sucked into a time warp and come out as a teenage werewolf in bobby socks and green hair. But last June—was it the call of the 17-year cicadas, or a yearning for some of that Indiana drawl?—I began thinking about Indianapolis and those Broad Ripple days, and how Dave's oddball sensibility, which was not widely appreciated back then, had been my teenage inspiration.

In July the hankering for some Indiana summer tomatoes and a State Fair corn dog got mighty strong. In August I was on a plane. I was going to make a little pilgrimage to the old house on Kessler Boulevard where I'd lived from ages two to nine, and the old Broad Ripple neighborhood. I'd go back to the house on Delaware Street (built and bomb-proofed by the Kurt Vonnegut family) where Dave had banged his head; the house where Dave grew up a 20-minute walk away (on a quiet tree-lined street that rhymes with a cooking oil, but I won't tell); to the Atlas Supermarket where he worked after school, stacking cans and playing pranks on shoppers like announcing fake car raffles, and bogus mah-jongg tournaments and fire drills; and to our old alma mater, Broad Ripple High.

Please, Mister. Let me in. I only wanna switch lanes so I can turn right onto what I think must be Keystone Avenue, even though it's not marked. Hunk was glaring down at me from his battered pick-up truck. I hate to pander in stereotypes, but he had the backslung baseball cap, biceps, ponytail and tattoos to go with the part. I might as well have been aiming a submachine gun at his tires. After ducking a sneer that made me wonder if he had a gun, I tore in front of him and screamed around the corner, and he shot off into space.

Tear in front. Leap lanes. Don't signal. Floor the pedal. Spin those tires. Squeal those brakes. Yippeeee! We're in Indianapolis!

Back home again, in Indiana—*dah dah dah*—and I'm nearly fainting in the tropical humidity. But it seems that I can see… A three-fold population leap. A gorgeous spiffed-up downtown. Gleaming new museums and a dazzling sports complex. An alternative arts and entertainment weekly called *NUVO* and a Greenwich Village of sorts, and new pride for Naptown, the amateur sports capital of the world, and the "Crossroads of America" within a day's drive of half of the U.S. population.

And am I imagining it? No I don't think so. Race driving INDY 500 style is not just the featured activity in the largest one-day sporting event in the world that sells out a tickets a year in advance. It's the way to get around town. How I remember the merry month of May, growing up on North Kessler Boulevard within beer-can throwing distance the Speedway. It sounded like giant killer bees and screaming velociraptors as the race cars droned and whined around the track doing 160+ at qualifications. And our street, being the main drag on the way to the racetrack, was a pile-up of cars as everybody from Gary to Rising Sun succumbed to race fever.

I never actually saw the race myself. Nobody ever saw it, because on a two-and-a-half mile oval track, it was impossible to tell who was ahead of whom. But I journeyed to the outer edges of the infield once, and watched acres of people with cases of beer sitting on top of cars or snoozing on blankets, waiting for the race to begin. The race that drove 400,000 reserved-seat spectators to crowd into the Indianapolis Motor Speedway 24 hours before the Memorial Day event. Moments before the race began, hearts pounded as the chorus of scratchy radios sang the Star-Spangled Banner, then recited a eulogy for those who'd given their lives "unselfishly and without reservation, to make racing America's most spectacular spectator sport." That is, died in crashes. And then the volume blasted up and a million checkered flags were raised for "Gentlemen, start your engines…"

I haven't driven around Indianapolis since high school, so call me a tourist. But it looks to me that the race has overflowed its 2.5 mile perimeter, and the city's green traffic light bulbs should be replaced with black-and-white checkered ones, and we should call it Laptown. And play down the fact that Indy has the third largest cemetary in the U.S., Crown Hill, pop. 170,000. It's hard to speed around town at 180 mph when you don't know where you're going, and when you're used to driving an old banger with no get-up-and-go. But after a day at it with my rental car, I really caught the *Vroooooom!* mood. Next time I'm in town, I might even grab a lesson at the Fast Company Racing School, one of the few racing schools where passing other cars is allowed.

I probably picked the worst time for a return visit. Sweltering August heat, with the Shriners in town for a convention, and all the hotels booked but one at the airport, and the downtown torn up with construction for the new $300 million Circle Centre Artsgarden and Mall, and traffic jams for the Indiana State Fair, going strong since 1852. But that's what I came back for—the good ole' Indiana State Fair. The smell of cows. The fluttering blue ribbons. Draft horses with braided manes and tails tied up with gay ribbons. The 4-H kids with their prize pigs. John Deere tractors. The gaudy neon Midway. Funnel cakes and foot-long hot dogs, corn dogs and corn-on-the-cob and chick-on-a-stick. But getting to the State Fair had challenged my lingering Hoosier pride.

The night before, I had settled into my room at the Ramada Airport Hotel and opened the curtains to check out the view. A UFO had landed on the roof a few feet from my window. The humongous bulbous thing was smoke-colored and I couldn't quite see into it. But eventually the overhead drone of the airplanes echoing my childhood memory of the droning race cars put me fast to sleep.

Around 3.a.m. I found myself dreaming that it was 1958 and The BLOB was coming through my window. Oozing through the air conditioner and onto the carpet and sliming over my bed. I woke in a panic and couldn't breathe. The room was filled with noxious gas. I staggered out into the hallway. I heard strange clicking noises from the room next door, posted with a Do Not Disturb sign. When it's 3 a.m. and the UFOs have landed and The BLOB is seeping through your window, you don't know where you are. Suddenly the door opened and a man spilled out with all his luggage. The manager was moving him to a room on the sixth floor, just in time.

"What's going on here?" I muttered.

"They're painting the swimming pool with toxic acrylic paint. I almost didn't wake up."

"Yikes—So that's what's outside my window! What if we'd just died in our sleep?"

"I know."

"They've got nerve doing this when the rooms are full."

"I know."

I spent the whole next day with a 500-mile-an-hour headache. It didn't help my driving performance, especially to and from the airport. I followed the sign for downtown, but saw nothing telling me to keep in the right lane. The left lane suddenly veered back into the airport and up the ramp of the high-rise parking tower.

Oh no! ROUND and ROUND...like A. J. Foyt... ROUND and ROUND, and feeling nastier with each lap. ROUND and ROUND, taking the turns like a killer hornet going for the sting. ROUND and ROUND and ROUND and ROUND! And then—ROUND and ROUND back down. Until I...ROUND and ROUND...finally reached the ticket booth, hissing like a Marmon Wasp and waving my 12-minute parking stub like a black flag.

"Don't worry, I won't charge you," laughed the ticket lady. "Everybody does this. The airport layout is kind of confusing. The lanes aren't marked. Next time, keep to the far right."

After that little warm-up, it was quite an adrenalin drive uptown. Indy now encompasses 3,088.73 square miles, and all of its occupants had converged upon the Indiana State Fairgrounds. I parked my car near the smell of pigs. I walked across acres of parking lot, past the Swine Barn and into a huge exhibition hall booming with auctioneers' mile-a-minute voices. The first thing to hit my eyes was a bunch of sheep's asses. A little boy from Charlottesville, Indiana was tending to his fluffy white Dorsets with sweet black faces.

"I bet you don't eat lamb," I said to him.

"Oh no, I love it," he said with startling enthusiasm. "We make them into lamb burgers, lamb chops, legs of lamb, lamb stew, lamb roast, lamb sausage, lamb—"

"But they're too cute to kill," I blurted. "I held a baby lamb in my arms once, on a farm in Canada," I started to say, when his mother, a lady sheep farmer, turned around and said, "Oh you're from Canada? Do you know Dick Assman? That Regina, Vagina?—or is it Winnipeg—gas station owner? Saw him on *Letterman* last night."

I'd seen Dick Assman on the CBS *Late Show with David Letterman* too, before The BLOB had attacked. Not having cable TV in Montreal meant I'd missed most of the last ten years of Dave's shows, so I watched it whenever I was south of the border. Last night Dave had announced, "It's time for another Dick Assman Update," as if all the eyes and ears of the world had been following every drop of gasoline pumped by this Petro-Can Station owner since he had been "discovered." Dave knew that they had. Dave Letterman had brought overnight celebrity to this man with the embarrassing name—because of his embarrassing name, and because he was Mr. Everyman, Canada. By showing how gosh darn easy it was to turn even a gas station owner into a celebrity—with Dick Assman T-shirts and mugs and bumper stickers and all, and even a home page on the World Wide Web—Dave was merrily mocking the celebrity-making process and the trappings of stardom.

"We've known this mild-mannered Canadian for almost a month now," Dave continued. "Let's give a nice warm American welcome for Dick Assman, ladies and gentlemen." And out came the little man himself, onto the big stage, with two glittering bombshell babes, one on each arm. While the band played a fanfare and the audience gave him a standing ovation, Dave presented Assman with a ridiculous armload of flowers and asked, "What are you doing this weekend?"

"Probably go home," said the red-faced celebrity.

"Probably go home," Dave laughed. And that was it.

Dave followed the Assman caper with video clips of "Small Town Commercials," one of my favorite *Late Show* gags. One of them perkily announced "Hi, I'm Ben Dover from Computers Northwest," and Dave jumped in, "Remember ladies and gentlemen, if your last name is 'Dover,' you might want to think about 'Bob' or 'Bill.'"

Another commercial featured Don's Guns in Indianapolis—three great locations open seven days a week, on Keystone, Lafayette Road, and Loews Boulevard. The white-bearded proprietor explained his "business philosophy" as Dave called it. "Five millimeter for only $149.95! A 38 Special only $119.99 and a 25 automatic for only $69.99! *Why?* You know *why*, folks. I don't care about makin' money— I just love to *sell* 'em!" And Dave said, "Guns don't kill people; Don kills people."

My evening at the Indiana State Fair warmed the cockles of my heart. I saw and smelled the world's largest boar and petted fluffy white llamas cooling their hides under blowing fans, and chatted with lady cow farmers about the benefits of socialized medicine. Then I went for glitter to the tacky Midway, for the salt water taffy booths, cardboard spook houses, and rowdy shooting galleries. My eyes were riveted by the neon colors in the air, the ferris wheels and towers of lights—and that Bullet! With pendulum swings it sliced the sky like an electric tomahawk. But the people inside it were safely bolted down. I thought of the night I climbed into the old Riverside Amusement Park Bullet, not knowing what it was. It went up, then down, then up a little higher, then all the way up until I was completely upside down with the concrete and crowds rushing up at me, and the dead weight of my upside down body and stretched head pulling against the only thing that kept me from tumbling through the sky and landing in a mash of bones and blood—the old leather strap around my waist. And it looked like it was just about ready to break. I'll never forget it.

And I'll never forget the drive back to the airport hotel. Coming off High School Road, I kept looking for the entrance to the Ramada. It was hidden behind a floodlit highrise that looked like a hotel. I was in the far right lane. When—Oh no!—ROUND and ROUND again…like Mario Andretti… ROUND and ROUND, and feeling stupider with each lap. ROUND and ROUND and then—ROUND and ROUND back down. Until I…ROUND and ROUND…sped like a Gasoline Alleycat to the finish line.

"Not you again," she said.

That was my first day back home again in Indianapolis.

The next day I decided to take a walk around downtown and get my bearings. It was deliriously hot and hideously humid. I staggered over the steamy streets. They were deserted. The city felt like a mirage. Was that waterfall on the Monument Circle gushing real H_2O? Yes—and the The Soldiers and Sailors Monument was still there. On his talk show on Indy's WNTS Radio in 1974, Dave announced one night that the city's centerpiece—the 234-foot-tall, spear-shaped monument erected in 1902 to commemorate the Indiana soldiers and sailors killed in the Civil War—had just been sold to the island of Guam. And that the government of Guam was going to paint the monument green in honor of their national vegetable, the asparagus. And that the Indianapolis City Fathers (there were no mothers in those days) were going replace the monument with a miniature golf course. And some listeners actually believed it!

I circled around and around the newly bricked Monument Circle, remembering on the second round to pay homage to the Circle Tower Building, the fake Babylonian ziggurat where my father had worked. Now I understood why this Midwestern city, which in the summer felt like the Middle East, had so many Assyrian, Babylonian and Egyptian architectural motifs. I staggered past the Circle Theatre, Indy's first "movie palace," looking for a restaurant or sandwich shop. Everything was closed. Naptown officers workers lunch from noon to 2 p.m.

I drifted east. Through the heat haze, the dome of the Statehouse looked as grand as the Taj Mahal. The renovated, expanded, 1886 City Market, where my mom use to shop for fresh kale and collard greens, felt as vast as the Roman Forum. I decided to investigate the old Union Station for signs of life. This grand Romanesque building stood on the site of the country's first union railway depot, which saw over 200 trains a day in the 1800's. Abraham Lincoln himself, on his way from Illinois to Washington D.C. for his 1861 inauguration, had stopped and given a speech. Union Station was certainly hopping now, but the dignity of its old cast iron girders has been painted over in artsy-cutesy pastels. I bought a giant-size iced tea and something ethnic. Then on my way out, I was held up. A man in one of those folksy craft booths was selling rubber-band shooters and he convinced me to try one. I was alarmed at what a sharp-shooter I was. I hit the bulls-eye dead center every single time. *Thwap!* His $8-12 hand-carved wooden firearms—rifles, pistols, derringers, muskets, six-shooters, bazookas and breechloaders and blunderbusses and what nots came in all gun shapes, gun styles and gun sizes. A five millimeter, a 38 Special, a 25 automatic, just like at Don's.

Wandering back outside, I was surprised to find a rustic-looking guitar player sweating under a cowboy hat. I dropped a dollar in his case and introduced myself as a happily retired street performer from Montreal.

"My name's Tom Merle Gowens, very nice to meet ya," he said. "I'm the only street musician in town. They think I'm a beggar. I get called names, but I've been doin' this for five years. I'm defiant as hell!"

"Yeah, of all cities to panhandle in…" I said. "It's been renovated to the hilt, but the downtown streets are still deserted—or is it just the heat wave?"

"The big crowds come in for the games," Merle said. "I play for all the Pacer Games. One night I made $200 in 45 minutes. The losing team's fans don't tip, but the winners tip big. Last month I was singin' "The Old Rugged Cross" and a guy pulled out his wallet and gave me a $50 bill. That's great for Indianapolis."

"That's great, period," I said. And then I said how great it was to be back home again in Indiana, heat and all, and how I planned to go back to Broad Ripple High School for a visit.

"Broad Ripple? *You* went to Broad Ripple? *I* went to Broad Ripple! Class of '64. We must be the only Ripple grads who are street musicians! Remember Norman Stewart? I beat him up. Remember Marcia Levinson?"

"Remember David Letterman?"

"Yeah, no kidding. Who'd have guessed he'd end up a trillionaire?"

I told Merle that the dollar I'd given him was a lucky dollar because I'd found it lying on a brick at the Monument Circle. And he took it out of his case and said, "Here—why don't you autograph it?"

"To a fellow busker—and Broad Ripple grad," I wrote over George Washington's head.

"Well, I'll be darned," said Merle. "I didn't know that's what I was." And he sang me away with "Oh Danny Boy."

I limped up Pennsylvania Street. Past the *Indianapolis Star/News* building, where I'd spent two summers writing up descriptions of wedding lace and seed pearls as a *Star* Women's Department reporter. Past the marble mausoleum paying homage to Hoosiers killed in the last four wars. Into a deafening sizzle of cicadas. The park benches were empty but the jungle was alive. The lusty shrilling of these horny tree-climbing male homopterous insects sang from every leaf. The beating of their abdominal membranes had lulled me to sleep over fifteen summers, but was it ever this loud? I sat for a contemplative while, amazed at the perfectly orchestrated rise and fall of its cadence. Then I sauntered up the steps of the old Indianapolis Public Library, for one last view of it all—the circles, domes and monuments I'd always felt embarrassed to call home.

My parents moved from Nashville to Indianapolis when I was two. Our first home was on North Kessler Boulevard. But there was also an East Kessler Boulevard and a West Kessler Boulevard, and none of these above-mentioned Kessler Boulevards had anything in common. I seem to have criss-crossed the city like a pair of pinking shears looking for it. The old street. The old house. I felt I was getting warm after crossing Cold Springs Road, but the street I thought must be Kessler, even though it didn't look like a boulevard, wasn't marked. The teenage blonde in the tight shorts at the filling station I stopped at said it best—"Yeah, Indy sucks for street signs."

Yeah. Another house I'd been trying to find was the old house known as The House of Blue Lights. I'd forgotten about it all these years, but it all came back to me the moment I drove across the Fall Creek Road. It had been our teenage rite of passage to go there after midnight with a strong-armed date who had plenty of nerve and a fast car. Because old Skiles Test, the reclusive millionaire who lived there, might leap out with a hatchet and hack our arms off, or drown us in the swimming pool, or bury us alive in the cat cemetery, or so we feared... But fear, when you're an adolescent, is a cheap aphrodisiac.

My memory is dim. I remember shivering in the dark with my date beside a high fence, which was on our left. I remember a crunch of gravel under the jalopy. And a haze of blue... The old man who lived in the shabby house lit with blue lights, surrounded by trees strung with blue lights, at 6700 Fall Creek Road was eccentric for sure. The three-day auction after his death on March 18, 1964 attracted 50,000 people to the old estate. It confirmed that he had been a hoarder—stockpiling crates of Aspirin and bottles of ketchup and canned goods and boxes of shoes and tons of junk. And that he had a pet cemetery for his hundreds of dead cats. But as for the dead wife...

They said he'd had three wives, and one of them was dead. They said he kept her in a glass coffin surrounded by blue lights, because blue had been her favorite color. He put up the fence to keep people out. To keep them from seeing the coffin. Which he kept at the bottom of the swimming pool.

Thank my stars there's no South Kessler Boulevard. After knocking on doors on East and West, I finally end up on the old street, and am amazed to see that the location of the old house is, after all, exactly where I had intuitively inked a red dot on the rental car map the day I landed. Sadly, the orchard and all the apple trees I used to climb have been cut to the stumps, and the flagstones on which I practiced my skipping are entombed under grass. But the two story brick house has been carefully maintained by the young African-American couple living there now. It's been spiffed up with a new front porch, but the driveway has not been touched. It's still the old concrete slabs seamed together with weeds sprouting from the cracks. My eyes are drawn to the concrete near the side door of the house, to a series of deep, silver dollar sized holes concentrated in a ten-foot perimeter. I stare at them for a long moment... until I'm struck dumb when I realize what they are. Still here after all these years...now a parody of the Footprints of the Stars preserved in cement in front of Mann's Chinese Theatre in Hollywood—the holes made by my father jumping on his pogo stick!

Broad Ripple Village is hip now. By day, this neighborhood adjacent to Broad Ripple High buzzes with students knoshing sandwiches, guzzling Cokes, running photocopies, returning library books, and shopping for munchies and groceries at Kroger's. By night, its bistros and clubs, casually chic restaurants, umbrella cappucino cafés, funky retro shops, and comedy clubs and repertory theatres listed in the spicy alternative news weekly *NUVO*—turn into a Yuppie Greenwich Village.

And where do these Yuppies shop for groceries? At the Atlas Supermarket at 54th and College, the old grocery store where Dave Letterman used to work as a stockboy after school. The Atlas is celebrating its 50th Anniversary this year, but it still has the same old sign out front, a broken neon Indian chief with a tall neon feather. Owner Sidney Maurer's father named the store after Chief Atlas when he opened it in 1945 and after that the tribe made his father an honorary member.

What a funky, eclectic Midwestern anomaly it is. Its contents rival London's Fortnum and Mason's for exotic variety, but its signs are hand-painted cartoons as corny as Roy Rogers peanut brittle. Sid and Lil Maurer's store has every conceivable munchie a Gourmet Couch Potato could dream of—from designer chef Paul Prudhomme's Majic Popcorn to Jalapeño cashew brittle to Kosher dill chips—and then Jalapeño bologna, island black bean soup, Tabachnick's Boil-in-the-bag Kosher Soups, lamb pasta sauce, Big Daddy Louisianna gourmet popcorn rice, Indiana State Fair shoulder roast, cinnamon crumpets and hogwash glaze. You name it, Sid's got it.

Sid and his wife Lil, who've worked side by side all these years, poke their heads over the counter to chat with me. Where did they find all this stuff, I wonder. Sid tells me proudly that he was the first grocer in the city—or was it the country?—to sell canned tuna fish and frozen foods, and mandarin oranges, and sardines. I can tell that he really loves food. And that he's a visionary. If he'd been working in fashion or car design, he'd be a millionaire by now.

Sid and Lil have followed Dave Letterman's career every step of the way. When Dave made the move to CBS, all the Atlas employees posed for a group photo to wish him well. But I'm sure none of them are up to the kind of pranks Dave used to play in the store, like stacking cans of food into a tower all the way to the ceiling, and emptying a box of breakfast cereal, stuffing it with corn husks, and putting it back on the shelf just in time for a customer to buy it. Dave's days at the Atlas Supermarket have been the origin of many a strange food joke. Like the Soldiers' and Sailors' monumental asparagus... and the hailstones the size of canned hams that he reported falling one night, on his Channel 13 TV weekend weather report.

Sid thinks it's too bad Dave hasn't had any kids. "It must be so hard, having to make it as a comedian," Sid reflects. "That's what broke up Dave's marriage to his college sweetheart. And you never hear of him being with another woman since. It must have been true love."

Back to school. The school that J.S. Puett started with seven pupils in 1886, along the riparian banks of the White River, which has always been a muddy brown. After a nostalgic meander through the halls of BRHS, I sit down to rehash old times with Mrs. Marilyn Dearing, an English teacher of Dave's and mine who I was always afraid of. Mrs. Dearing tells me now she wasn't exactly fond of David, or terrifically impressed by his performance, academic or otherwise. (I won't ask what she thought of mine...)

"If there was ever a definition of a nerd, it was David," Mrs. Dearing says with an ironic smile. "And he wasn't too bright, was he? What's listed about him in the yearbook, that he was a senior hall monitor?" [The chief responsibility of a hall monitor was to sit in the hall. Sometimes he watched pupils walk back and forth in the hall. And sometimes he fell asleep.]

"I love that scholarship Dave founded for telecommunications majors at Ball State University—to qualify, you have to have a C average!" I say. But so much for high school academic ratings, I'm thinking. I had been a C student in high school, and so had Dave, but look at his ratings now. And look at the Internet *alt.fan.letterman* talk group with postings like "Dave for President," and "Dave worship." And Aaron Barnhart's weekly electronic *Late Show News* on the World Wide Web, e-mailed free to 8,500 subscribers, with behind-the-scenes gossip, news, TV ratings analysis, and politics about The Show... And look at all the rip-offs of *The Late Show*, from Quebec to Australia. Yes, Australia. On my Ansett Airlines flight between Sydney and Melbourne, I'd sat with Gerry Connolly, a popular Australian TV and movie political satirist and comedian who told me about the *Clone Show*, down to the Davesque hand gestures of the host, and the look-alike of jazz band lead Paul Shaffer!

"...and Dave had a mean streak," Mrs. Dearing continues. "People thought he was being satirical, but he meant all those nasty things he said. But now that he's wearing these $500 suits, he's matured and his comedy has matured, and I enjoy him more. Especially those small town commercials."

"Did you see Don's Guns the other night?" I ask.

"Oh yes—and Don was written up in the paper here after that, and his phone has been ringing ever since."

Mrs. Dearing recounts an anecdote about Bob Ludlow, Dave's old track coach. Dave had pestered Ludlow for a pair of the new lightweight Nike track shoes, to replace the old clunkers he was running in. "I know I'd be a better track man if I just had those shoes," Dave kept insisting. And he pestered Coach Ludlow every single day for a whole month. But Coach Ludlow only had three pairs of new shoes for four students. And Dave was not one of the students he gave them to. Mrs. Dearing said Coach Ludlow still says, "If only I'd given Dave those track shoes, think where I'd be now! All those doors would be open for me today."

As our chat winds down, I have one more question—
"Do you remember The House of Blue Lights?"
"Yes, yes," she says. "But it's all been torn down."

Driving around the old Ripple neighborhood, I'm amazed how every street triggers the name and face of the classmate who'd lived on it. I drive up North Delaware Street, stopping for a long while in front of our second house, and gaze into the window of the living room where Dave banged his head. Everything on the street looks the same, except for sign on the house next door which says "FOR SALE $150,000," and the two men stopping to look at it—arm in arm, with shaved heads and braided pigtails, nose rings and tattoos.

I roll over to Mazola Avenue. Naw, that's not the real name of it, but I'm not going to give away the name of the street that Dave grew up on. I shyly pull up in front of the simple one-story frame Post-War suburban house on the small lot. It's freshly painted and an American flag is waving out front. I sit staring from my car for a few minutes, until a couple opens the door and comes out onto the front lawn.

"Just reviving some memories," I call out, embarrassed to be caught staring at what fans would probably call The Shrine of David. (This isn't Beverly Hills, folks. It's plain old Indianapolis.) "I'm an old Ripple grad," I explain.

They know why I'm here, of course. As owners Mary and Ken chat in the driveway about Dave's fabulous fame and fortune, they tell me that every so often they have bouts of people driving by the house real slow, staring and taking pictures. "A *National Enquirer* photographer came by a few years ago and shot the house, and my truck is in the picture," Mary says. "They didn't ask permission, but they didn't publish our address. We still get mail for Dave's mother, after five years. Dave comes back to Indy every May for the Race Day, but he keeps a very low profile... We'll keep the house... Who knows? One day it might become a museum."

"To Dave—Thanks for letting me exploit your Broad Ripple High School *Riparian* autograph and make a whole book chapter out of it. Love, Nancy Lyon"

I'm terrible about not throwing out old papers and junk. They just follow me around every time I move. But now I'm not sorry. Back home again—in Montreal—I find the old shoeboxes of tattered Broad Ripple memorabilia. I had never wanted to look at the stuff—flakey dry prom corsages...hay from hayrides...first kiss lipsticks...drive-in movie stubs, until now. In one box there's a pack of mildewed notes and letters written and passed around in Study Hall 219, including—

"How do you like L.Z.'s hair? It's O.K. but what a shock! What did you do to yours? It looks lighter. I put a brown Miss Clairol on mine and ruined it. I didn't do it right and it smells!"

... and

"Nancy Loins, (hee hee) are you still trying out for cheerleading? I'm so glad this Q. T. didn't streak on my face. Last year Susie R. used a whole gob and her skin turned orange."

At the very bottom of a box, along with a list of boys I'd kissed my freshman year, I find what I'm looking for: a yellowed scrap of three-ring notebook paper, circa 1962.

Decades before the advent of Dave's Top Ten List, I had, in my adolescent obsession, pencilled a list of 12 reasons why I was sure Dave Letterman secretly had a crush on me. Two of the reasons ("He laughed at Susie when Fred told him she wanted to ask him to my party" and "Susie didn't know if Dave would go to my party with her") seemed not only nonsensical but redundant. And so I'll eliminate them. Dave will never know.

10) He was the one who called me that night the boys got together instead of Fred.

9) He asked for me twice at a party.

8) He always burns me down in art class.

7) He and Bob came over the night they called from Fred's house.

6) He didn't want Fred to like me.

5) He signed his yearbook autograph "love."

4) He always looks at me when I'm at Rivi.

3) He showed off at Rivi and acted real funny about his foot cramps.

2) He wanted to stay at Rivi until he got all dried off when he could have used the towel.

1) He remembered my biology grade.

All my gratitude—un gros merci...

...to Benoît Ethier for the spark; to Denise Roig for the push, and all the other fertile minds in our writer's group—Joel Yanofsky, Janet Kask, Pauline Clift, Joe Fiorito, Gord Graham, Janice Hamilton, and Brenda Zosky-Proulx; to my colleagues in the Society of American Travel Writers, for nitty-gritty help and support; to Paul Waters, *Montreal Gazette* Travel Editor, for launching "Innocents Abroad" and encouraging quirkiness in travel writing over the years; to Peter Scowen, *Montreal Mirror* Managing Editor, for having the "alternative" vision to launch the X-rated travel column "GONE" with me, (and to the Editors of other alternative news weeklies for jumping on board); to Pierre Trudel—my "sounding bag" at the Québec Ministry of Tourism; to the editors of *enRoute* for sending me off in search of Arthur (and to friends Suzanna and Terry Knott in Cobham, Surrey, for helping me find him); to François Beaulieu, sober-minded Montreal UFOologist, for his flying saucer faxes; to E. Jean Guérin, film critic and David Letterman scholar extraordinaire, for inspiring me to go "back to school," and for valuable voodoo instruction; to Karen Yakovac of the Indianapolis Project, for helping me go back home, and to David Letterman, for teenage inspiration; to Mark, wherever you are, for taking the photo of me on a Tory Island cliff, used in the cover montage; to the good people of Inishbofin for keeping me sane through gale force 10's; to Stéphanie MacSheain for her thorough reading of the Irish material; to Maureen McCoy, wild Irish Midwestern spirit and renegade novelist, for long-distance hand-holding over the years; to Ciaran O'Reilly, co-founder of New York's Irish Repertory Theatre, whose desire to play "Miss Mullen" in "Pies" hooked me on dialogue; to Bill Ochs, (of The Pennywhistler's Press and *Clarke Tin Whistle* tutor noblesse) for that very first tin whistle lesson, and what came after; to Clément Demers for dual-citizenship, steady help and generosity—and teaching me to swear in French; to my editor, Karen Haughian, a superwoman after my own heart, for her unflappable good humor and patience, and her subtle eye and ear. And lastly, to Peg "Mega-Mom" Powers for the writing bug and her Rock of Gibraltar faith; to Elmer Lyon, Tennessee historian, for preserving the Lyon family history and photo archive—and to all those people along my way who have helped me travel, over land and through inner and outer space.

Photos

page	
8	Halloween photo of author with Indianapolis grade school friends
15	Delaware Street house where Dave Letterman hit his head
16	Self portrait in a Fifth Avenue Christmas window
19	Blueprint of harp plans, Robinson's harp shop, 1974
25	Busking on Fifth Avenue, taken by Doug McGee
28	Chuck O'Donnell, Bill Ochs, Nancy Lyon at Irish Arts Center, photographer unknown
29	Zabriskie Point, Death Valley
32	Death Valley Helen, Death Valley
36	Mushroom Rock, Death Valley
38	Tailor's Hall, Dublin
39	Lena Hanrahan's pub, Feakle, County Clare
42	Blackpitts bakery, morning tea break
51	Going to the fish market, Ireland
52	Enchanted white cow, Inishbofin
55	Inishbofin Harbor, with Don Bosco's Castle
59	Henry Lavelle, Inishbofin school house
62	Author's cottage window, Inishbofin
70	Mail boat skipper Paddy O'Halloran and Christie O'Halloran, Inishbofin
72	High Road, Middlequarter, Inishbofin
74	Marionette playing the violin, on the streets of Europe
77	Nancy and Peg in Paris; photographer unknown
87	Nancy in Paris; photographer unknown
90	Gay Village, Montreal, "Priape" store window
93	Calèche drive, The Mountain, Montreal
100	Busking on rue Prince Arthur, 1986: "Shenanigans": Reinhard "Golo" Görner, Bob Cussens, Paul Legrand, Guy Berniquez
112	L'Habitée village, Guadeloupe
114	Morne-a-l'eau, graveyard, Guadeloupe
117	Stained glass, King Arthur's Great Halls, Tintagel
118	Midsummer's Druid Rites at Stonehenge, June, 1968
126	Tintagel Castle, Tintagel, County Cornwall, England
127	Madame "M," UFO traveller, with her daughter
131	Gulf Breeze, Florida
135	Ogham Stone, County Kerry
142	SoHo, NYC
149	The Apollo Theatre, Harlem
150	Opryland, Nashville, Tennessee
152	Nashville Taxi "Elvis"
154	Bull's Gap, East Tennessee
157	Author's great, great, great grandparents, Leroy Lyon and Margaret D. Fugate Lyon, circa 1880
158	David Letterman, Nancy Lyon; Broad Ripple High School *Riparian* yearbook photos
162	David Letterman and Jeff Eshowsky shelving cans at the Atlas Supermarket; Broad Ripple *Riparian* yearbook, 1965
164	Nancy at the Indianapolis Motor Speedway Museum; photo by Karen Yakovac
166	Indiana State Fair Midway, Indianapolis
170	Atlas Supermarket, hand-written sign

All photos by Nancy Lyon unless otherwise noted

• Cap-Saint-Ignace
• Sainte-Marie (Beauce)
Québec, Canada
1995